MW00532345

DIANE CAPRI

BET ON JACK

Perpetually, for Lee Child, with unrelenting gratitude.

BET
ON
JACK

CAST OF CHARACTERS

Kim Otto
Carlos Gaspar
Charles Cooper
Jake Reacher
Samantha Vaughan
Maureen Tolliver
Jeffrey Willard

and
Jack Reacher

NOTHING TO LOSE
By Lee Child

"My conscience is already clear," Reacher said. "If people leave me alone, I leave them alone. If they don't, what comes at them is their problem."

Vaughan said, "You see something you don't like, you feel you have to tear it down?"

"Damn right I do. You got a problem with that?"

"No."

Chapter 1

Monday, May 9
Olympic TBI Center, CO

From Colorado Springs, you take I-25 toward
Pueblo, and turn off right on a state four-lane north
of Fort Carson that seems way too wide for the light
traffic. You drive about a mile on Department of
Defense property and turn through the pines.

It's sunny and clear and much too warm, but the heat
feels good on your skin. Unlike a lot of other places
you've been, the air quality is some of the best in the
world. Your sunglasses block the glare and the wreck
you're driving has reasonable air-conditioning. So far,
so good.

During your recon, you checked existing security
systems. There are no traffic cams out here. No

residents or businesses with cameras, either. A full tree canopy covers the road, preventing precision in satellite surveillance.

All of which means you are as close to invisible as it's possible to get in twenty-first-century America.

Two miles down the road you turn right into a half-hidden driveway and travel between a couple of squatty brick pillars. You pass a billboard that says *Olympic TBI Center* and below that, *Authorized Personnel Only*.

A smile lifts your lips and you keep going. Almost there. Almost done.

You come to a circle of old blacktop in front of some low brick buildings probably built in the 1950s. All of which was Army property once upon a time. You can tell by the architecture. Brick and tile painted with unmistakable Army-green accents, including the window casements and the tubular handrails.

Back when the place was built, there was green grass and graded parking no doubt. Not anymore.

Now it's all weeds and dry dirt and tumbleweeds.

If the Army still owned the place, it wouldn't be so decrepit and neglected. There were thousands of soldiers available to clean and shine. Which could only mean the place had long ago been deemed surplus and sold off when the Army didn't want it anymore.

Luckily, the Army didn't watch it anymore, either.

The thought brings a smile to your lips.

The Army was once a great institution. The lean, green, fighting machine. No more. Now it's run by bean counters and social justice warriors, making it weaker and less effective. All of which is just fine with you.

You pull the rented wreck into the small gravel lot and park at the end of a row of five old, dirty vehicles. All sported local plates. None were manufactured less than ten years ago. All six might bring two hundred dollars each when sold to a scrap yard. Maybe less.

Your wreck is indistinguishable from the others. You wouldn't pay two hundred dollars for it, either.

You circle the drive and move your wreck to the first curve in the road, hiding it from view.

Another quick check for surveillance cameras, just in case, confirms that there are none. As expected.

The place feels abandoned, but it isn't. It has merely been repurposed.

Staying in the trees and the shadows, you walk along the gravel road until you reach the open area at the front of the building. You walk across, up three steps, and over the threshold onto the Army-green mottled tile floor.

A distressed wood table at the right of the door is unoccupied. Which could be good or bad.

You'd expected Neske, the sloppy civilian in a grubby brown sweatshirt. You've seen him before. Scrawny and unwashed and you could smell him across the room. He chewed his cuticles, leaving his fingers raw and bleeding.

Where was he? Why had Neske abandoned his post? How long would he be gone?

You shrug. It is what it is. Good as long as he was gone. Bad if he came back.

A quick look around confirms there are no CCTV cameras in here, either.

You keep walking to the back of the hall and a big empty room that might once have been a waiting room or even an officer's lounge.

Ignoring the three young men, slack-jawed, obviously drugged, and strapped to wheelchairs, you keep walking through another dim and dirty corridor. You stop at a green door, dull and faded, battered and scratched.

A wax pencil had scrawled the occupant's name in the center: *D R Vaughan*. A string of eleven digits followed. Easily recognized as Vaughan's DoD benefits number reflecting his eligibility for the benefits that paid for his care here.

You pause to pull on a pair of surgical gloves, turn the handle, and open the door.

Vaughan's room is as dismal and depressing as the rest of the place. His gaunt upper body is raised to a forty-five-degree angle thanks to the bed's tilting mechanism. A tented sheet covers most of him. Several medical lines run down to his body under the sheet.

His skin is nicely pink. He is clean shaven. Full lips, and a straight nose suggests he might have been handsome back when his wife first fell in love with him so long ago.

Vaughan has a white bandage around his forehead to keep the fresh wound clean after his recent skull reconstruction. The swelling has finally improved enough to cover the open wound and protect his brain from further injury.

His blue eyes are open. They widen when he recognizes you.

"Hello, David," you say, as a test, because you've been told he's awake and talking now, which is the problem. "Good to see you again. It's been a long time."

Vaughan blinks and runs his tongue over dry, cracked lips. He tries to speak, but no words come. He nods shallowly instead.

"I heard you're feeling better. New medicines, better treatments, right?" You reach into your pocket to retrieve the syringe as you approach his bedside, keeping your hand out of view.

Vaughan nods again and pushes a breathy "yes" through his lips.

He would have felt significant pain, but they have him on so many painkillers that he doesn't seem to feel anything at all.

"I'm so glad to hear it. We've been very worried." Your calming hand cups his shoulder.

Vaughan moves his head carefully, as if he might disturb his bandage or his damaged brain behind the gauze, to glance at the Styrofoam cup on his bedside table.

"Water," he says with a push of breath. "Please."

You reach for the long, soft line and follow it to the PIC catheter to be sure the catheter is inserted into a large vein headed to the heart and not somewhere else in his body. You continue talking to him about nothing in particular, like an old friend. Which, once upon a time, you were.

Quickly, you push the contents of the big syringe into the line, cap the needle, and return the syringe to your pocket.

"It's a lovely day. Are they taking you outside for fresh air regularly?" you ask, uncaring, watching, waiting for the injection to do its job.

Which doesn't take long.

Blood stops flowing to Vaughan's vital organs.

His respirations slow and stop. His eyelids fall closed and his head sinks into the pillow.

You check his carotid artery to confirm that his heart has stopped. Sudden cardiac arrest isn't painful, but it is fatal after eight minutes, so you wait for ten minutes. And then another five, just to be sure.

Once you've confirmed his death, you take a few quick strides across the room and slip into the corridor, pulling the door securely closed. Reverse your path to the front entrance.

The grubby sentry near the front door has still not been replaced. A stroke of good fortune.

You walk outside and along the gravel street to return to the rental and retrace the route to the interstate.

A quick glance at the clock shows less than an hour of elapsed time since you arrived at Vaughan's facility. You enter the southbound expressway and drive toward Pueblo.

You drop the wreck at a truck stop where you'd left another rental earlier. You'd parked it in the very back of the lot, shielded from view by large bushes. In the second rental, you continue southbound to Albuquerque.

Mission accomplished. The thought makes you grin like you've won the billion-dollar Powerball.

Chapter 2

Four weeks later
Wednesday, June 8
Detroit, MI

Working the Reacher assignment made FBI Special Agent Kim Otto feel a thousand times more alive than her normal field work. The danger and the constant tension of hunting for Reacher had made her an adrenaline junkie. Normal work activities seemed bland by comparison.

Adrenaline flooded her body, which kept her alive. But the respite afterward caused her to crash hard, falling into a long, deep sleep. The groggy feeling lingered long after she awakened and mainlined two pots of hot, black coffee.

All of which meant she was returning to her desk at the FBI Detroit Field Office with the usual mixed emotions. Reacher was out there, and she wanted to be the one to find him. Spending time in the office seemed like an unnecessary distraction.

The office was bustling with activity, as usual. Agents at their desks, phones ringing, many conversations going on at the same time. A couple of conference rooms with glass walls sported whiteboards with photos and notes pinned in place, where small groups of agents were working together.

All of it seemed like a perfectly normal day in what Kim thought of as her life before Reacher. She hadn't experienced a normal day since that first 4:00 a.m. phone call eight months ago.

"Otto, I need you in the team briefing," her boss, Special Agent in Charge Robert Walker, said as soon as he spotted her filling her coffee mug. "We start in two minutes."

"Yes, sir," she replied, collected her coffee and her laptop case and followed him along the corridor to one of the many conference rooms in the building.

A wall of windows overlooked Michigan Avenue. Weak diffused light filtered through the dirty glass, casting an insufficient glow. On his way through, Walker flipped on the overhead fluorescents adding a slightly green wash to the room and everything in it.

The scent of fresh coffee lingered in the air. Every agent in the room had a fresh cup on the table.

Kim entered carrying her java. Her colleagues, some she knew and others she didn't recognize, were seated already. The low murmur of hushed conversations created a constant hum in the background. Shuffling papers, pens tapping, and keyboards clacking acted like a soundtrack to increase anticipation.

The size of the team and the feeling of urgency suggested the briefing was unusual. Kim leaned against the wall near the door, wondering what was going on and why she'd been ordered to join.

Walker stood at the front of the room, a stack of files on the table and a screen behind him. He cleared his throat and the agents snapped to attention.

"Good morning. Let's get right to it, shall we," Walker's deep voice filled the room. "As some of you know, the Albany Field Office has identified what they believe are related murders. The deaths were originally classified as heroin overdoses. For reasons we'll get into shortly, we now believe otherwise. This is Special Agent Genevieve Johnson from Albany. Her team has isolated two victims. It appears we have confirmed a third victim here in Detroit."

He nodded to his left. An agent passed out files to each team member. Kim opened hers to find pictures of the three female victims. The images were heart-wrenching.

"Albany believes we may be dealing with the same killer in each case. Could be an organization or group or an individual at this point." Walker continued, his words cutting through the air like a chilling breeze. "Code named *Hornet* because of the kill method, which involves injecting the victims to deliver a venous air embolism. Our experts say it's a rare cause of death, usually resulting from criminal intervention."

Kim's stomach flipped over as she realized the magnitude of such an investigation. Identifying potential victims was itself an overwhelming task. She grabbed an antacid from her pocket and slipped it into her mouth.

Walker explained, "Right now, we have no witnesses. No confirmed connections, although the victims identified so far have broad things in common."

He identified each with a raised finger. "To start, all three known victims are military veterans, but not from the same branch of service. Next, they were homeless at the time they died. Third, all were heroin addicts. Finally, all three were initially believed to have died of heroin overdose."

"So the number of victims could be significantly greater," Kim said, standing away from the wall. "How do we know these women were murdered and not accidental deaths?"

"You're right that homeless drug abusers do die from overdose, accidental and intentional. At first, all three of these deaths were thought to be accidental. They've got track marks from drug use, so pinpointing the site of the fatal injections is difficult," Agent Johnson replied. "At this point, after significant investigation, our sophisticated best guess is that these three women were murdered by intentional injection of air emboli into their veins. We'll explain further as the briefing continues."

Confirming air embolus as the cause of death didn't necessarily mean foul play. But there were few alternative possibilities.

Kim's mind raced with the implications of simply detecting fatal air embolism during an autopsy. Special precautions and equipment, like an aspirometer for the detection, measurement, and storage of gas originating from the heart ventricles, would be required.

Why did Johnson's team believe these women were murdered?

"Meticulous procedures are now in place to confirm or exclude potential additional victims," Walker said. "We've asked law enforcement around the country to notify us when a homeless female is thought to have died by heroin overdose. We're fielding those calls and following up. When and if we identify possible victims, a specialized pathologist will perform special autopsy procedures to confirm or rule out Hornet."

"Have we ruled out male victims?" Kim asked.

"At this point, it's too early to rule anything out. Keep an open mind," Walker said, his voice unwavering as he announced the roles of the team members. "Special Agent Otto, you're a key member of the investigative unit, reporting directly to Agent Johnson, who will be leading the team."

Kim nodded, accepting her role. She was surprised to be tapped for the case, given her ongoing Reacher assignment. Had Charles Cooper, the man upstairs who was directing her off-the-books assignment to find Reacher, decided to terminate the quest?

"Welcome to the team. A task force has been assembled in Albany," Special Agent Genevieve Johnson, the team leader, chimed in. "We have experts in behavioral analysis, forensics, and military backgrounds. We'll pool FBI resources and bring Hornet to justice."

The room buzzed with a renewed sense of purpose as they began discussing strategies and sharing insights. The urgency intensified, like a growing storm gathering on the horizon.

Johnson pushed a couple of buttons on the remote and images of the first victim were displayed on the screen.

Ten minutes into Johnson's briefing, Kim felt a tap on her shoulder. Walker tilted his head toward the door, indicating that Kim should follow him into the hallway. The agents were riveted by Johnson's presentation.

Walker led the way to an interior conference room. He opened the door and waved her inside. "Wait here."

"Yes, sir." Kim took a seat at the table.

Walker left and closed the door behind him.

He returned with a file folder and a flash drive and a fresh mug of hot, black coffee. He placed all three on the table in front of her.

"What's going on?" Kim asked.

"The Hornet investigation has a potential connection to an ongoing classified operation. We want you to handle that aspect of the Hornet case," Walker said.

"Why me?"

He leaned against the wall with his hands in his pockets. "Not my choice."

"You were told to give me the assignment? Told by whom?"

"You're smart enough to figure that out on your own, I'm sure." He arched one of his eyebrows and lowered his chin to stare over his readers. "Think about it."

Walker tossed a small, padded envelope across the table.

The envelope was a brand and size the US government ordered by the gross. Which meant it could have come from any of a thousand supply rooms around the country and the world.

Still, she didn't need to open it. She already knew who it came from and what was inside. The Boss, Charles Cooper, had sent her an encrypted cell phone.

There was only one reason Cooper would have brought Kim into this case. He believed the Hornet investigation was somehow connected to Reacher. Which was not a reason he'd disclose to Walker or anyone else.

"Understood," she said to Walker.

"I like you, Otto. I'm looking forward to having you back in the office on a permanent basis. Finish this business so we can get you back on our team where you belong," Walker said as he left her alone with the file and the flash drive and too many unanswered questions.

Kim pushed the padded envelope aside, opened her laptop and inserted the flash drive. A moment later, the contents came up on her screen and, simultaneously, the padded envelope began to vibrate on the table signaling an incoming call.

Chapter 3

Jake Reacher waited for the woman, as ordered. Dressed in his uniform, he sat with his back against the wall in the far corner of Benning's Diner watching the entrance.

The diner was busy. Intensely focused customers hurried inside, consumed fried food faster than a star-nosed mole colony at an earthworm banquet, and rushed out again. Plates and flatware clanged, loud voices exchanged lively conversation, and kids shouted among themselves as if everyone within two miles of the diner needed to hear them.

One family of five filled a table near the entrance, adding more than their fair share of chaos to the mix.

The kids were out of control. Jumping, screaming, throwing food. The mother looked too exhausted to rein them in. The father was oblivious, staring at his cell phone, texting or something.

Benning's Diner was not Jake's favorite. It was the kind of place where kids could misbehave and parents could ignore the bad behavior and no one asked them to leave. Since the diner was jammed to the gills with locals, Jake could only assume the miscreants weren't negatively impacting business, either.

Jake ignored the cacophony and lowered his gaze to his own business. The clock in his head established that the woman was late. How long was he required to wait?

He'd swallowed two mugs of spectacular coffee poured by the pretty waitress. The cup was white, perfectly cylindrical, four inches high and two and a half inches across. It was made of fine bone china as thin as paper.

No way could he get his huge fingers through the fragile handle, so he wrapped his hand around the whole mug. The vessel seemed delicate in his paws, as if he might unintentionally crush it.

This fancy china was the opposite of the thick, heavy mugs the Army provided. Which wasn't great. He loved the Army, and he loved Army coffee. He drank about a gallon a day. Someday, years from now, he'd have a home with a kitchen and heavy mugs and all the coffee he could possibly drink.

Jake pulled a ten-dollar bill from his pocket and handed it to the pretty waitress with the sparkly smile when she refilled his cup. She thanked him profusely for the generous tip and hurried away, flashing a suggestive glance over her shoulder.

He gave her an interested smile in reply. Spending time with the pretty waitress could be fun. But he'd never get the chance. His goals were focused, and they didn't include getting sideways over a pretty woman.

Jake had been buried under a never-ending mountain of work since he'd arrived. He wouldn't have any free time for a good long while. Pretty girls could wait.

Which was more than okay. Jake didn't want free time. He'd had plenty of that already. He itched to complete his Army officer training and launch what he thought of as his real life. The life his father and his uncle had lived. Travel. Adventure. Excitement. Eventually, he'd make it to the military police and excel there, as his uncle had done. He craved it all.

Jake scanned the diner again. The clock in his head insisted he was due on base in less than thirty minutes. He could make the trip in twelve if he ignored all speed limits.

Which meant Samantha Vaughan only had a seventeen-minute window to show up and tell him who she was and what she wanted.

Jake tapped his forefinger on the plastic tabletop like a metronome, as if he might hurry her along by sheer force of will.

She'd contacted him three days ago through his CO. "She's a Gold Star wife, Reacher. Lives in some Podunk

Colorado town called Hope. Lost her husband to Iraq. The ultimate sacrifice. She wants to talk to you."

"Why me?"

"She'll explain her reasons. Go to the Benning Diner. Meet with her. Be polite. Courteous. Grateful. Find out what she needs, and we'll try our best. It's the least we can do." He returned his attention to his work. "We owe her, simple as that."

"Yes, sir," Jake had responded with a sharp salute before he'd returned to work.

The first rule of Army life was to follow orders. He couldn't have refused to see Mrs. Vaughan or dishonor her husband's service, even if he'd wanted to. Which he didn't. So he went to the diner and waited, as ordered.

Eventually, a woman matching the photo he'd seen of Samantha Vaughan stepped into the diner and strode his way like she was on a mission.

Jake sized her up as she approached.

Arms at her sides. Nothing in her hands. She was slightly built under her crisp white shirt and jeans. Maybe five-six. Probably less than a hundred and thirty pounds. No jewelry at all. No makeup, either.

She was attractive and self-assured in a way that suggested she could take care of herself, and he'd be smart to remember that.

"Sorry. Got held up," she said as she slipped onto the bench across before he had a chance to stand. "Samantha Vaughan. Call me Vaughan. Everyone else does."

"No problem."

She watched him for a moment as if he were an unusual specimen. Which, he supposed, he was. At six feet five and two hundred fifty pounds, he was imposing and intimidating to both men and women. Which was totally okay sometimes. Not so okay other times.

"You look like him," she said, after giving Jake a thorough appraisal.

"Think so?"

"Well, if he were younger and less damaged. But yeah. Same size, same shape, same icy blue eyes." She paused before she added, "Same grin."

Which caused him to nod and flash the grin for her benefit. "His brother, Joe, was my father. Two years apart. They looked like twins, people say. Guess the apple doesn't fall too far from the orchard."

"That's what I'm hoping," she said as she pushed a strand of hair behind her ear. Her hands were supple and her fingers long. No wedding ring. No white line indicating she'd ever worn one. "Do you know your uncle well?"

"Not as well as you probably do."

Her eyes widened and her lips rounded and her cheeks grew pink before she said, "What makes you say that?"

"You hunted me down because he's my uncle. Not likely you'd have wasted your time if you didn't know him, is it?" Jake replied easily, as if her reaction hadn't confirmed his guess.

Jake didn't know a lot about his uncle, but he knew women were attracted to Reacher like moths to flame.

Sometimes, they got too close. Vaughan could be one of those.

They stayed quiet while the pretty waitress delivered a second china coffee mug and filled them both. She looked at Vaughan and said, "Can I get you anything?"

"No, thanks." Vaughan shook her head. She tried the coffee, but it was too hot to drink.

The waitress gave Jake another meaningful glance and turned to walk toward the kitchen.

"Reacher has that effect on women, too," Vaughan said with a smirk.

"Is that why you're here?"

"Because I want a date with Jack Reacher?" she deadpanned briefly before all the light left her face. "No."

"I've only got twelve minutes until I need to return to Fort Moore. I can't be late getting back. I'm lucky they let me leave at all. You know how it is," Jake said with a shrug, looking directly into her eyes, which were deep brown pools of tragedy. "Tell me what you need and if I can do it, I will. But if you're looking for Reacher, I don't have a clue where he is."

Vaughan gave him a hard stare. "You know how to find him, though, don't you?"

Jake chewed the inside of his lip. He wanted to say no. But he couldn't lie to her. Nor could he turn her away. She was a Gold Star Wife. And even if she hadn't been, the CO had stated his orders plainly enough.

She'd made a big mistake choosing Jake, though. If she were really in trouble, she should have kept hunting for the real deal.

"I might look like Jack Reacher." He felt duty bound to warn her. "But that's where the similarities end. He's smarter and harder and better than me in every conceivable way. He's got age and experience, and I don't."

"You're not giving yourself enough credit," she stated flatly.

"Trust me. I don't have an ounce of humility in my entire body. In that way, I'm exactly like him." Jake shook his head with a grin. She rewarded his humor with a small smile. "Reacher is one of the best the Army ever trained. I'm just starting my career. I'll get there, but I'm not there yet."

"I already believe that, so stop trying to convince me," Vaughan replied. The fierce glare she leveled was enough to prove she was dead serious.

Jake said nothing. He'd warned her. That's the most he could do. His conscience was clear.

Before Vaughan had a chance to say more, the busboy dropped a tray full of dishes onto the hard tile floor. Flatware, busted plates, and shattered glasses flew everywhere.

For a brief moment, the raucous destruction silenced the entire diner.

Until a young girl jumped up from her chair, holding her hand to her cheek, screaming as if she'd been hit with shrapnel or something. She ran toward the restroom, blood dripping through her fingers and down her arm.

"You jerk! What the hell's wrong with you?" the girl's mother yelled at the young busboy as she followed her daughter into the restroom.

The busboy looked mortified as he tried to apologize and bent to pick up the mess.

The two younger children at the table began wailing like banshees.

Which was when the father lost it.

He stood up fast, knocking his chair over in the process. He kicked aside the plastic tub full of destroyed tableware and lunged for the terrified busboy, still fumbling to collect the shards on the floor.

The pretty waitress knelt nearby helping with cleanup.

The father swore as he grabbed the busboy by the front of his shirt and jerked him to his feet, knocking the waitress off-balance.

She plopped down into the mess and yelled at the top of her lungs. "Stop! Stop! Stop!"

The father, undeterred, pulled his fist back to punch the kid in the face.

Jake stepped out of the booth and took three quick strides to reach the boy just in time to catch the father's fist before the punch connected with the kid's nose.

Startled, the father glared at Jake. "What the hell's your problem, soldier?"

The waitress scrambled to her feet. The seat of her trousers was stained with eggs and gravy.

With the father's fist gripped firmly in his palm, Jake stared into the man's eyes and gave the fist a hard squeeze. The father winced and tried to break free.

Jake squeezed the fist tighter as he warned, "Leave the kid alone. Accidents happen. Let it go."

"What's it to you? That kid's unfit for the job," the father said, glaring, nostrils flared, attempting to shake his fist free from Jake's hold. "My daughter will have a scar *on her face* forever."

"Let the kid go," Jake said again, squeezing the guy's fist tighter yet. Jake gave the boy a reassuring glance and spoke to the father again. "I'd rather not be forced to explain your blood on my uniform to my CO, but I will."

The outraged father blinked. He was smaller, older, leaner than Jake. And not in great shape, either.

Jake squeezed tighter. One quick twist. He could snap the guy's wrist and bring him to his knees.

The father finally calmed enough to realize his situation. He released his hold on the busboy's shirt and the terrified kid scrambled into the kitchen.

Jake softened his grip on the fist.

The pretty waitress rushed forward with a broom and dustpan. "It's okay. We're fine."

"Go on," Jake said to the deflated father as he released the fist with a little shove. "Collect your family. Take your daughter to the hospital. I'll cover the cost of your meal."

"The hell you will," the father said belligerently. He jammed his swollen hand into his pocket, pulled out a wad of bills, and dropped them on the table. "I'll sue you and this place to hell and back."

"You can try," Jake said, standing aside to clear a path to the door. "Now get going while you still can."

The wife and daughter emerged from the restroom. The daughter's cheek had stopped bleeding. The wound was barely more than a scratch. Teenagers. So much drama.

The father gathered his family and pushed them toward the exit. "Let's go."

Unnatural stillness continued inside the diner until the young family left and then for another full minute before noisy conversations started again.

Jake lifted the heavy plastic bin filled with broken dishes and greasy food and turned to the pretty waitress. "Where do you want this?"

"Oh, I can take it. Give it to me," she replied.

He titled his head toward the kitchen. "Lead the way."

He followed her toward the back and placed the plastic bin where she told him to. Then he stopped in the restroom to wash the sticky mess off his hands.

Vaughan cocked her head when he returned to the table. "What was that about?"

Jake shrugged. "I don't like bullies. And I don't like to see a kid so worn down that he's willing to take it."

"You see something you don't like, you have to tear it down?" Vaughan asked as if she already knew the answer.

Jake shook his head. "If people leave me alone, I leave them alone."

"And what if they don't? Leave you alone?" she challenged. "Do you ignore the provocation and keep the peace?"

Jake shrugged and Vaughan let the matter drop. For now. He sensed she'd raise the question again soon enough.

She'd come a long way looking for a man notoriously impossible to find for reasons Jake still didn't know.

Which probably meant Jake was her only option.

He was dead certain that Samantha Vaughan was a woman with nothing to lose.

Chapter 4

Wednesday, June 8
Columbus, GA

"Let's go for a walk," Vaughan said, sliding out of the bench and heading for the exit.

Jake followed her outside. The sun was obscured by heavy clouds and the temperature had dropped a few degrees. Wind had picked up, too.

He noticed the town was moderately busy for mid-afternoon. School had ended for the year, leaving children with empty hours to fill. Flocks of teens huddled outside the movie theater staring at their phones. A few couples strolled along the sidewalk, stopping to look in the shop windows.

Traffic moved at an orderly pace, advancing only when permitted by the light at the intersection of Main and First.

"Fort Moore's a much bigger place than I'm used to," Vaughan said as they walked into the gusty wind.

"Yeah, unbelievably huge to me, too. Something like 120,000 people living on base. I grew up in a small town in New Hampshire," Jake said, trying to draw her out by sharing more about himself than he normally would. "This is my first post since basic. I'll be here a few weeks. Then they'll ship me somewhere else."

"My husband was there briefly. It was called Fort Benning back then." She glanced away and blinked a few times and kept walking.

Wind whipped the grit off the sidewalk like angry gnats biting his ankles while he waited for her to continue.

When she spoke again, she recited the words as if she were reporting to superiors. No tears this time. Just the facts, as if her feelings about them were much too personal to share with a stranger.

Bluntly, she said, "David was National Guard. They extended his tour. Didn't armor his Humvee. He and his squad were blown apart by an IED in Ramadi."

"I'm sorry for your loss, ma'am. Your sacrifice will never be forgotten." Jake murmured with quiet sincerity.

He had suffered his share of losses and many people had said similar things to him at the time. Nothing anyone said would bring David Vaughan back to life. Still, he felt honor bound to continue the ritual and hope she was comforted by it.

"Thank you." Vaughan bowed her head for a moment and then raised her eyes to look forward. "David wasn't killed in Iraq. He should have died when his Humvee was hit, but he didn't. He suffered a serious traumatic brain injury. Which was worse than death in some ways. He was kept in a medically induced coma for years while I prayed for a miracle."

Vaughan glanced toward Jake as if she wanted to be sure he was paying attention.

Jake shook his head in sympathy. "It must have been a very difficult time for you both."

"Yeah. Until my prayers were answered. New treatments became available. They reduced the swelling in his brain, and then they woke him up," Vaughan said. "It truly felt like a miracle."

Jake had read online that better treatments for brain injuries were coming, but a full recovery after several years' time seemed like a miracle for sure. Still, David Vaughan must have been unusually strong and resilient simply to have survived.

"David was finally awake. He couldn't speak yet." Vaughan paused to clear her throat and blink away her tears. "But he could hear me. Understood what I was saying. Responded to questions by squeezing my hand or blinking his eyes."

Jake gave her time to get the words out mainly because he could think of nothing helpful to add. The wind gusts were stronger now and he'd felt a few raindrops.

"They did surgery to replace the portion of his skull they'd removed when his brain was so swollen. The last time I saw him, the doctors were telling me that he could be moved to a better rehab unit once his surgical wounds had healed." Vaughan paused to gather her emotions.

They walked another half a block before she inhaled deeply and continued as if she needed to finish in one quick breath. "But none of that happened. He never left his bed. David died."

"Do they know what did happen?"

"Sudden cardiac death, they said. Which just means his heart stopped." Vaughan cleared her throat and put more energy into her words. "There was an autopsy. Results were inconclusive. They couldn't pinpoint a specific thing that caused his heart to stop beating."

Jake didn't know much about cardiac arrest, but that answer was unsatisfactory, even to him.

Everybody dies of the same thing. At the end, your heart simply stops.

But a man as young as David Vaughan, who had already survived so much? Surely, he shouldn't have just died like that, without warning, because his heart simply gave up the battle.

"Have you asked for a second autopsy?" Jake asked. "Maybe they missed something the first time."

"I don't need a second autopsy. I'm a cop. I already know what happened," Vaughan said flatly. "David was murdered."

They had reached a busy intersection. While they stood waiting for traffic to clear, lightning flashed across the dark clouds followed by a deafening clap of thunder.

A moment later, the sky opened up and dumped rain straight down in heavy sheets.

Quickly soaked to the skin, Jake grabbed Vaughan's hand and hustled her into the hardware store on the corner. They stood near the exit, dripping pools of water to the floor.

Jake dropped her hand.

Vaughan flashed an easy smile and pushed her wet blond hair behind her ears. Raindrops streamed down her face, neck, and arms. Her wet shirt clung to her body like a second skin in the cold air-conditioning.

As far as Jake was concerned, she looked spectacular. With a lot of effort, he managed not to stare at her. She was more than ten years older but at the moment, she looked about eighteen.

He blinked hard to clear her body from his imagination. He had no time for women, even if she were interested. Which she probably wasn't.

The rain had started strong and intensified as the wind gusted. Darker clouds gathered. Lightning and thunder came faster and louder. A few more soaked pedestrians rushed inside seeking shelter.

Hearty souls fighting the weather on the street had given up on their umbrellas after the wind turned them inside out. Heads down, hats off, hands in pockets, they trudged against the storm.

"We have hard storms in Colorado," Vaughan said, a hopeful tone in her voice. "Usually they blow over quickly."

"First Georgia storm I've experienced," Jake replied. "In New Hampshire, rain like this can last for a couple of days or longer. Where's your car?"

"Not too far. Couple blocks down," Vaughan said with a smile as she tilted her head in that direction. "I won't melt. How about you?"

Jake opened the door and Vaughan stepped into the storm. Jake followed. They walked along the sidewalk at a brisk pace toward a rented Toyota 4-Runner parked at the curb. Vaughan pressed the key fob to unlock the doors and they climbed inside while the storm continued unabated.

"I feel like I just took a long, cold shower," Vaughan said, teeth chattering, while she started the engine and flipped on the heat.

Their warm breath and wet bodies promptly fogged up the windows. Jake's view through the opaque glass blurred everything outside. Only a few pedestrians, partially shielded by umbrellas, braved the storm, scurrying quickly along the sidewalk.

"I'm overdue returning to base. My Jeep's down the block. Can you drop me off?" Jake pointed straight ahead.

"Of course." Vaughan slid the transmission into drive, buzzed the window down so she could see, and pulled into the slow-moving traffic making its way through the puddles.

She was a good driver. Jake felt comfortable with her behind the wheel.

"You never told me why you wanted to meet with me," Jake said. "How can I help?"

"It's a longer story than we have time for now. But you guessed it. I'm looking for Jack Reacher."

"Why?"

"Because he met David. We talked about David's situation a lot. He wouldn't like where we are now," she said as she moved the SUV close to Jake's Jeep. "When Reacher sees something he doesn't like, he destroys it. That's the kind of help I need."

The rain pelted the SUV's roof, a hard and fast staccato beat, like a soundtrack for her urgency.

"How long will you be in town?" Jake asked. "My CO might let me or someone else follow up on this."

"What about your training? The Army's pretty strict about its schedules and procedures."

He winced at the hopeful tone in her voice as he pulled out his phone. "Give me your number. I'll call you."

He punched her digits into the phone as she recited them. Then he opened the door to hop out. Standing outside, cold rain pounding his wet clothes and sluicing to the ground, he stuck his head into the SUV.

"Go back to your hotel. Get a warm shower and a bite to eat. Get some sleep. I'll check in with my CO and make a few calls and we'll go from there."

His CO had said the Army owed Samantha Vaughan. A debt that could never be repaid.

Jake took the point to heart.

He closed the door and dashed through the raging storm, which felt like a metaphor for the promise he'd made.

Chapter 5

Kim wasn't ready to talk to Cooper. Not yet. She ignored the vibrating cell phone until she was better prepared to deal with him. Meaning, after she learned more about Hornet and tried to figure out why Cooper wanted her on the Hornet team.

And, as always, why and how Reacher was involved.

When she'd started the Reacher assignment, Kim had believed Cooper was the kind of leader she could follow into Hell and back out again. After seven months on the hunt, she knew better.

The one man she could always count on was her former partner, Carlos Gaspar. Cooper? Not so much.

She turned to her initial review of the flash drive's harrowing contents. As she studied the files, her heart pounded, and the familiar metallic taste of adrenaline surge filled her mouth.

There was a lot to unpack here.

She copied all of the files and sent them to her secure server, just in case. Then she encrypted them again using her proprietary software and sent them to Gaspar.

Whatever the connections were to Reacher, she wouldn't find them all on the first pass. Gaspar had the resources to dig deeper.

The first group of classified files on the flash drive contained sensitive information about Hornet's victims. Each entry was meticulously documented with details of how and where the victim was found, along with the possible reasons each had been included on the killer's list.

Kim shook her head. "So much wasted life and destroyed potential."

The first identified victim was Melody Bennett, a thirty-six-year-old former Marine. She'd served two tours in Afghanistan. She was found in a rundown motel room in Albany, New York, eighteen months ago.

Could Reacher have been in or around Albany back then? Of course he could have. Eighteen months ago was long before Kim started trying to find him. But *was* he there?

Bennett had been dead for several days before the cleaning crew found her. According to her devastated sister, she had been living on the streets, battling the heroin addiction she brought home after military service.

At first, Bennett's death was presumed to be an overdose. She never married and had no children. Both parents died long ago. Her sister, seeking answers, had offered Bennett's body for medical research.

Bennett was sent to a medical school where eager students conducted an exhaustive autopsy examining each and every puncture wound that riddled her body. Their thorough diligence eventually revealed the cause of death.

Bennett, the autopsy concluded, had been injected with a fatal dose of air.

The injection site was most likely one of her jugular veins.

Which meant she couldn't have performed the stick herself. The neck was an awkward location for self-injection. She was an experienced IV drug user by the time she died, and she'd had much easier options if she'd wanted to kill herself.

So the injection was probably administered by another person.

Kim paused to consider how the fatal dose might have been delivered. Death by injection was an up close and personal method for murder.

Bennett was five feet eight inches tall, which would make it awkward to hit the artery in her neck if she were standing at the time. She was probably seated or lying down, vulnerable, unable or unwilling to defend herself.

Kim reasoned that she must have been unconscious, restrained, or she knew and trusted her killer enough to let him get too close to her.

The thought sent a shiver through Kim's body.

Reacher had a habit of seducing strong, capable women. Often, they were law enforcement or military and still in uniform. It was one of his quirks.

Had Reacher known Bennett? Had sex with her? Possibly.

Killed her? Kim shook her head. She could think of no good reason why he would have done so.

No suspects and no apparent motive to kill Bennett had been located thus far. Although the thick file of witness interviews proved the FBI's Albany Field Office had spared no expense when working the case.

Kim went through the remaining file materials more quickly, now that she had absorbed the facts on the first victim and had a better idea what to look for.

The later files were not as well developed as the Bennett case. Which probably explained the formation of the task force. More manpower had been needed.

The second body identified as a potential victim was Emma Fonda. A twenty-nine-year-old Navy veteran discovered lifeless in a vacant warehouse in Miami, Florida, six months ago. November. Shortly after Kim was tasked with finding Reacher.

Kim made a mental note to follow up with Gaspar about Fonda. He'd retired from the FBI, but he'd been assigned to the Miami office for several years. He might know something. Or know someone who knew something. And if he didn't already know, then he could find out.

According to the file, Fonda battled post-traumatic stress disorder after her discharge. She couldn't hold a job or a relationship. She ended up homeless, self-medicating with heroin to keep her flashbacks under control.

Ultimately, the pathologist declared Fonda's method of murder was the same as Bennett's. Fatal injection of air to the jugular vein.

Kim shivered. The cold-blooded killer had exploited Fonda's struggles and loneliness as she fought her demons over and over.

The third victim was Lydia Harmon, a forty-year-old Army veteran. She was found dead in a desolate alley in Detroit's Cass Corridor last week. Her family had given permission to exhume her body for the second autopsy.

She had been suffering from depression and addiction, a heartbreaking consequence, her mother believed, of Harmon's service-related injuries.

Harmon had suffered a traumatic brain injury when her Humvee triggered an improvised explosive device. The same IED had damaged her left leg, which was later amputated. When her body was found, her prosthetic leg was missing.

Like the others, Harmon's initial autopsy had failed to discover that an air embolus had killed her. Cause of death on her death certificate was listed as heroin overdose.

One detail raised the hair on the back of Kim's neck. Harmon was buried in Detroit's Mt. Olivet cemetery. The cemetery was famous and infamous. Crime bosses, celebrities, athletes, and captains of industry rested there.

Mt. Olivet was also an excellent place to hide both people and things. Kim had used it for that purpose herself. She expected her secret to remain undiscovered indefinitely. Harmon's killer probably believed her murder would be buried with her, too.

As Kim went through each file, she hypothesized that the killer's victims had been methodically chosen. Each victim had four things in common. Military service, homelessness, and drug addiction. All three were female.

While the commonalities were broad and general, Kim had to agree that the odds against random victim selection were too high.

Which meant Hornet had some twisted reason for choosing these victims.

Nor were these crimes of passion or the acts of an enraged lunatic.

Kim had to agree with Agent Johnson's conclusion. Brave, competent women, who had sacrificed so much for their country, were being systematically, intentionally eliminated.

Kim believed the facts suggested Hornet was a single killer. The team might find more evidence that these murders were the work of a criminal organization. There were plenty of resources being deployed to investigate that theory.

But for now, Kim focused on a single unidentified subject.

Although the killer of multiple unrelated victims could certainly be a woman, such killers were usually male. Occam's razor. The simplest answer was usually the right one.

For a working theory, Kim hypothesized a single male, taller than Bennett, who had a reason for choosing these particular victims. He was stealthy, highly organized, clever, and for some reason, the victims had trusted him.

While Reacher certainly fit that profile, Kim couldn't see him in the role. She'd need more solid evidence before she'd even consider it.

So who was the real killer? And why did he kill these particular victims?

She ran quickly through the list of recognized motives for murder. Revenge, jealousy, greed, mental illness, and anger were the basics.

The other personal motives were crimes of passion, domestic violence, and self-defense.

Less common but still somewhat likely were gang violence, mercy killing, contract killing, ideological or political.

Common but not likely here were serial killing, accidental murder, and accidental homicide.

Kim tried to identify the motives and connect the dots between the classified operation and the public one as she studied the intel.

The classified op files on the flash drive involved a shadowy international organization. They called themselves Piranha because like the fish, they moved in aggressive, lethal packs, viciously killing without remorse.

Piranhas were suspected of exploiting and trafficking contraband of all sorts across borders and state lines, as well as recruiting the homeless with military backgrounds into their criminal network.

Possibilities came at her like a series of quick gut punches.

The Hornet might not be a sick serial killer. What if he was a contract assassin, ideological or political, targeting those whom Piranhas considered a potential liability or threat or enemy?

Still a single, male killer, most likely. Female serial killers were rare.

But the motivation for serial killers and assassins was completely different.

"Dammit," Kim muttered under her breath. "What the hell is going on here?"

The team investigating Hornet was operating in the dark. She knew what that was like.

She'd been operating off the books for months. From experience, she knew working in the field when critical intel was deliberately withheld was beyond dangerous.

She was torn between loyalty to her new team, desire to stop Hornet, the urgency of taking the Piranhas down, and finding Reacher.

Would Cooper be interested in having Kim on the case if Reacher wasn't a part of the equation? Definitely not.

She didn't believe Reacher killed these women and she doubted Cooper felt otherwise. Then how was he involved?

Determined, she stepped into the conference room. She caught Agent Johnson's attention and subtly gestured for her to step aside. Johnson followed Kim into the hallway.

Johnson returned Kim's steady stare. "What is it?"

Kim kept her voice low but firm. "It's possible Hornet is an assassin connected to a larger organized crime operation."

Johnson's eyes widened and she lowered her voice. "What makes you say that?"

Kim cleared her throat. "I'll need approval to say more. But these murders could be the Hornet eliminating potential threats to protect a crime syndicate."

Johnson nodded her understanding the gravity of the situation. "How sure are you about this, Otto?"

Kim cocked her head, her mind racing with the implications. "At the moment, it's nothing more than a reasonable hypothesis."

Johnson studied Kim, taking the new intel on board, probably filtering it into known facts so far.

Before Johnson could say more, Walker approached from the opposite direction, a stern expression on his face. "We have new developments in the Hornet case."

Walker opened the door, ushered them into the room, and called for attention. "We just received a lead on Hornet. Detroit PD has located a new witness. Says he saw a suspicious individual near the Harmon crime scene. They're bringing the witness in for questioning now."

The team dispersed and Kim returned to the conference room where she'd left her laptop.

The hunt for a highly organized killer like Hornet could easily fail. He'd proven repeatedly that he could kill by stealth, up close and personal, and get away with it. Three times so far, at least.

Which meant he could probably kill even more effectively from a distance.

Kim ripped the padded envelope open. Cooper had called three times. He'd left no messages.

Chapter 6

Wednesday, June 8
Detroit, MI

Kim slipped Cooper's latest encrypted cell phone into her pocket, grabbed her laptop case, and headed out in search of privacy. She took the elevator to the parking garage in the basement where she'd left her vehicle.

After tossing the laptop onto the passenger seat, she slid behind the wheel and started the engine.

She flipped on the electronic surveillance disrupter she'd had installed and drove up the ramp to the exit onto Cass Avenue.

The scene of the Harmon murder, the third victim, was only a few blocks away. She turned in that direction.

The witness had already been removed, but she wanted a good look at the scene.

Traffic was heavier than usual. As she approached, she saw that Detroit PD had the street blocked off.

Kim parallel parked her SUV a block away. With the engine running, she fished Cooper's cell phone from her pocket and hit the redial button.

Charles Cooper was near the top of the food chain at the FBI. His office was in DC. Kim had been there a couple of times. It wasn't as impressive as she'd assumed it would be.

Still, for a long, long time, she'd planned to sit behind the director's desk one day. But Cooper had to get out of the way first.

He picked up the call. "Couldn't resist getting a look at the Harmon crime scene, Otto?"

"Good to know you're still watching me." Kim frowned.

She'd need a stronger signal blocker than the one she had now if she wanted any privacy at all. Cooper was always watching. Which was simultaneously comforting and alarming.

"Why'd you want me on the Hornet case, anyway? You think Reacher's involved?"

"We can discuss that later," Cooper replied. "You're expected in DC. A helo will pick you up at your apartment in thirty minutes."

Kim glanced at the clock on the dashboard. "Why am I going to DC? Why'd you put me on the Hornet case if you meant to send me out of the jurisdiction?"

She heard someone talking in the background. Cooper's privacy had been compromised. "Helo's on the way. I can't hold this thing forever. You've got thirty minutes." Before he hung up, he added, "Don't be late."

Kim shook her head as she disconnected on her end and dropped the phone into her pocket. Thirty minutes wasn't much time. Maybe she should give up here and head back.

Or she could see the Harmon crime scene first.

Her bag was always packed, and she wasn't far from her apartment.

If Cooper wanted to show her something, he'd wait until she got there. Probably.

After half a moment's hesitation, she shut down the engine and climbed out of the SUV. She hustled toward the uniformed police officers standing at the alley's entrance. Deeper into the alley, near a dumpster, was the spot where Lydia Harmon's body had been found last week.

Why were the police here now? Most of the people milling around were homeless and most likely had no desire to help Detroit PD.

Before she reached the barricade, two FBI agents from the Albany office emerged from the alley. They recognized each other from the briefing earlier. A short man and a tall woman.

"What's going on?" Kim asked.

"Nothing much," the tall guy replied. "The witness was taken to the closest Detroit PD station for a formal interview. We questioned a few folks milling around. Most of them have only been hanging here a short time.

Nobody admits to being here at the time the body was discovered or knowing Harmon."

"Which is probably true," the woman said. "This group of homeless is transient. They don't stay here in the winter. It's too cold."

Kim nodded. Homeless people living on the streets like this were unlikely to be good sources of usable intel. Transients, addicts of all sorts, mentally ill.

The whole investigation was likely to be one series of dead ends after another.

"Okay. I've gotta run. Thanks for the update," Kim said.

"No problem," the tall man said as the pair peeled off in the opposite direction from Kim's SUV.

Kim glanced at her watch. Twenty minutes to get back to her apartment, collect her bag, and make it to the helipad on the roof of her building. She picked up the pace.

Before she reached her SUV, a man stepped onto the sidewalk from between two buildings, blocking her path. He looked older than he probably was. He hadn't had a shave, haircut, or a bath in a long time. His clothes were filthy, and he smelled like a brewery.

Kim moved to the outside of the sidewalk, intending to pass him and keep going. He stepped directly in front of her, forcing her to stop.

"You with those other cops?" he slurred, nodding his head toward the uniformed patrol at the alley. His breath was so bad it would stop a charging rhino at fifty paces.

"Why?" Kim asked in return, moving upwind, breathing through her mouth. It was all she could do not to gag.

"I didn't like those two in the suits. You with them?" His rheumy eyes peered as if he couldn't see well enough, even in the daylight. He couldn't be a solid witness to whatever had happened to Harmon, even if he wanted to help.

"I'm Kim. What's your name?"

"Billy."

"Was there something you wanted us to know, Billy?" she asked, trying to stay upwind and mindful of the passing time.

"I knew her."

"Who did you know, Billy?"

"Lydia."

Kim's breath caught. "Lydia Harmon?"

"Yeah. Saw her every day. Then she didn't come back. Haven't seen her for a long time."

"What happened to Lydia, Billy? Do you know?"

"She left with her boyfriend." Billy shrugged and shook his head sorrowfully. "Do you know where she is?"

Kim's pulse quickened. Maybe she'd been wrong about Billy after all. "Lydia had a boyfriend? Do you know where we can find him?"

Billy shook his head, letting his chin drop to his chest. "Lydia called him 'Buster.' She liked him better than me."

"She called him 'Buster'? Buster what? What was his last name?" Kim tried to lead him gently, but he didn't seem to follow the questions. His eyes wandered and his head moved as if he had no control over it.

"Buster was mean to Lydia. I was nice to her. Why she liked him more than me?" Billy said, the way a small child might.

Kim glanced at her watch. Billy could be a lead, at least, into the murder of Lydia Harmon. She couldn't simply leave him on the street and hope someone else would find him another time.

Cooper's helo would wait for her, but not indefinitely.

Should she take Billy in now? He felt comfortable with her. Would he talk to someone else?

Another moment's indecision before Kim retrieved her cell phone. She called Special Agent Johnson, who promised to send a car immediately when Kim reported Billy's comments.

"Billy, would you like a bite to eat? My friends will take you to get a hot meal. Maybe a shower, too. Might be able to scrounge up some new clothes as well. Would you like that?"

His eyes seemed interested, but the rest of his face didn't get the message. Billy shook his head and shrugged and shuffled his feet.

"What's your last name, Billy?" she asked him gently.

"Boy."

"Your name is Billy Boy?"

He nodded. "Yeah."

An unmarked Bureau car pulled up at the curb and an agent got out of the passenger seat. He came around the front of the sedan.

Realizing he could spook the witness, he was careful not to approach until he asked, "Can I help?"

Kim placed her hand on Billy's arm and guided him toward the agent. "What's your name?"

"Peter Phillips."

"Peter, this is Billy Boy," Kim said pleasantly, like introducing two friends at a party. "Billy needs a hot meal and a shower, some clean clothes, and a place to sleep for a few hours. Can you get him all set up for me?"

"Yeah, sure," Phillips said, playing along.

"Billy, my friend Peter here will help you. Okay?"

Billy nodded, keeping his eyes down.

"I'll check on you later, okay?"

"Okay."

"Come this way, Billy. We'll get you settled," Agent Phillips said taking Billy Boy's arm and leading him to the car. Billy shuffled along, head down, without objection.

When Billy was settled in the backseat of the car, she gave Phillips a quick report on what Billy had told her.

"Johnson's waiting for you and I've got a plane to catch," Kim said. "You okay to take it from here?"

"Yeah. Thanks. We've got this." Phillips climbed into the vehicle's front seat and drove Billy away.

Kim watched the car's receding taillights for a moment and then hustled to her SUV. She made a U-turn and sped toward her apartment. She saw Cooper's helo landing on the roof of her building as she reached the entrance to her underground parking.

She rushed down the parking ramp to her reserved space. Jumped out of the SUV, grabbed her laptop case, and scurried into the building. She took the express elevator to her floor, ducked into her apartment to retrieve her travel bag, and hustled up to the roof where the helo was waiting.

She stowed her bags and climbed into the cabin, flashed the pilot a thumbs-up as she donned her headset and found the straps to her harness.

"Hold onto your seat." The pilot grinned and lifted off before she had fully secured her harness.

Kim slipped the buckles into place and offered him a weak smile in response.

Whatever Cooper wanted, it had better be good. She hated helos. Damned things were unstable as hell.

Chapter 7

Wednesday, June 8
Fort Monroe, Georgia

The storm hadn't let up. Rain pounded the street, turning it into a river. Jake's boots squelched as he made his way to his Jeep, but his mind was far away from the weather. Samantha Vaughan's story had ensnared him, and her desperation was palpable.

She had obviously loved her husband. She needed help. He couldn't just walk away.

What would Reacher do?

Jake had no idea. But he knew she didn't deserve what had happened to her and he couldn't ignore her pain. If he could help her, he had to do it. Simple as that.

He slid into the driver's seat, his wet clothes seeped into the upholstery and the carpet. He started the engine, but his thoughts were on David Vaughan's mysterious death and his widow's insistence that her husband was murdered.

Jake could feel her grief like a physical weight in the car with him. He knew what loss felt like, and he knew that her pain was real.

A loud crack of thunder brought him back to the present. He looked out at the rain-lashed streets and realized that this was no ordinary case. It was personal. He felt called to action. Perhaps he was more like his uncle than he'd realized.

"I'm looking for Jack Reacher," she'd said, *her voice echoing in his mind. "When Reacher sees something he doesn't like, he destroys it. That's the kind of help I need."*

Jake shook his head, trying to clear the lingering image of Vaughan's wet shirt clinging to her body. He had to focus.

He had a duty, a promise to keep to a Gold Star widow and her husband and to the Army.

And, if he was honest, to Reacher, who had been concerned, somehow, with all three.

Jake pulled out into traffic, his windshield wipers working furiously to clear the rain. The city lights were blurred, the streets slick with oil. He drove carefully through the storm, even as his mind worked on Vaughan's situation.

He made his way back to base, thoughts on David Vaughan's sudden death, the inconclusive autopsy, the military's lack of interest.

None of it added up in his head. Something hidden and dangerous was going on here. What was that something?

Jake went straight to his CO's office and laid out the problem. Reluctantly, his CO agreed that Jake needed to see this Vaughan thing through. Provided he could do it quickly.

"Do the job, Reacher. And get back here. Not one minute more than absolutely necessary," his CO said.

Back in his quarters, Jake changed out of his wet clothes and took a hot shower. His body was still chilled when he finished.

But he couldn't shake the cold feeling in his gut that David's death was bigger than Jake and his wife could handle alone. They were up against forces they couldn't see, fighting a battle they didn't fully understand.

How could they possibly find David Vaughan's killer in just forty-eight hours working alone?

Vaughan said Reacher would have taken care of this thing efficiently and effectively.

Jake wanted to handle it on his own, too. But he needed help, connections, resources, someone who understood the way things worked and how to move around the roadblocks.

He picked up the phone and dialed FBI Special Agent Kim Otto's number. It rang, and he waited, his heart pounding hard.

This was the first step, the beginning of something that might change the trajectory of his life. Which he wasn't quite sure he was ready to do.

"Otto." She sounded preoccupied when she picked up the call.

"It's Jake Reacher," he said, his voice steady.

He could hear the surprise in Otto's voice when she replied. "Good to hear from you, Jake. What's going on?"

"I need your help."

He told her about Samantha, about David and his mysterious cause of death. "I need to help her find out what happened. But I don't really know where to start."

"I'd start with Jack Reacher," Agent Otto said. "From what you've said, he's dealt with both Vaughans before. He knows them better than you can hope to."

"I've talked to the guy twice in my life. Both times, he helped you get my ass out of trouble. I'd really prefer not to ask him to do it a third time," Jake said flatly as embarrassment warmed his face. He was glad Otto couldn't actually see him.

"But you're willing to ask me? You think I'm not as scary as he is?" she teased, which made him grin.

Agent Otto was every bit as scary as Reacher, but in a totally different way. Jake wouldn't want to run up against either of them in a dark alley.

"No offense," he said.

"None taken."

"Between the two of us, we should be able to handle this one. We don't need Reacher," Jake said. "All she wants is some answers about her husband's death. And she's a cop. So she can help, too. Three of us should be enough, shouldn't it?"

Otto paused a moment before she replied. "You *can* contact Reacher, can't you? If you were so inclined?"

Swiping a palm across his hair, still close cropped from basic training, Jake cleared his throat. "Not exactly."

"What do you mean?"

Jack Reacher used pay phones or a borrowed land line. He didn't own a cell phone.

When Jake asked why, Reacher said he liked to travel light. He carried nothing that wouldn't fit in his pockets. He didn't want to be tethered to anyone or anything. He'd made that clear.

All of which was weird to Jake, but he didn't push the point. He had his own reasons for not connecting with Reacher.

Such as Reacher's reputation as a trouble magnet with only one defense setting—apply deadly force.

Reacher never solved problems through peaceful negotiation and smooth diplomacy. Over the years, he'd made more enemies looking to exact revenge than Genghis Kahn.

"My CO says I can help Vaughan but only for a few days. I'm not really entitled to extended leave, and I'll have to work harder to catch up. He said to do it fast, do it right, stay out of trouble, and get the hell back to base," Jake replied and then paused a moment. "See the problem?"

"I see a lot of problems." Otto laughed. "But you're probably right that getting Reacher involved wouldn't help to avoid trouble, if that's the goal."

"Exactly," Jake replied.

Beyond that, Reacher was a legend in some circles. Inside the Army, people loved or hated the guy. If his name came up, which didn't happen often, reactions were always odd and unsettling.

Calling on his uncle would make Jake look weak and incapable of fighting his own battles and building his own reputation the way he wanted it to develop.

No thanks.

Jake preferred to keep his head down and his name out of Reacher's business.

When it came to Reacher, Jake's goal was don't ask, don't tell. Worked great so far. His plan wasn't broke, and he saw no need to fix it.

All of which meant he didn't have the faintest clue how to find his uncle, even if he'd wanted to.

"I've got to go, Jake. I'll poke around a bit to see what I can find in the official places," Otto said. "I'll call when I've got something to report."

"Thanks," Jake waited until she disconnected and slipped his phone into his pocket.

He'd been uneasy about calling Otto, but what choice did he have? His CO had made it clear that he'd get no help from the Army. David Vaughan was no longer the Army's problem, he'd said, and their resources were stretched thin as it was.

The rain continued to pour outside, the wind howling like a wild beast. But Jake was in this now, and he had something to prove to himself.

He wanted to follow in Jack Reacher's most successful footsteps and avoid repeating his failures. One of which was washing out of the Army after only thirteen years of service.

Jake intended to make the Army his life. It was way too early to be making a nuisance of himself.

So, under the circumstances, what would Reacher do?

Jake looked out at the storm, the rain streaming down the window, and knew he was on a path that could go bad and lead him into the lonely place where Reacher dwelled. Among thugs and thieves and killers of all stripes with no family and few friends.

Could he handle the challenges as well as Reacher had while still avoiding Reacher's defeats?

Truth was, Jake didn't know. But he knew he had to find out. He was all in at this point. No turning back.

His mind was already working on the next move.

He called Vaughan. She'd rented a room at a cheap motel. Time was short. He couldn't afford to waste any of it.

"I'm on my way. Be there in twenty," Jake said as tossed a few things into a duffel and stepped out into the night, head down, buffeted by the rain and wind, headed toward the Jeep.

Jake parked outside the Dewdrop Motel, an old place on the outskirts of town where the rooms were cheap and often rented by the hour. He knocked on the door to Room 112 and Vaughan let him in.

Chapter 8

The familiar smell of booze and sweat filled Maureen Tolliver's nostrils as she sat in the deep shadows of Bull Gator's, a dive bar in Arlington, Virginia. The owner had fought a twelve-foot gator in the Everglades, he claimed. A plastic version of the defeated beast was mounted behind the bar, above the bar's neon sign.

The place was filled with ex-military, rough men and women who lived through tough times and came out of the military to live rough lives. Raucous voices, arguments and fights were layered over music and blaring televisions to produce a background of constant pulsing, high decibel camouflage.

Jeffrey Willard, eyes hidden beneath heavy brows, his face betraying nothing, sat next to Tolliver. Both had their backs to the wall and kept a vigilant watch for the point when violence boiled over into an all-out brawl, as it often did.

"You've seen the latest reports." Tolliver kept her voice low and steady, but something was gnawing at her gut.

"I have," Willard replied, tinged with defiance.

A sudden crash from the front of the room was followed by shouted curses. Her eyes darted to the back exit, but Willard seemed unfazed.

"Small fight," he said, his tone dismissive. "They do that several times a night in this place. Nothing to worry about yet."

Tolliver forced herself to focus, pushing away the nagging threat of vulnerability. She wasn't worried about personal safety. She could defend herself. She'd been doing it her entire life. She simply didn't want to be discovered here.

"We need to act faster, Willard. Time is not on our side."

"The operation is risky, and you know it. Planning and financing are key," he countered, leaning his chair back on two legs to rest against the wall. "I'm not doing this for fame and glory. Money, Tolliver. And lots of it. That's why I'm here. Did you get the funding or not?"

She looked at him, something cold settling in her chest. "We need to trust each other."

"Trust?" he said, hard and bitter. "Trust is a tool. You had it before you screwed me over. After that, you show me the cash first. So where is it?"

Tolliver's hands tightened into fists under the table. The tension in the room was a living thing that seemed to feed on hard words and hard feelings. She felt her entire body vibrating with it.

"What's going on over there?" she demanded, her voice rising to be heard over the cacophony in the bar.

"Nothing to worry about," Willard said, but his eyes flicked toward the front door.

The fistfight had turned into a brawl. One guy had pulled a sidearm and was waving it in the air.

A moment later Tolliver heard the distant wail of sirens, cutting through the night like a knife.

"We need to leave. Now," she said urgently.

The walls of the bar seemed to close in around her. When the cops showed up, she'd be exposed, vulnerable. She couldn't be arrested, and she couldn't be seen here, either. Her carefully constructed world would come crashing down. Which she would absolutely not allow.

"It's not time to go yet. We've got things to discuss," Willard said. "This operation is too important. Don't let your emotions get in the way."

She turned to face him, eyes blazing, anger raising her heartbeat to the tempo of the blaring music. "Don't you dare lecture me. I know what's at stake here. And I know what you've done. Those secrets you're hiding? They won't stay buried forever."

His eyes narrowed. "Just get my money. Then we'll talk."

She flipped her hoodie up over her head and stood. "Is there a back exit? Can we reach it?"

"Yeah. Follow me." Willard pulled his hoodie up, too. He led the way.

The sirens were closer now, a reminder of the dangers they faced, balancing on the edge of a volatile precipice. If Willard could execute the plan, he'd be an obscenely wealthy man and she'd be promoted to the Joint Chiefs.

If he failed...

Tolliver was a hard woman, tough as nails, but she was not invincible. Willard, with his defiance and greed, was an unknown variable. No time to think about that now.

Willard took long strides toward the back exit, Tolliver close on his heels.

He pushed the bar across the door with his forearm to avoid leaving DNA or prints and they stepped out into the darkness. He shoved the door hard to close it securely behind them.

Blue and red lights flashed around the corners. Police cruisers had pulled into the front parking lot, and more were on the way.

"I'll be in touch." Tolliver strode past Willard and moved into the dark alley.

"The clock is ticking," Willard replied.

She ignored him and headed toward her vehicle parked six blocks away.

At the end of the first block, Tolliver paused and turned to watch Willard as he sauntered down the alley in the opposite direction.

She stuffed her hands into her empty pockets. What happened to her cell phone? She peered into the alley and found it on the ground. She bent to retrieve it and dropped it into her pocket and headed on her way.

Cold reality settled in her bones. Willard was the right man for this job, but she didn't trust him.

He didn't trust her, either.

Which wasn't ideal, but it was okay. She didn't intend to marry the guy. Her plan was to use him for his skills and resources and pay him well to deliver both.

But Willard wasn't the only man in the world who could do this job. She wouldn't hesitate to move on if he failed.

Chapter 9

Samantha Vaughan's room was filled with photographs, documents, and a dry-erase board covered in notes. Vaughan was pacing, her face drawn and her eyes wide with intensity.

"My husband was a wonderful man. I've been trying to figure out why anyone would want to kill him," she began, not wasting any time. "Local authorities and military police say they investigated but found nothing to suggest that David's death wasn't natural causes."

"They'll keep looking, won't they?"

Vaughan shook her head. "They've held the file open as a courtesy to me. But they're not really doing anything now, budgets and manpower being what they are."

Jake stood looking at the board she'd assembled. She had photos of the facility where David had lived these past few years. Off to one side was a snap of David in his hospital bed.

His body was covered by a tented sheet. Otherwise, he looked like an emaciated teenager with a scruffy beard and a bandaged skull.

But his eyes were open, and his lips lifted slightly. His wife had probably asked him to smile for the photo and David had tried to oblige.

"This facility looks pretty remote. I mean, you're the cop. I've never investigated a murder," Jake said. "But if David was targeted, how did the killer even know to find him there?"

"Exactly. And that's only one of a zillion unanswered questions," Vaughan replied with a weak grin. "Cops have a lot of questions. It's how we find answers."

"Such as?"

"How did the killer know that David had a private room and where it was inside the facility? How did he make it all the way to David's bedside without anyone noticing? How could he have killed David and gotten away?" Vaughan recited, as if she'd memorized the list. "And that's just for starters."

"You think the killer had inside information," Jake nodded as he examined the board and listened carefully. "Are you saying David's death was some sort of conspiracy?"

"We might have something bigger than my husband's murder going on here," she replied, not wasting time arguing about how to label it. "David died of sudden cardiac arrest. I've seen the autopsy report. No question about cause of death. It's possible he survived all those years and then died of natural causes."

"But you don't believe that. So what do you believe?"

"David was silenced. For a reason," Vaughan said quietly. "We find that reason, we'll be closer to knowing who killed him."

Jake's heart skipped a beat. "What do you mean?"

"David was the only surviving member of his unit in Iraq. He and his squad witnessed horrific things over there. Some of what went on wasn't strictly by-the-book. Other stuff would be called war crimes now, probably. He never told me exactly what happened, but I know he was troubled about it," Vaughan directed him to the board, pointing to a photo of David with his squad sitting together in a Humvee in a dusty lot halfway around the world. "One theory I'm following is that something David saw back then is related to his murder."

"How do you know all this?" Jake asked, stunned.

She handed him a diary. "I found David's journal. He wrote brief notes about what he saw, what he knew."

Jake took the small leather-bound book and flipped through the pages. David's handwriting was printing, really. Small, neat letters crammed close together on unlined paper. Some of the ink was smeared and some of the pages had been wet. The ink had all but disappeared in several places.

"Do you know who the other members of David's squad were? Names, addresses, family and friends?

Maybe we can track them down and get a better handle on what happened over there," Jake suggested.

"They started with ten and there were eight still alive when this photo was taken," Vaughan pointed to a group of soldiers gathered around a picnic table. "They're all dead now."

It looked like they'd just finished dinner. They were armed and wearing their uniforms. She pointed to each one as she recited their names.

"Do you have contact information for their families?"

"Last known addresses and the names of their survivors, as listed in their Army files," she replied. "They're all over the country. Talking to them in person would be better than cold calls on the phone. But with just the two of us working the case, that's not likely to happen. We don't have the budget for it, for one thing."

"It's a place to start, though."

Vaughan paused a lot longer this time before she continued, "David and the other members of his squad were part of something. He was worried about it. I don't know exactly what it was. But they all died when their Humvee hit that IED. David was the only one left."

Jake said nothing.

"When David—" she paused to clear her throat. "While David was comatose, he was no threat to anyone. But after he woke up, I think someone was worried that he might remember something and report it. It's the only thing that makes any sense to me. There's no other reason why anyone would want to kill him."

As far as you know, Jake thought.

The reality of the situation sank in. The guilt, the horror, and the pain in David's journal were palpable, even to a first-time reader who hadn't known David or his squad.

"What did they do, exactly? I mean, why now? If the old crimes didn't come to light after all this time..." Jake asked.

Vaughan shrugged. "I have no idea. I wish I did."

Jake shook his head and pointed at the hospital picture. "Looking at David in this photo, I can't see anybody feeling threatened by him, even now. He wasn't a big guy to begin with. And at this point, I mean, what could he actually do? Didn't you tell me he wasn't even able to speak?"

"Not yet," Vaughan said. "But that's where he was headed. We were hoping for a full recovery. We thought it might take a couple of years, and he'd certainly have residuals. But the docs offered us hope and we clung to it like a man overboard clings to a life raft, you know?"

Jake nodded. He did know. He understood perfectly.

"What's the plan?" he asked with hard determination.

"We need to find David's killer. Bring him to justice," Vaughan said, her voice shaking with resolve. "I've contacted some of my old colleagues, and I'm digging into military records. We can start by identifying everyone who served with David and track movements after they returned from Iraq."

Jake looked at the board, his mind working rapidly. "We'll also need to find out who the killer is connected to now, who might be protecting him, who he has power over."

"Exactly," Vaughan nodded. "I've started building a profile, but we need more information. We need to find out where he's vulnerable."

"Okay."

"We have to be smart about this. He's dangerous, Jake. Any man who would do that to David…" She shivered like a naked woman in an ice storm.

"I know," Jake said, his voice steady.

They spent the next few hours working through details, creating a strategy, and identifying potential leads.

"I need to see where David died," Jake said.

"Why?"

"I don't know. Something about the way I'm visualizing this just feels off. Maybe the killer is local and they just haven't looked in the right places." He pulled his phone from his pocket and pulled up flights to Colorado Springs. "Flight time is three hours. There's a flight leaving Columbus tonight. Looks like I can get on it."

She offered a weak smile as she teased, "Reacher would walk all the way. Or hitch."

Jake flashed a responsive grin. "Yeah, and it would take him a week to get there. We don't have that kind of time."

"Okay. You go. I'm driving up to DC. I've got a meeting with a senator."

"Wow. Go for the big guns right out of the gate, eh?"

Vaughan said, "It's not what you know in life, Jake. It's who you can persuade to help you."

Which was why she'd come looking for Reacher. And ended up with Jake, a poor substitute.

"Okay. Send me all the files you have collected so far. I'll have three hours on the plane to get up to speed," Jake said. "Keep in touch."

As Jake left the motel room, he looked back at Samantha, her face etched by grief and determination.

What would Reacher do?

He'd helped Vaughan once before. No way in hell Reacher would turn his back on her now.

Chapter 10

Jake's plane touched down in Colorado Springs under a heavy, clouded sky. He rented an SUV and followed the navigation south on I-25 toward the remote facility where David had spent his last years. Without Samantha's guidance and the exact address, he'd never have found the place.

He took the exit off the expressway and followed the winding roads. The Olympic TBI Center was north of Fort Carson, located on property owned by the Department of Defense, even though the facility was operated by private contractors.

David Vaughan had been a veteran injured in war. That gave him certain rights and benefits. One of which was lifetime medical care. Which was more than okay. It was the least Uncle Sam could do.

The sad truth was that VA healthcare was uneven, which was not okay. Not even remotely. Some VA healthcare was outsourced to excellent providers. And some of the private contractors were motivated by profit rather than duty, loyalty, and honor. None of that was okay with Jake.

As he pulled into the dusty parking lot, Jake saw the place as Samantha's photos depicted. Decayed, unkempt, and ignored. The remnants of Army décor were comforting. Surrounded by thick forest and isolated from prying eyes, the location itself felt ominous. Maybe because of what had happened to David Vaughan here.

Jake shook off the foreboding, parked, and squared his shoulders to face what lay ahead. He didn't bother to lock the rental. No one was wandering around here. Chances of losing the SUV to grand theft auto while he was inside were slim.

He strode across the dusty parking lot and took the steps up to the front entrance two at a time. The door squeaked on its hinges as he crossed the threshold to the inside.

Jake recognized the mottled green tile on the floor. There was plenty of it all over the place back at Fort Moore. He'd walked a lot of miles on that tile during basic training, too.

The desk clerk was a sloppy civilian in a grubby gray sweatshirt and wrinkled jeans, scrawny and unwashed.

Jake could smell the fear on him across the room.

Recognition flickered in his eyes, followed by fear. He stood up quickly when Jake approached the oak hutch where a busy duty sergeant would have once sat.

"You!" he exclaimed, backing away from Jake's long reach.

He had never met the guy before, but his reaction was amusing and proved Jake was on the right track.

"I'm here about David Vaughan." Jake moved closer to the desk where he could read the nameplate. "You're Neske?"

The guy nodded furiously.

"I need to know what happened to Vaughan, Neske."

Neske's gaze darted toward the door, around the room, and back. Probably looking for reinforcements, but none materialized.

He snapped to attention. Stood up straight, snapped his feet together, shoulders back, head up, gaze level, arms straight, hands by his sides, thumbs in line with the seams of his pants.

"I don't know anything," he whined.

Jake slammed his hands down on the desk, leaning in close. "Don't lie to me, Neske. You were stationed at the front desk the night Vaughan died. What did you see?"

"I wasn't here!" Neske blurted, his voice shaking and a string of drool leaking from the corners of his mouth.

Jake grabbed him by the collar, his face inches away. "Why not? You left your post?"

"I had something else to do," Neske stammered, his eyes wide with terror. "Please, don't tell him. He'll kill me!"

"Who are you so worried about?" Jake demanded.

"You know. You look just like him. He didn't tell me his name. He's gotta be your brother or something, right?" Neske said. "He came here with Vaughan's wife. Said he'd send someone to check up that we were taking good care of Vaughan. That's you. He sent you. Right?"

Reacher came to visit David Vaughan? He was with Samantha? The truth hit Jake like a two-by-four to the face. Vaughan could have told him Reacher had been here. She didn't. What else was she concealing from him?

Jake covered his surprise and tightened his grip. "Tell me what you know, and I'll think about not telling him."

"I didn't see anything, I swear! But..." Neske hesitated, glancing around nervously.

"But what?" Jake growled.

"There was a car. I saw it when I left. It was down the road, just out of view. I didn't think much of it at the time, but it was strange," Neske said, pushing the words out through Jake's hold at his throat. "W-we don't get many visitors and it wasn't a c-car I recognized."

Jake released him with a backward shove, knocking Neske into the wall. Jake's mind was racing. "Describe the vehicle."

Neske rubbed his neck, still shaking. "Beat up old model black sedan. Paint was sun-damaged. Couple of dings in the quarter panels. Tinted windows."

"You're describing thousands of cars on the road. Give me something specific."

Neske scrunched his nose and squeezed his eyes shut. After another moment, he opened his eyes and said, "I caught the license plate, but only the first few numbers. It started with 'TR.'"

"What state?"

Neske shrugged. "I don't know. Colorado, probably? I mean, the wreck didn't seem like it could have traveled far, you know?"

Not much to go on, but better than nothing. "Anything else?"

Neske shook his head, his eyes pleading. "That's all I know, I swear."

"I need to see your CCTV video," Jake demanded.

"W-we don't have cameras here," Neske whined.

"No? Seems negligent at the very least," Jake snarled. "How do you keep track of the safety of your patients?"

Neske shrugged. "I don't make the rules, man."

"What about military satellites? Anybody check those?" Jake balled his fists by his side, itching to punch the guy, just because he was such a worthless piece of scum.

"No, man. I don't know." Neske's eyes grew wider, noticing Jake's waning patience. He shook his head. "I didn't know there were satellites. They're not ours. We wouldn't be allowed to check them even if we wanted to."

Jake stared at him, weighing his words. "You left David Vaughan unprotected. He died on your watch. You know what that means?"

"He was okay. I mean, he was never any trouble. Like a brain damaged lizard. IQ of a goldfish. He'd been here for years with no problems. I didn't mean for anything to happen to him," Neske said, his voice breaking. "Vaughan had a heart attack. How was I supposed to know? I couldn't do anything even if I'd been here. Really."

Jake continued to glare.

"Vaughan would have died anyway, man," Neske sniveled like a six-year-old.

"If I find out you've lied to me…" Jake frowned.

"I swear. I'm telling the truth," Neske blubbered. "Please, just don't tell him. He'll kill me. He said he would, and I believe him."

Jake grabbed Neske by the collar again and shoved him toward the hallway. "Show me."

"Show you what?"

"I want to see Vaughan's room. Now."

Neske nodded furiously like a fast-action bobble head. He wiped drool from the corner of his mouth with the back of his hand.

"This way, sir," he said, shuffling ahead, leading the way.

Jake followed, absorbing everything he saw and smelled and heard along the way.

The place was unnaturally quiet. A couple of young men were tied to wheelchairs staring slack-jawed through the windows. Neither one could give a decent description, even if they'd seen someone suspicious the night Vaughan died.

At the end of the hallway, Neske turned and eventually reached Vaughan's room. He pushed the door open and stood aside.

Jake went in alone. The room hadn't changed much from the photos he'd seen on Samantha's white board. Except the bed had been stripped and all of the medical equipment removed.

Nothing relating to David Vaughan remained in this room. There was nothing more Jake could learn here. He returned to the hallway.

Jake grabbed Neske's grimy sweatshirt again and leaned in close, his voice a menacing whisper. "You better pray that Vaughan died a natural death, and nothing could have been done to save him. Because that was on you. To keep him safe. You're a disgrace to the Army and I intend to report your employer and get this place cleaned up. Do yourself a favor. Find another job before I come back here."

Jake gave him a push that landed Neske on his ass on the floor. He made no effort to stand.

Jake wanted to kick him about two hundred times. Reacher would have.

He turned and left while he could still control his fury. A few dozen steps returned him to his rental where he started up and retraced his route to the interstate, still fuming.

He glanced at the rearview mirror, half hoping to see the facility explode in Reacher-like fashion. But all that lay behind him was Neske, the shadow of a man more afraid of Reacher than the severe penalties for dereliction of duty.

David Vaughan had been National Guard. Infantry. Assigned to the First Armored Division. He'd served two tours and come home a damaged hero. He deserved better than this and so did his wife. They all did.

Neske and the others assigned to care for patients like David Vaughan were a disgrace. Jake vowed to get them shit-canned. Court-martialed, if he could possibly make that happen. Although Neske was already discharged from the Army, so probably not.

He'd learned two new things, though. The first was that Jack Reacher and Samantha Vaughan had been a lot closer than she'd admitted to Jake. Which somehow felt like a betrayal. She should have told him. Why didn't she?

The second thing? An old black sedan was nearby at the time. Neske's memory of the partial license plate was a lead. Perhaps an insignificant one. But still, a lead he didn't have before.

He gripped the wheel tighter and accelerated down the winding road. First things first. Finding the driver of that black sedan.

Chapter 11

Wednesday, June 8
Near Fort Carson, CO

Jake's phone buzzed with incoming messages and emails, but he ignored them all as he dialed Vaughan's number. The rhythmic tapping of his fingers on the steering wheel was the only sound in the car as he waited for her to pick up.

"Jake? Is that you?" Vaughan's voice was hurried, a touch of worry lacing her words.

"Yeah, it's me," Jake replied steadily. "I've got something for you. A lead."

"What is it?" she asked, her tone sharpening.

"An old black sedan, banged up in prior accidents, tinted windows, partial license plate starting with 'TR.' Could be a Colorado plate. It was spotted near the facility the night David died. Guy at the duty desk said he noticed the black car that night because it didn't fit the area."

There was a pause on the other end of the call, and Jake could almost hear Samantha's mind working.

"That's something," she finally said. "I'll get on it right away, see if we can track down that car. How's everything else?"

"I confronted the clerk, Neske," Jake informed her. "He's a disgrace. And curiously terrified of Reacher. Maybe because he left his post the night David died."

"Terrified of Reacher?" Vaughan's voice crackled with surprise. "What does he have to do with this?"

He briefly explained Neske's reaction when he saw Jake. "He thought Reacher sent me to check on David. And to beat his ass because David died and Neske didn't stop it. Believe me, I was tempted."

"Interesting," Vaughan murmured. "I took Reacher to see David once. But I didn't know he'd threatened Neske. Could explain why David's room and his body were cleaner and nicer after Reacher left. I'll keep that in mind."

Her explanation made Jake feel better. Maybe she wasn't hiding her relationship to Reacher, whatever it was. Now was not the time to follow up. But that time would come.

Jake grinned, even though Vaughan couldn't see him. "Whatever Reacher said to Neske, it definitely made an impression."

"I'll bet it did," Vaughan chuckled, and it was nice to hear her lighten up a little. "By the way, I'm almost to

DC. The senator owes me a favor, and I think it's time to pull some strings."

"That's perfect. I'll meet you in DC. We can regroup, compare notes."

"Let's do that. I'll text you the details once I've stopped driving."

Jake sensed the fatigue in her voice. "You holding up okay?"

"I'm managing." Samantha's sigh was almost inaudible. "Just need to keep moving, you know?"

"Yeah, I know." There was no time for breaks now. "We'll get to the bottom of this."

"I know we will." Her voice was firmer now, filled with determination, and a hint of righteous anger.

Which was good as far as Jake was concerned. She was entitled to be angry. And anger was a better motivator than the overwhelming grief she was carrying around.

"Another thing," Jake said while she was still listening. "That facility doesn't have any CCTV, as you know. But the place is located on property owned by the DoD."

"What are you thinking?"

"There's a possibility that Uncle Sam has satellites watching the place," Jake said.

"You think so?" Vaughan's tone was hopeful. "It's pretty remote and the Army doesn't have anything much to do with the place, they tell me. Why would they watch it?"

"They might not be watching the hospital, exactly. But general surveillance satellites are not that precise. They're watching Fort Carson because they watch military bases around the world," Jake said, in a long speech for him. "They might have caught something without trying to. It's worth checking, anyway. Do you have any contacts you can ask about government satellite imagery?"

Vaughan paused a good long time, as if she were running through her mental list of contacts. "Can't think of anyone. Unless the senator might know. Once I find him."

"Meanwhile, don't Colorado agencies have traffic cams posted in this area?"

"Possibly. Our department is smaller, but I've worked a couple of cases with Colorado Springs PD. Their jurisdiction doesn't stretch that far south. I haven't had to deal with that sort of thing much. I'll make a call," Vaughan said.

"I'll check around, too. Between the two of us, we'll find something."

"Thanks, Jake. I'll see you in DC."

"Copy that." Jake disconnected the call, his mind already racing ahead.

They had a new lead, however slim, and a plan coming together. Meeting with Vaughan in DC made sense. Maybe he could connect with Otto there, too. His forty-eight hours were rushing past. He had no time to waste.

But something nagged at the back of his mind.

When he'd first entered the hospital, Reacher's name had come up with Neske too quickly. Reacher hadn't been around for a few years. No matter what Reacher had said to Neske back then, his terror now seemed too fresh after such a long passage of time.

Was there more to Reacher's involvement than Neske admitted? Had Reacher been around again, more recently? Checking up on things?

Reacher wouldn't have killed David Vaughan. That idea was too crazy to be considered.

Jake tried to smack it down as instantly as it had popped up. But he couldn't simply forget about it.

The idea was there. It wouldn't go away on its own.

He pushed the thought aside for now. Multi-tasking was a myth. The brain could only work on one thing at a time.

The black sedan's image loomed large in his mind. It was a thread, one he intended to pull. It wouldn't unravel the whole story surrounding David Vaughan's life and death. But it was a start.

He'd checked the flight schedules. No flights out of Colorado Springs to DC tonight. The fastest option was a nonstop departing from nearby Pueblo.

He merged onto the highway heading south and stepped on the gas, the road unwinding before him.

They were one step closer to knowing what happened to David Vaughan. Jake could feel it. But they needed help.

The next call he made was to Agent Otto. She worked for the feds. And she had friends in high places. Which meant she had access to intel he couldn't reach.

Otto's phone rang several times before kicking over to voicemail. He left a cryptic message. "It's Jake. Please call me back."

He'd been driving on the interstate for miles, checking every pole and watching the license plates. The area was sparsely populated and much of the land belonged to the government.

The Colorado plates he saw fit a familiar pattern. Three letters followed by another letter and two numbers. Six digits separated by a square green icon. Plates were mounted on the front and back of the vehicles. Front plates made it easier and more reliable to collect tolls, he figured.

Still, car crashes, crime, and vehicle breakdowns were common everywhere. Some government agency should be patrolling the road. Which should include traffic cams.

Less than a mile later, he saw the first one. The next was two miles south of the first. And another was posted two miles after that.

Who owned those cameras? How could Jake access the video?

The clock in his head said he would miss the only flight to DC leaving tonight if he turned around to drive north and check for cameras on the way to Colorado Springs.

Something Vaughan should be able to find out.

He'd confirmed the traffic cams existed. He felt fairly confident about the satellites, too. Someone would have video surrounding the area on the night David Vaughan was killed.

All he had to do was find it.

Chapter 12

Wednesday, June 8
Washington, D.C.

Kim's personal phone buzzed with a message when she stepped out of the helo onto firm ground in DC. She glanced at the caller ID. She picked up the message and then pushed the redial. He answered like he'd been holding the phone in his hand. Perhaps he was.

"Jake? What's going on?"

"I've got a lead. Could be connected to Reacher, so I thought you'd be interested."

"What is it?" she asked, heading across the tarmac to a waiting sedan that would take her to her meeting with Cooper.

Jake quickly filled her in on the details of his visit to the facility near Fort Carson, the black sedan, and the frightened clerk's reaction to Reacher's name.

"Sounds promising," Otto said as she tossed her bags into the backseat and slid in behind them. Cooper was waiting, and the man had zero patience.

The driver pulled away from the curb and blended in with the usual heavy DC traffic.

"The facility where David was recovering has no CCTV," Jake said. "There are traffic cams along I-25. And there could also be government satellite surveillance of the area. Can you find out?"

Otto leaned back in the plush leather seat, considering. "It won't be easy, and it could take some time. But I'll try to find anything I can."

"Thank you," Jake said with gratitude. "I'll be in DC tomorrow. We can meet up."

"Sounds good. I'll call you later," Kim said. "And Jake, be careful. If this does connect back to Reacher, you could be stirring up something way more dangerous than you're prepared for."

"I know," Jake replied.

Kim disconnected the call without saying more. She didn't have time right now to explore all the ways Reacher could be up to his neck involved with the Vaughans.

The limo pulled up in front of the Hoover building and she got out with her bags. Cooper was waiting upstairs. She had no idea how long she'd be tied up once she stepped inside or where she'd be going next or when she'd have another chance to connect with Jake.

The familiar thrill of excitement mixed with foreboding roiled her stomach. Jake's lead could be something big in her hunt for Reacher, or it could be a dead end. Either way, she had to follow it.

She pulled a fresh burner from her laptop case and dialed Gaspar as she walked toward the Hoover building. He'd retired a while back due to medical issues that prevented him from physically doing the job.

But there was nothing wrong with his mind. Or his skills. Or his resources. Quite the opposite. Gaspar was more valuable to Kim now that he wasn't FBI.

He'd landed a great job with Scarlett Investigations in Houston, which gave him broader and deeper access to almost everything Kim needed. Even better, he'd never refuse her anything. He'd started the Reacher assignment with her, and he meant to see it through, whether he was on the FBI payroll or not.

"Good evening, Sunshine," he said with a smile in his voice when he picked up the call.

Kim came straight to the point. "We might have something on Reacher."

"You're always so optimistic…" Gaspar deadpanned. "If I had a dollar for every time you've said that these past few months, I'd be a rich man."

"You are a rich man. You've got a great job, five kids, and a wife who's a saint to put up with you. Plus, you have this amazing former partner who can't seem to let you go. What more does one man need?" Kim jousted back and Gaspar laughed, which was always good to hear.

She quickly filled him in on Jake's call, the black sedan, and the possible surveillance.

"So you want me to find the surveillance, if there is any. Maybe locate the black sedan. Perhaps get a usable photo to ID the driver," Gaspar said, already clacking the keys on his keyboard.

"Yes," Otto replied firmly. "And keep a close eye on Jake. I'm stuck dealing with Cooper at the moment. But if Jake's onto something, I want to be there when he finds it."

Or when Reacher finds Jake, she thought but didn't say. She'd learned that Reacher would do everything within his power to keep his friends alive. Of course, he'd do that and more for his one and only nephew.

"Got it. I'll start working on the satellite angle." Gaspar hummed. "If Reacher is involved, whatever this is will be complicated. And deadly. Watch your back, Suzie Wong."

"Copy that, Chico," she said. "One more thing."

"There's always one more thing with you, isn't there?" He didn't bother to disguise his amusement.

"One of the murder victims was Emma Fonda. Body was found in a Miami warehouse. I sent you all of the intel we have about the case. Look into it for me, will you?" she asked, picking up the pace.

"What are you looking for, exactly?"

"At this point, we don't know what we don't know," Kim replied.

"I'll do what I can," Gaspar said before he disconnected.

Kim dropped the burner into her pocket, grabbed her bags, and marched toward the Hoover Building's main entrance and went inside. The guard checked her ID and waved her toward the elevator bank.

She strode through the maze of corridors that made up the Hoover Building. Her heels clicked a steady staccato beat on the polished floor, emphasizing her determination.

Jake's call was unsettling. The black sedan, the facility near Fort Carson, the connection to Reacher—these were important facts, but they were pieces of a larger puzzle. Nothing was ever simple where Reacher was concerned.

And now, she had been tapped for the Hornet murder case with Cooper pulling the strings. Which meant the Hornet case was anything but ordinary.

Cooper was waiting in his office. For the first time, she noticed how old and tired he looked. The job was wearing him down. She understood how that felt.

"Agent Otto, please have a seat," he said, motioning to a chair across from his desk. "I brought you in on this Hornet case for a very specific reason."

"I figured. It's not like you to operate on a whim."

He cut right to the chase. "As you know, the three Hornet case victims we've identified so far were all military, all female, and all killed in the same way—by air embolus injection into the jugular vein."

"What does this have to do with David Vaughan?" she asked, her voice steady.

·

Cooper's expression was grave. "David Vaughan breaks the pattern because he wasn't female or homeless, exactly. But he was military and killed by air embolus. My intel says the four cases are all connected, loosely, perhaps, but connected nonetheless."

He paused, letting the information sink in.

"What intel?" Kim asked. "I've seen all the files. There's nothing in them about David Vaughan."

Cooper's lips turned up at one corner. Not a sneer, but not a smile, either. "You doubt my word?"

She ignored the question. She didn't trust him. He knew it. And she knew he knew it. No benefit to belaboring the point.

"And Reacher?" Kim asked, her mind racing. "How is he involved in whatever this is?"

"These murders are connected to Reacher if they are connected to Vaughan." Cooper's eyes darkened. "Reacher had an affair with Vaughan's wife."

"Were they married at the time?" Kim asked, adding the new information to what she already knew.

"Yes. Vaughan was comatose. Had been for a while. All but dead," Cooper continued. "She probably justified the affair that way. I'm sure Reacher did, if he thought about it at all."

"How do you know?"

"Because I know Reacher. He lives in the moment. Takes everything as it comes. He had a pretty, willing woman within reaching distance?" Cooper raised both eyebrows and tilted his head. "That's a no-brainer for him. One of his mottos is never look back."

"How does that justify having an affair with a dying veteran's wife?" Kim's mind was spinning. The implications were enormous.

"Another reason I wanted to see you. To be sure you haven't romanticized him. Have you?" Cooper wagged his head and grinned this time, for real. "You have. You think Reacher is some sort of what? Knight errant? He slips on his tarnished armor and travels the country putting the bad guys in their place and saving damsels in distress? Is that it?"

She didn't admit anything, but she didn't deny it, either. Her views about Reacher had changed.

And Cooper was sharp enough to figure that out. He didn't need any help from her on that score.

Her voice calm and controlled. "What do you want me to do?"

Chapter 13

"I want you to find the connection," Cooper said, leaning forward, his eyes intense. "Find out how the female victims are linked, how their deaths connect to David Vaughan's, and how all of it ties back to Reacher. If he's involved, we need to know how, and we need to know now."

"Why? Why is it so important to find out if Reacher's involved?" Kim asked, pressing him harder than she usually did.

Maybe she wore rose colored glasses where Reacher was concerned, but her days of hero worshiping Charles Cooper were long over, and he should know that, too.

Cooper's response was gruff. "You know Reacher's being considered for a classified assignment. We can't use him if he's under arrest for multiple murders."

"Reacher didn't murder those women or David Vaughan. We already know that," Kim said.

"You're clairvoyant now?"

"Victimology. Reacher doesn't kill people weaker than himself."

"You think not? Everyone is weaker than Reacher and he kills and maims whoever he chooses. Without a second's hesitation." Cooper chewed the inside of his lip. "What else?"

"Manner of death. Reacher wouldn't waste time injecting air emboli like that. If he wanted to kill them, he'd just break their necks and be done with it," Kim said, realizing the truth as she said it.

But just because she believed Reacher didn't kill David Vaughan or the female victims, didn't make it so.

Truth was, it was all too possible that Reacher killed them. Reacher did what he wanted, when he wanted.

Still, she couldn't see Reacher wanting to eliminate these particular victims. What would be the point?

"Maybe you're right. Hard to know in the abstract," Cooper replied, as if he'd conceded the matter when they both knew he had not. "But consider this. Reacher had an affair with Vaughan's wife while they believed the guy was practically a vegetable. What if Reacher wasn't the only man she's been involved with since her husband went to war?"

Kim blinked.

Jealousy.

The suggestion took root in that moment, just as Cooper had known it would. If Vaughan's wife had a new man, her lover might want the husband out of the way, too.

Beyond that, wives and husbands killed each other all the time. For a whole host of reasons. Mercy killing was one. David Vaughan wasn't supposed to wake up, but he never actually died. How long was a man supposed to suffer? And how long should a wife's world revolve around a husband in that situation?

Okay, so it was completely possible that the wife, or her jealous lover, took David Vaughan's life.

Connecting David Vaughan's death to the other three victims didn't fit that paradigm, though. Did all of these women have jealous lovers, too? Unlikely.

As Kim processed the new intel and acknowledged the feasibility of Cooper's theories, he smirked and then his expression turned sour.

Crisply, he ordered, "Find Reacher. That's been your assignment for a while now. When you find him, you can ask all the questions you like about David Vaughan and his wife. He'll tell you the truth."

"You think so?"

"Of course. Why wouldn't he? Reacher thinks absolutely everything he does is justified. He'd have no reason not to tell you. I know the guy. You don't," Cooper said flatly. "Right now, I'm wondering if I chose the wrong agent for the job of finding him."

"Success would be more likely if you'd give me some support," Kim shot back, tired of taking the brunt of his frustration. "I don't even have a partner again. No office. No assistance. No access to databases or experts or even archived files. It's like you want me to fail. Is that it?"

"If you can't handle it on your own, you should just say so," Cooper replied. "I'll find someone else. We've got a lot of competent agents on the payroll eager to work off the books."

Reacher wasn't the only person Cooper knew well. Mrs. Otto's daughter, Kim, would never admit defeat or lack of confidence in the face of a direct assault. Certainly not to him.

Kim said nothing. Cooper gave her a curt nod to acknowledge that her defiance was noted and disregarded.

Cooper pushed a brown folder across the desk. "There's a potential new victim. A homeless female veteran. Her body's still fresh. Police are holding the crime scene for you for another half hour."

She opened the folder. Photos of the crime scene were on the top of the slim file.

Cooper said, "Found her a few hours ago."

"Same manner of death?" Kim asked, flipping through the few papers contained in the file before she stuffed the folder into her laptop case.

"I've uploaded everything we have at this point to your secure server. We'll have more once we make a positive ID. You need to get going," Cooper said. "We can't hold the crime scene any longer. The driver who brought you here will take you to the body."

Kim closed the folder and stuffed it into her bag. "How do the Piranhas fit into all of this?"

"Another thing to figure out," Cooper said flatly. "I'll send you what I have that's relevant."

The Hornet murder case was not just another assignment. It was a chance to unravel a web of lies and deceit, a chance to find the truth for these victims and maybe, just maybe, to find Reacher.

As she left Cooper's office, Kim's mind returned to Jake's call, the black sedan, the terrified clerk. These were not isolated events. Perhaps everything was connected, and Reacher was at the center, as Cooper claimed.

Kim believed Reacher didn't kill these women or David Vaughan. Not his style. Not even a little bit.

But was she right?

And what if she was right? If Reacher didn't kill them all, who did?

Chapter 14

Wednesday, June 8
Washington, D.C.

Kim Otto stood in the grimy alley behind a dive bar, shielded by the yellow police tape. The victim lay sprawled on the ground, lifeless eyes staring into oblivion. A team of forensic experts worked around the body, and local police officers cast resentful glances her way.

The detective in charge, a bulky man with a thick mustache, approached her, his eyes narrowed.

"You're FBI?" he asked, his tone more accusatory than curious.

"Special Agent Kim Otto," she replied, extending a hand and displaying her credentials.

He ignored the gesture. "Detective Joe Friday."

"Seriously?"

Joe Friday was a fictional police officer featured in an old television show Otto's parents watched in reruns when she was a kid. This guy looked nothing like the guy who played the role.

"My mother was a fan of the show and names are destiny," Friday replied curtly, flashing a deep frown in her direction. "We've got this under control. We need help from the Feds, we'll ask for it."

Otto ignored the slight, focusing on the task at hand. "I've been following similar cases. All the victims have common—"

"Yeah, yeah, I've read the reports," Friday cut her off. "Military veterans, homeless, drug addicted. We've got a handle on it."

"I need to see the body."

Friday's phone rang. He picked up and told the caller to hold, clearly not thrilled with Kim's request, but he had more pressing things on his plate. "Fine. You can look. But don't touch anything. And don't get in the way."

Friday stepped away for privacy to take his call. Otto approached the team working on the body, the smell of garbage and decay heavy in the air.

She crouched down, scanning for details. The team of forensic experts gave her a curious glance and continued their work. They had hours of processing to do.

The body was an adult female, excruciatingly thin. Dirty dark hair, nails chewed to the quick. Her clothes were several sizes too big for her, as if she'd borrowed them or snagged them from a shelter.

Track marks marred her arms, hands, and feet, indicating she'd been using drugs for a long time.

"Any idea how long she's been dead?" Kim asked.

"Won't know for sure until we do the autopsy, but I'd guess at least a couple of days. Maybe longer," one of the men said.

"No ID on the body?"

"Not yet," the man replied.

A woman working to preserve evidence on the body's hands glanced up toward Kim. "What are you looking for, specifically? I'll check for you."

"Any indication she'd been injected into her neck recently?"

The woman's eyes widened. "Strange question. She has a lot of needle marks all over her body. But let me see."

She paused her work on the hands and retrieved a small flashlight from her pocket. She moved to examine the dead woman's neck, shining the LED light on the neck from the ear to the collar bone on the right side and also on the left.

"There are four carotid arteries, a pair on each side of the neck," the woman said as she worked. "Internal and external carotids. They deliver oxygen rich blood from the heart to the head and the brain. An air embolus will kill when it gets into the blood. But if you want an injection site that will cause sudden cardiac arrest, faster to choose a jugular vein. Goes straight to the heart."

"Who would know that besides a pathologist?" Kim asked.

"Almost anybody with some medical training. It's a commonly used procedure to insert catheters for central venous access into a jugular vein," the tech explained as she continued her meticulous searching.

After a few tense moments, she pointed her flashlight and a gloved finger to a mark on the victim's skin on the side of her neck. "These are far from ideal conditions. We'll know more when we get her back to the morgue. But it's possible she was injected here."

"Thank you for checking." Kim knelt down to look at the mark. She could barely see it in the dim alley, even with the flashlight.

"What's that?" Kim asked, pointing to something reflective in the bottom of victim's shoe she noticed as she was moving to stand.

One of the other forensic experts, a young woman with a sharp gaze, reached into the shoe and pulled out a small stainless-steel rectangle. "Looks like a dog tag."

She put the dog tag into an evidence bag and handed the bag to Kim. "Be quick. Friday won't like you touching the evidence, even if it's inside the bag."

Kim examined the metal. It was definitely a dog tag. The size, shape, and color suggested Army or Air Force since both tags were the same these days.

If this tag belonged to the victim, her name was Skinner, Suanne A. The other lines on the tag were DoD ID number, blood type, and religious affiliation. Skinner's blood type was listed as "O Neg" and she was Catholic.

Kim snapped a couple of photos of the tag with her phone's camera and returned the evidence bag to the tech. Then she made a brief video and more snaps of the body and the crime scene.

She was preoccupied and didn't notice Detective Friday approaching until he was at her side again. "Told you, we've got this under control. Everything here says she was just another druggie who went down the wrong path."

Kim straightened, facing him. "That's a simplistic view, Detective. She's a veteran. All of these women served their country. Now they're being killed. Something more than a simple overdose is going on here."

Friday scoffed. "They served, then they fell. Happens all the time."

"Nothing harder to open than a closed mind, Detective," Kim said flatly. "I need everything you've got on this victim. Fast."

"Happy to be of service," Detective Friday said. "But I expect the same from you. Are we clear?"

"I understand. We're all on the same side here. We want to catch this killer, don't we?"

His gaze softened for a fraction of a second but hardened again quickly. "Yeah, well, just remember that."

As Kim left the scene on her way back to the limo, she dialed Gaspar's number again. When he picked up, she said, "We've got another victim. That's four women now. And David Vaughan."

"What about suspects? How many of those have you got?" Gaspar asked, preoccupied.

"Too many, Chico. Way too many."

Chapter 15

Thursday, June 9
Washington, D.C.

Maureen Tolliver's eyes were bleary from hours of paperwork, but the soft murmur of the television news station in the background kept her awake.

The grandfather clock's persistent ticking was a constant reminder of the relentless march of time. It was 2:00 a.m., yet sleep was a luxury she couldn't afford.

A sudden chime from her laptop caught her attention. Her breath caught as she read the notification.

A body found behind Bull Gator's. A woman. A veteran. Identified by a dog tag found in her shoe.

She leaned closer, squinting at the flickering images. Yellow crime scene tape, flashing police lights, and a journalist holding a microphone standing amid the officials. Everyone was wearing a serious expression.

Tolliver turned up the volume on the news report. The victim wasn't shown, of course. But the setting was familiar. Bull Gator's, the dive bar in Arlington, Virginia, was a place Tolliver knew well. She'd met Willard there only a few hours ago.

"In a tragic story, a woman was found dead in this alley tonight," the reporter said from the scene. "She was a veteran and a hero. Now she's gone. The police are asking anyone with information about what happened here to call the number on your screen."

The words hammered into Tolliver's brain, each one a cold, heavy weight.

She silenced the volume on the broadcast but left the captions on screen to follow the report at a glance.

Bull Gator's was popular with military veterans. People who should know the value of life but lived as if they were bulletproof. All of which meant this victim wasn't the first to die at Bull Gator's and, sadly, she wasn't likely to be the last.

Tolliver knew only too well how precious each veteran, especially the female officers, should be.

Building a strong fighting force by adding more female officers was a constant struggle. Despite millions spent on recruiting, the armed forces had fallen short on recruiting goals the past few years.

Losing the up-and-coming junior officers to combat injuries was an expected consequence of service, a fact of life Tolliver and the rest of DoD had internalized and attempted to manage.

But when the best of the recruits survived combat only to be murdered at home? That was another whole issue.

One she could exploit as she moved further up the career ladder herself, if she played this right.

This was the fourth victim. Tolliver shouldn't have known about the murders. But keeping secrets among governmental agencies was impossible, regardless of the procedures in place for handling confidential intel.

She assumed dozens of people probably knew about the murders by now, even if the full story hadn't reached the nightly news yet. Four women killed, all decorated veterans with bright futures now extinguished.

Her hand rested on the phone. She hesitated only a moment, even as she realized the call would open a Pandora's box of demands and questions she wouldn't answer.

She needed information and the best place to get it was from the top of the food chain. But she had to be careful, circumspect.

Charles Cooper, special assistant to the Director of the FBI, could be a prickly, relentless S.O.B. The last thing she wanted was to arouse his curiosity, but it couldn't be helped.

She called his private number.

"Cooper," he said when he answered.

"Tolliver," she replied, holding her voice steady despite the turmoil in her gut. "I just saw the news about the body near Bull Gator's. What can you tell me?"

Cooper's voice was guarded, suspicious. "Do you know these women?"

"You didn't seriously think you could keep these four related deaths under the radar?" Tolliver chose her words carefully. "The victims were all military. It's a matter of concern to me and to the Joint Chiefs if our veterans are being murdered. Even you should respect that."

Cooper asked, his voice tinged with challenge. "You're suggesting we've got a serial killer here? Some psycho is eliminating female officers specifically?"

"I didn't say that." Tolliver kept her voice cool. "But I need to understand what's going on. Read me in."

"You're sticking your nose where it doesn't belong," Cooper shot back. "Unless you know something I don't."

"If there's a pattern, if there's something we've missed... we owe it to them," she said.

There had been a time when Tolliver's appeals to Cooper's better nature were persuasive. That time was long gone. After years of professional sparring, they were wary colleagues at best.

"This is a law enforcement matter. There's nothing to be gained by spreading false information to the public," Cooper stated with conviction. "When we know something definitive, we'll report to DoD in the usual fashion."

"DoD is interested when our veterans are targeted," Tolliver told him firmly. "And you know as well as I do that there could be broader implications. We need to get ahead of this thing. The PR alone will be a nightmare to manage, given the current anti-war climate in the country."

"Broader implications?" he said, incredulously. "Sounds like your own personal interest to me. What's really driving these questions, Tolliver?"

A cold chill settled in her bones. A warning that he could get way too close to truths she would never reveal. She needed to be careful.

"My concern is for the safety and welfare of our military personnel, past, present, and future," she replied vigorously. "How easy do you think it will be to recruit great women when they end up drug addicted, homeless, and dead? What kind of thank you is that from a grateful nation for their service and sacrifice?"

"Don't play patriot games with me, Tolliver. You don't have an altruistic bone in your body," he snapped. "What aren't you telling me?"

"I don't report to you. You'll have to trust that I'm acting in DoD's best interests." Her voice was as icy as she could make it. "We both know you don't want me kicking this request upstairs."

"I'll consider it," he said grudgingly. "But you're treading dangerous ground. Be careful what you ask for."

"I know what I'm doing. And I expect your cooperation." With that, she hung up.

Charles Cooper was as insufferable as ever. The years had not mellowed him one bit.

He was right, though. This situation was dangerous. But she wouldn't back down. Quitting was out of the question.

She looked at the image of the most recent crime scene still dominating the local news.

Not so many years ago, she could have been one of these murdered women. Cooper had revealed more than he realized.

Could some misguided psycho believe killing the weak ones was doing a service to the remaining women in uniform?

The truth was a slippery thing, and one wrong move could unravel everything she'd spent years building.

Tolliver leaned back in her chair, heavy with the weight of secrets and lies.

The wars, foreign and domestic, were far from over. She'd spent years climbing her way to the top and she didn't intend to give up now.

Chapter 16

Thursday, June 9
Washington, D.C.

The early morning sun was just beginning to light up the streets of Washington, DC as Jake and Vaughan walked to the restaurant. They were silent at first, each lost in their thoughts, but the weight of the upcoming meeting hung heavy between them.

Finally, Vaughan broke the silence, her voice filled with determination. "We need to know what he knows, Jake. Senator Wilson's son was a member of David's squad in Iraq. He must have some information about what happened over there. That could help us. Give us another place to look, at least."

"Think about this, though." Jake glanced at her, his eyes filled with a mix of resolve and concern. "If someone really did kill David, then this thing goes deep. David's location wasn't a secret, but he'd only be found if someone was already looking for him."

She cocked her head as she listened to him. "I've interviewed more than one suspect in my life, you know."

"Asking the wrong questions of the wrong people could be painting a target on our backs," Jake said quietly.

Vaughan paled but she agreed. "Maybe you shouldn't come with me. You didn't even know David. There's no reason to put your life on the line. But I have to try. You understand that, right?"

"We'll find out what happened. But let's be smart about this." Jake reached over and gave her bicep a brief squeeze of reassurance. "We need to ask the right questions but be subtle about it."

"What do you mean?" Vaughan asked, her brow furrowed.

"Since David's entire squad was killed, we can't interrogate the people actually involved in whatever it was they were doing," Jake said. "Maybe Senator Wilson had direct contact with his son or other members of David's squad while their activities in Iraq were still happening. Someone might have filed reports, for example."

"True."

"Has anyone else has been asking questions about David or the squad itself recently? Or whether there have been other unexpected deaths tied back to that time."

Vaughan bit her lip, her mind working. "War is inherently political. Let's ask about political connections, any new players or unknown entities who might have a vested interest in the squad or its activities."

Jake nodded. "Right. And we need to watch his reactions closely. If he's hiding something, or if he's scared, we might be able to tell."

They fell into silence again as the restaurant came into view. Jake turned over questions in his mind, rehearsing what he might say, given the chance.

Vaughan's hand trembled slightly, and Jake gave her another reassuring squeeze. "We'll get through this. We'll find the truth."

As they approached the restaurant entrance, a chill wind whipped through between the buildings, and Vaughan shivered, pulling her coat tighter around her. She looked up at Jake, her eyes filled with uncertainty.

"What if we're wrong, Jake? What if David's death really was just his time?" Vaughan inhaled deeply, as if she drew courage from the oxygen. "We talked about dying, you know. David and me. He believed that when it's your time, it's your time, you know? He thought there was nothing you could do to change it."

Jake's jaw tightened, and he looked away for a moment before meeting her eyes again. "We're not wrong. There's something bigger at play here."

They entered the restaurant, the warmth and the smell of coffee enveloping them, but Jake doubted Vaughan felt comforted.

As they were led to the table where Senator Wilson was waiting, Vaughan's phone buzzed in her purse. Her face paled as she glanced at the screen.

"Jake," she whispered, showing him the phone.

It was an anonymous message: "Stop asking questions."

Someone was watching them. Someone knew what they were doing.

"Too late for that." Jake gave her a reassuring grin and kept walking.

The dining room was filled with the gentle clinking of cutlery and low murmurs of conversation as Vaughan and Jake were ushered to their table. Vaughan's eyes were haunted, but there was nothing Jake could do about it.

Senator Wilson, a tall man with a dark tan, a strong jawline, and a politician's practiced smile, stood to greet them. He extended his hand in friendship and Vaughan reciprocated. "Mrs. Vaughan, my condolences once again. Your husband is with the angels now."

He turned to Jake, offering his hand again. "And you must be Jake Reacher. I've heard about you."

"Sir." Jake nodded and shook hands, his eyes never leaving the senator's face.

They took their seats, and after a brief exchange of pleasantries while the waitress delivered coffee, Vaughan was the first to speak.

She cleared her throat, voice trembling slightly. "Thank you for meeting with us. Your son and my husband were close. David admired you very much.

We won't take a lot of your time and we wouldn't have asked if we'd had any other options."

"Not at all," the senator grinned. "I eat breakfast every day. Happy to share my table with you. But we're short on time. How can I help?"

Vaughan took a deep breath and gripped the chair arms tightly. "I need you to help me find David's killer."

The senator's eyes widened slightly, and he looked genuinely taken aback. "Killer? The autopsy report said, 'sudden cardiac arrest.' What makes you believe—"

"It wasn't natural causes," Vaughan interrupted, glassy-eyed. "Someone killed him. I don't know how, exactly. But I know it's true."

Senator Wilson's face was a mask of concern, though Jake noticed a brief flicker of something else in his eyes. Was it fear? Recognition? Doubt?

"I'm deeply sorry for your loss," the senator said, reaching across the table to place a reassuring hand on her wrist. "But you're making difficult accusations. Do you have any proof?"

"We're working on it," Jake replied, his voice steely. "We just need a little help."

The senator leaned back. He looked thoughtful for a long moment before speaking.

"David was a good man and a good soldier, and he was a good friend to my son. If there is any truth to the idea that he was murdered, I'll do everything in my power," he paused. "But I have to say that I haven't been briefed on any of this and I don't know where to start looking."

"We believe the reason David was murdered has to do with something he witnessed or maybe even participated in while he was deployed to Iraq. That's the place to start," Jake said.

"Iraq was a long time ago," the senator said, cocking his head as if he were considering the question seriously. "David's been a vulnerable target in that hospital bed for years. Why did the killer wait so long?"

Vaughan narrowed her eyes, and her voice was hard. "We don't know. Not yet. But we will."

"Let me look into it. I'll get back to you as soon as I can," Senator Wilson said.

Vaughan, Jake, and the senator finished their breakfast. The dining room hummed with quiet conversation. The senator's assurances were still ringing in Jake's ears, but he couldn't shake the feeling that something was off.

"Thank you. Your help means the world to us," Vaughan said, extending her hand to him as they prepared to leave.

The senator smiled warmly, grasping her hand. "I'll do my best."

As they made their way to the door, Jake glanced back to see the senator watching them, his expression inscrutable.

Then, without warning, Senator Wilson looked past them. His eyes widened and his face blanched.

Vaughan and Jake turned to see what had alarmed him.

Chapter 17

As usual, Gaspar couldn't sleep and gave up the effort about three o'clock in the morning. He'd spent the dark hours at his desk, bathed in the light of his computer screens, while his family slept in the back of the house.

He accessed all of the databases available to Scarlett Investigations and tapped a few favors from former contacts. After several hours, he had a pretty good picture of Emma Fonda. Her story was definitely a tragedy.

After he helped his wife get the kids fed and out the door, he swallowed a couple of Tylenol with cold Cuban coffee to sand the edges off his constant pain.

While on an FBI case, he had been shot twice. Once in the right side and once in the right leg. The wound in his side had damaged the muscles and sitting was painful. The weight of his upper body crushed his organs, literally, as if his ribs and his pelvis were the jaws of a vise.

His doctors weren't concerned. They were like mechanics who had rebuilt a totaled car, and they weren't about to listen to complaints about a scratch in the paint.

His leg wound had been dismissed as trivial. The bullet hit his shinbone and didn't even break it. But day to day it was far worse to deal with than his side. The leg ached constantly, like someone was in there with a drill from the hardware store.

Tylenol barely touched the pain, but he wouldn't allow himself anything stronger, although his wife worried about his liver.

Gaspar refilled his coffee cup, returned to snag Otto's latest burner phone off his desk, and pressed the redial.

She picked up quickly, which told him she'd been awake for hours, too.

"Morning, Chico. How goes the day in paradise so far?" Otto said with more energy than he'd expected. She'd probably downed at least one pot of coffee already.

"Sunny. Humid. Going up to ninety-five later. Pool water is perfect. You should come down," Gaspar said, sipping the sweetened coffee from which he metabolized most of his energy.

Otto laughed. "I'm convinced you're part lizard."

"Indeed," Gaspar wasted no energy defending his preferences. "I've been working on Emma Fonda. Thought I'd catch you up. Is this a good time?"

"You have my full attention," she replied. "We've got a new victim to add to the mix. Suanne Skinner. Army or Air Force. We're running that down now."

"You think Skinner's death is related to the others?"

"It's something we need to rule out," Otto said. "The more potential victims we find, the less likely these cases are unrelated."

"And let me guess. Cooper thinks Reacher's involved."

"Something like that."

Gaspar had returned to his study, which was now the remote but fully functional satellite office of Scarlett Investigations, surrounded by the files and evidence that painted a picture of Emma Fonda's life.

The LED lighting cast a soft glow over the discussion as Gaspar tried to piece together the why and how of Fonda's murder.

"You've seen Fonda's record," Gaspar said, leaning back in his chair. "Academic excellence, tactical brilliance, leadership skills. She was headed for great things. Until a friendly fire incident in Afghanistan. Can you pull up the report I sent?"

"Yeah, looking at it now."

He gave her a couple of minutes to skim through. "According to her medical records, the incident led to her PTSD, self-medication, and the rest of her downfall."

"You think the whole thing was engineered?" she asked.

"It's a possibility." Gaspar shrugged and adjusted his position in the chair. "The timing, the players involved, the subsequent cover-up. Could be someone wanted her out of the way."

"You're stressing the 'could be' bit, aren't you?" Otto asked. "Sometimes a cigar is just a cigar. You tell me that all the time."

Gaspar ignored her objections. "The question is why. Can't find a motive that makes sense."

Otto replied, her voice neutral. "If Fonda was a threat back then, why kill her now, when she's already been neutralized by her own behavior?"

"Maybe she didn't stay neutralized," Gaspar suggested. "Maybe she found or did something that made her a threat again."

"Like what?"

Gaspar waited to give her time to consider the idea. Otto was a thinker. Her mind was sharp and well trained, but her methods were not at all the same as his. Which was one of the reasons they made a good team.

Otto said slowly, "Like evidence, information, something that could expose the ones who destroyed her?"

"It's a possibility that explains some things," Gaspar said.

"It is. You're right. We need to find the motive. Motive will lead us to the answer," she paused. "Eventually."

"I've spent hours poring over the details of Fonda's life, looking for any clue that might point to motive," Gaspar said. "No luck."

Otto's phone buzzed. He waited while she read the message.

A moment later, she said, "An anonymous source claims Fonda discovered something that got her killed. They want to meet."

Gaspar's expression soured. "Could be a lead. More likely, it's a trap."

"I know. But it's the only thing we have," Otto said as she replied to the message. "No harm in talking, right?"

He heard another buzz from her phone indicating she'd received a reply.

Otto read the message verbatim. "Fonda wasn't alone. There are others."

"Others?"

Otto continued reading the message as it came in. "Others like Fonda, destroyed by the same people. We have proof."

He heard her thumbs moving rapidly over the virtual keyboard followed by the whishing noise indicating her message was sent.

"What did you say?"

"Asked for a time and place to talk," Otto said. "Catch me up on the friendly fire thing that might have started it all for Fonda."

"Friendly fire incidents are not uncommon. We worried about this constantly in the Army, but it plagues all military services," Gaspar said, warming to his subject. "Fonda was in charge of a group of Navy exercises. All the proper notifications were issued, but mistakes were made. Nineteen sailors died and fifteen others were injured. All on her watch."

"Since Fonda wasn't court-martialed, or even discharged because of the incident, I'm assuming the investigation concluded she was not at fault," Otto said.

"Roger that," Gaspar replied. "But Fonda couldn't live with the weight, according to her medical files. She carried a lot of guilt over the deaths. The PTSD started then and progressed. She repeatedly relived the trauma."

"She was honorably discharged, wasn't she?" Otto asked.

"Yes. And treated by the VA and released," Gaspar replied, skimming the reports on his screen. "But she never really recovered."

After a long pause, Otto said slowly, "So family and friends of the wounded and the dead could be looking for vengeance, I suppose."

"That's a lot of suspects. You'll need a big team of people just to track them all down and get statements. Checking alibis will take a while, too," Gaspar said. "You should turn this over to Cooper or the Albany Field Office. We don't have the manpower to handle a big job like that alone."

"Good point. I'll contact Agent Johnson. She's leading the team assigned to solve these murders."

"Ask Johnson to compare what we know about Fonda's service record with the other victims, too. If they were all rising stars, that might be a thread she can pull to unravel more," Gaspar suggested.

"Will do," Otto said, sending a text to Johnson while she was thinking about it. "Anything else that jumps out?"

Before he had a chance to reply, her phone buzzed with another message.

"Now what?" Gaspar asked.

"The meeting is set. The Christopher Hotel in Colorado. Tonight. Want to come along?" Otto replied.

"Yes, but no," Gaspar said with a grin she couldn't see. "Take Jake Reacher with you. He's a good man to have along in a cage fight. Samantha Vaughan can take care of herself, too, according to her service records. Not to mention Reacher likes her. He might want to participate if you've got both his nephew and his former lover tagging along."

"Now you're thinking like Cooper. Jake's got two jobs going at the moment. I can't read him in on everything about the Hornet case, but sure, I can ask him to come along," Otto replied. "I don't suppose your pal Flint is in the neighborhood?"

"Last I heard, he was somewhere in the Caribbean or Switzerland or Italy or somewhere." Gaspar shot a brief note off to Flint, just in case. "Cooper's got a few thousand agents reporting to him. Can't he dig up a partner for you?"

"Apparently not," Otto replied angrily. "Cooper's not inclined to sacrifice another agent to the Reacher case. He's lost two already."

Gaspar didn't bother to point out that Cooper always had more than one reason for everything, and none of his reasons were intended to shelter Otto from disaster.

Gaspar stretched his bad leg out and crossed his ankles. Man, he was tired. If only he could get a few hours of painless sleep. But that hadn't happened for years.

No reason to believe things would magically change.

"What about the black sedan Jake asked us to find? Any luck with that?" Otto asked after Gaspar failed to reply. "Jake thinks the sedan has something to do with David Vaughan's death."

"Good news first. I found the vehicle in the vicinity on video the day David Vaughan died. Took some digging. And I had to piece it together from satellites and traffic cams and a few CCTV cameras installed on private buildings," Gaspar replied, sitting up at the keyboard and shifting his view to a different screen.

"What's the bad news?"

"How much time do you have?"

"You're hilarious, Chico," Otto deadpanned.

"I'm opening for Seinfeld in Vegas next week," Gaspar replied.

"Yeah, yeah."

Gaspar grinned and swallowed the last of his Cuban coffee before he relented. "The black sedan was abandoned at a truck stop on Southbound I-25. It stayed there for a couple of weeks. Then it got towed to an impound lot."

"Is the sedan still there?" Otto said hopefully. "We can get it picked up and put forensics on it."

"Possibly. The impound lot is inside a closed garage. No cameras inside or out," Gaspar replied. "I called. The owner claims the black sedan is not there. But who knows?"

"Which means we'll need to find out the old-fashioned way," Otto said. "I've gotta run."

"Yeah," Gaspar replied. "One more thing. I know the Miami PD detective who caught the Fonda case when the body was first discovered six months ago. Agent Johnson asked the locals to exhume the body, which they did. Detective Martinez sent me her files and I'm meeting with her this afternoon. If I learn anything helpful, I'll let you know."

"Good. And forgot to ask, what about the license plate on the black sedan?" Otto said, but he could tell her mind was already moving on to other issues.

"Running it down now. Colorado plate numbers are randomly assigned. They don't have any particular meaning to them. But once the plate is registered to a specific vehicle, they've got good records in searchable databases," he said.

"And?"

"Looks like the black sedan's plates were stolen off a green Toyota Camry from a Walmart parking lot near the airport in Colorado Springs," Gaspar replied. "Later, the owner of the Toyota got pulled over and ticketed. Claimed he didn't even know his plates were missing."

"Didn't even know? Was he high?"

"Most likely."

Distracted, Otto said, "Anybody believe that stolen plate story when he floated it?"

"Locals might have. But the guy had a record for grand theft auto, so…" Gaspar let his voice drift off. "Still checking."

Chapter 18

Before Jake could identify what Senator Wilson had seen that alarmed him, a deafening crash filled the room. A dark sedan had smashed through the restaurant's large front window, shards of glass spraying everywhere.

Screams filled the air as patrons dove for cover. Jake grabbed Vaughan and pulled her behind a pillar. He scanned the room, looking for Senator Wilson, who was momentarily lost in the chaos.

People were scrambling, running in all directions, as four masked assailants stormed through the gaping hole in the windows. They were armed, moving with precision, eyes scanning the room.

Jake's gaze locked with the first man.

"Get down!" Jake yelled, pulling Vaughan to the floor. He felt her grip on his arm.

Vaughan drew her pistol from her holster. Which was when Jake saw she had been cut by flying glass. Blood was streaming down her arm.

"Find them!" the masked man yelled.

This was a planned attack. They were being targeted.

One of the invaders caught sight of Vaughan's bright red dress, a flash of color behind the pillar.

"There!" he shouted, pointing in Vaughan's direction.

A bullet struck the pillar inches from Vaughan's head. She cried out when a piece of shrapnel embedded in her leg. She reached down and yanked the sliver from her calf. A trickle of blood ran down to her ankle, but she ignored it.

"Stay down!" Jake yelled as he grabbed Vaughan's pistol and returned fire, hitting the shooter in the groin below his vest. The man went down. Probably dead, with luck.

Another attacker advanced, but Jake fired again and watched the second man fall when the bullet ripped into his belly. Only two were left.

Vaughan's breath came in ragged gasps. "Jake... they're after us. They know..."

Jake's voice was grim. "Let's go."

He glanced up just in time to see Senator Wilson slip out a side door.

How did the attackers know Jake and Vaughan would be here? Had the senator set them up?

The sound of sirens wailed in the distance, getting closer.

"Can you run?" Jake asked, turning back to Vaughan.

"Absolutely," she replied.

He helped her to her feet, and they hurried to the back exit, gunfire still echoing inside the restaurant.

As they stumbled out into the alley, the sound of heavy boots quickly followed. Jake heard sirens coming closer, but they were not close enough.

Vaughan ran around the corner and stopped. It was a blind alley. Jake grabbed her hand and pulled her in the opposite direction. Before they could run, they were trapped.

"Drop your weapons!" a man's cold voice commanded.

Jake scanned the area quickly, seeking an alternative escape.

Who were these killers? What were they after?

"Drop your weapons!" the gunman yelled again.

The guy was big and bulky, like he was hopped up on steroids. Which he probably was. Jake wasn't worried. He could take more than one big guy, given the chance.

But how many more were right behind him? And what about Vaughan?

Jake shrugged. Seemed like a good time to find out what these guys wanted anyway. He needed to get back to work.

He dropped the gun and stuck his hands up. Vaughan did the same.

As the masked man advanced, Vaughan's phone buzzed in her purse.

"Take the call," the gunman demanded gruffly.

She read the message aloud. "Come now or die now. Your choice."

Jake stared into the gunman's cold eyes. He'd been looking for answers. Seemed he'd hit the jackpot. This guy knew something. Now was a good time to find out what it was.

"Let's go," Jake said, stepping closer to the gun and blocking Vaughan.

The gunman directed them to a black SUV. He'd moved his gun hand to the folds of his jacket. Still accessible, but out of sight of pedestrians on the street.

Inside the SUV, Jake and Vaughan were quickly bound and their heads covered by a cloth bag, the cold press of plastic twist ties biting into their wrists. The SUV's engine roared to life, and they were on the move.

Vaughan's hand found Jake's in a silent vow of solidarity. Jake gave her a reassuring squeeze. "Don't worry. They don't want to kill us."

"How do you know?"

"We're still breathing."

The SUV traveled like a rat in a maze. One sharp turn after another. The clock in Jake's head said elapsed travel time was thirty-two minutes. So far.

When the SUV came to a halt, the gunman yanked them from the vehicle and ushered them across an open, paved lot into a building.

As they walked, footsteps echoed inside what sounded like a cavernous open space. The air was cool but not air-conditioned. No breezes, either. Jake smelled oil and grease. He guessed they'd entered an old factory, or maybe a warehouse.

They were shoved into chairs and the cloth bags covering their heads were removed. Blinking against the harsh bright spotlight aimed at him from the ceiling, Jake saw they were positioned in a smaller room somewhere inside.

Their armed escort left the room, closing the door behind him.

Which left them facing a man seated behind a large desk. He appeared calm enough. He wore a black turtleneck with long sleeves, long black pants, and gloves. His face and head were unconcealed.

His eyes bore straight through them as he allowed Jake and Vaughan to absorb the futility of their situation.

"Officer Vaughan, Lieutenant Reacher," he said, dripping with insincerity.

Which confirmed the abduction was intentional. He knew their names and where they'd be having breakfast. What else did he know?

Jake demanded coldly, "What do you want?"

"You can call me Captain," the big man said, leaning back in his chair. "You've been poking your noses into places you shouldn't. Asking questions that are none of your business."

Vaughan's voice broke the silence with defiance. "David Vaughan's death is our business. If you had anything to do with it—"

Captain leaned forward, his voice dropping to a dangerous whisper. "Careful, Mrs. Vaughan. You're in no position to make threats."

He paused to let that truth hang in the air. "You want answers, and I'm willing to give them to you. After you do something for me."

Jake and Vaughan stared at the man behind the desk, his expression cold and calculating.

"I know what your husband did in Iraq," Captain said slowly, his eyes fixed on Vaughan. "He deserved to die in that Humvee bombing. Too bad he didn't. If he'd died back then, you wouldn't be in this situation now. Maybe you'd be living with Jack Reacher, eh?"

Which confirmed Jake's conclusions. This guy had way more intel about them than he should have.

Vaughan took a sharp breath. "What are you talking about? David was a hero. He served his country with honor."

Captain's lips twisted into a cruel smile. "Did he, Mrs. Vaughan? Or was he involved in war crimes?"

"What do you want?" Jake demanded.

He had assessed the situation. There were three armed men, but no posse within shouting distance. Three against two. He liked those odds.

Which meant he could end this here and now.

He didn't have the intel he came for, so he was willing to wait. But not forever.

Captain ignored Jake. He leaned back in his chair, steepling his fingers. "I served with your late husband, Mrs. Vaughan. We were part of a special operations unit. What David did back there... It was unforgivable. He should have been court-martialed. Then his Humvee hit that IED and he was all but dead anyway. So the Army gave him a pass for his crimes, out of deference to you and the other families involved. We did not."

"What do you want?" Jake asked again, his tone harder this time.

Captain paused, moving his head slightly to allow his stare to focus on Jake. "I want you to find the others who know the truth."

"So you can kill them?" Jake said.

Captain shrugged. "Justice must be served."

"What truth?" Vaughan whispered. "What did David do?"

Captain's eyes narrowed, and he leaned forward. "He was involved in an operation that went criminally wrong. Innocents died. Those responsible will be held accountable."

"That's a little vague, isn't it?" Jake said flatly.

Captain stood up, his gaze moving between Jake and Vaughan. "Find the others who have so far escaped justice and bring them to me. I'll give you the full story, including the identity of David's killer."

"We don't know what you're talking about," Vaughan said. "What others? What do you mean?"

Captain paused to let his words sink in. "Fail and the truth will die with you, Mrs. Vaughan. Succeed and I'll give you David's killer. You may do with that information whatever you like."

The room was silent, the weight of his words heavy in the air. He pushed a button on the top of the desk and the door swung inward to open.

The same pair of armed guards stood aside to escort them out.

First, they replaced the hoods. Then, Jake and Vaughan were escorted from the building, stumbling along the cluttered concrete. When they reached the SUV, they were shoved into the cargo area.

The SUV started up and reversed out of the building. Once again, the vehicle drove city streets, turning several times along the way.

Jake timed the trip, but the clock in his head didn't display and it wasn't an internet search engine, either. Questions without answers popped up and couldn't be settled.

Had Captain killed David Vaughan?

What had David Vaughan done that was worth killing him for after all this time?

Who was Captain and who were the others Captain wanted to expose?

Could Captain be trusted to keep his word? What about the others on his team?

The SUV slowed, turned again and again until it finally came to a stop. One of the gunmen left the passenger seat and walked around to open the cargo hatch.

"Get out, Reacher," he growled as he yanked Vaughan out of the SUV and onto her feet on the rough pavement. "Stand still."

Jake wiggled his ass until his legs were free of the vehicle. He stood, feet apart, still wearing the cloth bag over his head.

"Wait five minutes. Then get yourself free," the gunman said. He dropped something onto the pavement. It bounced and hit Jake's boot.

The gunman slammed the hatch and his footsteps moved around the SUV to the passenger seat. He closed the door, and the vehicle took off.

"Are you okay, Vaughan?" Jake asked inside the hood.

"Yeah. I'm fine." Her voice was angry and hard. "Who the hell were those guys?"

Jake swept his foot over the pavement until he hit the metal object the gunman had dropped on the ground. Then he squatted and picked it up. It felt like a box cutter in his hand.

"Come closer," he said from his position near the ground. Vaughan did as he asked. "Turn around. I'll squat low enough. Use your hands to pull this bag off my head."

Jake knelt low to the ground so that Vaughan could reach the top of his head with her hands bound behind her back.

After a couple of misses, Vaughan performed the maneuver. "Can you see?"

"Yeah." Jake blinked a few times to restore his vision in the dim daylight.

"Where are we?"

"In an alley. They've left us a box cutter to slice through the plastic ties binding our wrists," Jake said. "I'll cut you free and then you can pull off your hood and cut me free. Okay?"

"Yeah. Go ahead," Vaughan replied. "Try not to sever any essential parts."

"Why? You play piano?" Jake joked as he moved to stand back-to-back, close enough to maneuver the box cutter.

He entwined Vaughan's fingers with his to feel his way to the plastic tie cutting into her skin. Grabbing the narrow plastic band, he positioned the box cutter as well as possible. He nicked his hand and drew blood before he sliced the band.

Vaughan's hands were free.

She whipped her hands around and pulled off her hood, taking a few deep breaths of the fetid air in the alley. She massaged her wrists to get the blood flowing again. Then she collected the box cutter from Jake and cut his hands free.

"Now what?" Vaughan asked, rubbing her hands together and following Jake as he hurried from the alley toward the street, limping slightly.

Chapter 19

Thursday, June 9
Washington, D.C.

As soon as she hung up the call with Gaspar, Kim dug out Cooper's burner phone and pressed the redial. After five rings, he answered.

"I don't have much time. What do you need?" Cooper asked.

"I need to be at the Christopher Hotel. Colorado. Tonight at 9:00 p.m. Can you manage that?" Kim said getting straight to the point.

A long pause was his response. She heard nothing for several moments, wondering if he had disconnected or gotten distracted by something else.

Finally, he said, "Why do you want to attend the ball?"

"The what?"

"The Angel Ball is tonight."

"What's that?"

"Some medics call military personnel killed in combat 'Angels.' In this case, the 'Angels' are a private group of benefactors for survivors with medical needs and their families. The Angel Ball is their annual fundraiser, held at the Christopher Hotel," Cooper said. "Members and invited guests only. Which doesn't include you. So why are you going?"

Kim cocked her head. "Meeting with a witness who claims to have knowledge about the second victim, Emma Fonda. Working theory is Fonda uncovered something that threatened her killer. So he removed her from the equation."

"You're thinking anything you learn about Fonda's murder will inform the other cases," Cooper said.

"Something like that. Gotta start somewhere."

"Who is the witness?" Cooper asked.

"That's one of the things I need to find out." Barely holding onto her patience, Kim said pleasantly, "Unless you'd like to help me. Rather go yourself? You could take a full battalion, perhaps? Just blow the whole place off the face of the earth and solve all our problems?"

Cooper said nothing for such a long time she was tempted to hang up. But she waited, and eventually he said, "Do you own a ball gown? You'll stick out like a clown at a funeral if you don't dress appropriately."

"Let me worry about that. What I need from you is transportation. For three."

"Three?"

"Jake Reacher, Samantha Vaughan, and me."

Again the long pause, as if he were actually considering Kim's welfare. Which she knew he wasn't. And he knew she knew it.

"Okay," he said. "Three seats to Broomfield, Colorado, which is the closest airport. Less than four hours airtime from DC."

"We'll need a vehicle when we get there. A driver, too," Kim said, refusing to back down.

"You think you're ordering at McDonalds? Should I throw in some fries with that?"

Cooper was annoyed, which was just fine with Kim. He annoyed her constantly. It was long past time for him to be on the receiving end for a change.

"You want the job done or not?" Kim replied. "Okay with me either way."

"Your flight leaves Dulles at four o'clock. Don't be late. TSA Agent Mikowski will meet you at the checkpoint and pass your weapons through," Cooper said. "In the back of the SUV when you arrive at Broomfield, you'll find appropriate attire for the three of you. Driver's name is Cliff. Keep me posted."

"More weapons when we get there, and someone to wield them, would be helpful," Kim said.

He hung up, leaving Kim holding dead air and wearing a grin. She rarely got the better of Cooper, but she'd won this particular skirmish. The feeling was worth the payback he'd inevitably deliver later.

Her next call was to Jake Reacher. No answer. She left a message asking him to call back.

After that, she made a fresh pot of coffee and went over the list of victims and murmured her list of questions while she waited.

"What does all of this have to do with Reacher? What does Cooper know that he's not telling? Why were these women targeted? Was David Vaughan murdered, like his wife thinks? Why?"

Maybe Gaspar would get some good intel on Emma Fonda from his Miami PD contact. If the victims were connected in some way, focusing on Fonda could tell them how. Possibly.

Chapter 20

Gaspar met Miami PD Detective Olivia Martinez in the parking lot of the abandoned warehouse where Emma Fonda's body had been discovered. He had worked with her a couple of times back when he'd been assigned to the FBI's Miami Field Office. He'd found her to be a solid detective. Methodical, effective, well trained.

Dressed in a dark suit, yellow shirt, and flats, Martinez's dark hair was pulled into a tight bun, all of which only served to accentuate her attractive Latin features.

Like Gaspar, Martinez was Cuban-American. Their families moved in the same circles. Which meant he was as comfortable with her as he was with any colleague.

The sun blazed in the Miami sky, casting a harsh light on the dilapidated warehouse on the edge of Wynwood. Gaspar's shirt clung to his body almost as soon as he stepped out of his vehicle.

"How's the crime rate around here these days, Martinez?" Gaspar asked as he approached her on the street. "Still three hundred percent higher than everywhere else?"

Martinez grinned. "Last I heard, twenty percent of Florida communities are worse than Wynwood."

"Well, that's comforting," Gaspar laughed, cocking his head toward the graffiti-covered walls of the decrepit block building. "Fancy paint job on this place."

"Yeah, plenty of budding Picassos roaming the streets. Gets worse every day," she said, leading the way through a hole in the chain link fence that surrounded a string of abandoned one-story buildings.

All of the warehouses on this street had been constructed with concrete blocks. At one time, stucco had been applied over the concrete, but most of it had flaked off over the years.

As they approached, the pungent scent of decay mixed with body odors and salt air and the heavy, sweet stench of cannabis smoke reached them.

"This way," Martinez said, walking along the broken sidewalk and around the corner. "The body was found here six months ago. We get about one or two bodies a week in the buildings around this area. We sent her to autopsy and tried to investigate. You know what that's like."

Gaspar nodded. Homeless drug addicts died with distressing frequency and most of the deaths were caused by drug overdose, malnutrition, and exposure. Unless there were a reason to suspect other causes, law enforcement everywhere had precious little resources to devote to these cases.

When they reached an opening where a busted door was stuck in the up position, Martinez ducked under the door. Gaspar followed into the stifling stillness.

From inside, the sound of distant traffic mingled with barking dogs and squeaking rodents. Faint mutterings came from the vagrant population that had taken refuge in the warehouse's shadows.

"Why dump her here?" Gaspar wondered as his eyes adjusted to the warehouse's semi-darkness.

Heavy humid air coated his skin like a warm blanket too heavy for comfort.

"This place is isolated enough," Martinez shrugged. "Known to house vagrants and drug addicts. Perfect place to dump a body without facing too many questions."

"Which suggests Fonda's killer was familiar with the area," Gaspar said. "Otherwise, how would he know she'd blend in here?"

They walked carefully on the grimy floor, every footstep echoing, crunching on broken glass and garbage and discarded syringes. A rat ran from under a filthy pizza box into the deep shadows and two more scurried inside to replace it.

In the north corner, a man strummed a beat-up guitar which added to the eerie ambience. Addicts huddled in small groups. The sharp, acrid smell of burned plastic wafted over as they puffed makeshift pipes.

Martinez led Gaspar to the spot.

"Here," she pointed to an unused corner covered in dust and cobwebs. "This is where she was when we found her."

Gaspar crouched down, studying the ground. He pulled a flashlight from his pocket and shined it along the floor. "You said she was moved here post-mortem?"

"Yeah, that was our working theory. Forensics agreed that the body was dumped here after death." Martinez nodded. "We haven't found the actual murder scene, but I can't say we've been looking very hard."

While Martinez was speaking, Gaspar's hand brushed something embedded in the floor. He pulled out a tiny, crumpled piece of paper. Squinting, he spread it out, revealing a faded sketch.

It was a Navy Meritorious Unit Commendation Lapel Pin.

"Did your team find this?" he asked, showing it to Martinez.

She frowned, "If we had, it would be in the evidence locker now."

"Might not have been here six months ago. Either way, it would have been easy to overlook, mixed in with all this trash and debris. But for Fonda, this would've meant something." Gaspar said. "It's comparable to a Bronze Star. The real one would be nickel-plated with red and blue enameled surfaces."

Martinez stared, pulling an evidence bag from her pocket and holding it open while Gaspar dropped the sketch inside. "You think Fonda had that on her when she was killed?"

"It's a possibility. Maybe it fell onto the floor here during the transfer," Gaspar suggested. "Or maybe it has nothing to do with Fonda. She wasn't the only military vet in this place, if I had to guess. Unfortunately, too many vets end up homeless. It's just odd to find this sketch here, that's all."

A woman, her face lined and eyes sunken, approached them, the smell of stale alcohol and body odor preceding her.

"I saw the girl," she said in a raspy voice roughened by misuse. "I saw them drop her."

Gaspar and Martinez exchanged looks. The chances of this particular witness recalling Fonda's body being dumped here six months ago were slim.

Martinez stepped closer, her professional demeanor cutting through the woman's hazy focus. "Can you tell us what you saw?"

The woman clutched a grimy blanket tighter around her shoulders, her eyes darting around as if she were afraid of the shadows.

"It was late," she began, haltingly, leaving long pauses between phrases. "Most were asleep or... out of it. The nightmares... they keep me awake. They brought her in a black van. Two of them. Big guys."

"Did you recognize them, ma'am?" Gaspar asked.

She grinned as if she'd never been called ma'am before. Perhaps she hadn't. "Melissa. I'm Missy."

"Missy, I'm Carlos. This is Olivia," he said. "Did you recognize the men who left the girl here?"

Missy shook her head, using her fingers to pick lice from her filthy hair. "But I heard them. One called the other 'Mick' or 'Nick'... something like that."

Martinez took a notebook from her pocket. "Did you see the license plate on the van?"

Missy seemed to go inward for a moment, struggling to recall. "Not all of it. Just the last part... 019 or 091. Maybe. I can't be sure."

Gaspar nodded, "It's a start, Missy. Thank you."

"You've been a great help." Martinez pulled a few bills from her pocket, pressing them into the woman's hand. Missy nodded, her eyes glistening with unshed tears, and then disappeared back into the shadows.

Gaspar turned to Martinez, holding the drawing of the Navy pin. "Did Fonda receive any commendations when she was on active duty?"

"Dunno. We'll check. We'll check the sketch for DNA, too. And I'll run Missy's suggestion about the partial plate through the system, see if we get any hits," Martinez replied, shaking her head. "Not likely we'll find anything, but we'll try anyway."

Gaspar took another look around, but he didn't see anything else noteworthy. He pulled his phone from his pocket and snapped a few shots. Then he took a video. Otto might want to see it and there was no reason for her to waste time coming here to do it.

They left the building and had just reached their cars when Martinez's phone rang. She answered and listened to the caller.

"Thanks," she said and disconnected. "That was the lab. They found something on Fonda's body. Something we missed during the first autopsy."

Gaspar raised an eyebrow.

"A tattoo. A recent one. Probably inked not more than a week before she died. It's numbers. Coordinates," Martinez said.

"That's unusual. You think Fonda knew her time was short, and she was sending some sort of message?" Gaspar mused.

Martinez shook her head. "I don't know. Come back to the office and we can go over what we've got so far. It's too hot to stand here."

"Okay. I'll follow you," Gaspar said, as they parted to return to their vehicles for the drive to the station.

Chapter 21

Half an hour later, Gaspar sat across from Martinez in one of Miami P.D.'s cluttered interrogation rooms. Martinez had pulled the investigative file on Emma Fonda. She pushed it across the table to Gaspar.

"Take a look. You'll see that Emma Fonda was special."

"How so?" Gaspar opened the file and paged through it. The file was thicker than the one he'd received from Otto.

"Academic excellence, for starters. Fonda graduated top of her class at the Naval Academy," Martinez said. "Her professors said she was the brightest mind they'd seen in years. She could've taught maritime law or naval engineering with the smarts she had."

Gaspar added, "I've heard about her classified missions. People say she was exceptionally skilled in strategic planning."

Martinez nodded, "Exactly. Her tactics were unorthodox but incredibly effective. She was an asset in the field."

"Lots of exceptionally bright people don't adjust well when faced with extreme pressure on the battlefield, though."

"Not Fonda," Martinez continued, "She was an inspirational leader. The officers under her command said they would follow her anywhere. She wasn't just their commander; she was their mentor, their friend."

Gaspar considered the intel. "She might've been headed for admiral, or even higher."

"There was chatter about her stepping into a significant political role, given her combination of experience and diplomacy." Martinez frowned. "But not everyone was pleased with her. She was challenging the system."

"So she was making waves," Gaspar said. "Her push for transparency and holding people accountable probably ruffled more than a few feathers. The establishment saw her as a threat?"

"Possibly. And then came the incident," Martinez said. "We believe that 'friendly fire' situation wasn't an accident. Someone manipulated it to tarnish her, to use her sense of duty against her."

"It worked. It led to the PTSD, the drugs, the streets," Gaspar said, shaking his head. "Feels like they wanted to discredit her, remove her from the equation. But who would do that?"

Martinez shrugged. "And they succeeded, for a while. But she might've come across something. Something that could expose the very people who took her down."

Gaspar looked at Martinez sharply. "You think she had evidence?"

"It's a theory. She was reaching out to some old contacts before she died. We've been running those down as we have the manpower." Martinez said. "Maybe she found something she wasn't supposed to."

"And that made her a target again."

A beat of silence passed between them.

Gaspar said carefully, "If Fonda discovered something like that, we need to find it before it's too late."

Martinez met his gaze. "Agreed."

"Let's see that new tattoo. Might give me some place to begin."

Martinez pushed an enlarged photo of the tattoo across the table. "It's fresh. The skin is still slightly raised. The pathologist pegs it at about a week old, given the state of healing."

Gaspar examined the photo. "It's definitely numbers. Precise and clear."

"We believe they're rough coordinates, longitude and latitude," Martinez explained.

Gaspar frowned, trying to process the implications. "Coordinates? Like a location?"

Martinez nodded, passing another autopsy photo of the body showing the tattoo under her right breast. "Could be important. Or not."

"So you don't know what this means?" Gaspar asked. "The numbers are difficult to read. But it looks like somewhere around Taiwan, doesn't it?"

"Best guess is the South China Sea. Whatever it means, it was something important to her," Martinez nodded. "But so far, we don't know why. Hell, maybe it's the place she met her soulmate or something."

Gaspar said, "Or maybe the tattoo was a backup. She wanted to make sure it wouldn't get lost or destroyed. Or that she wouldn't forget. Drug addicts forget things. Only someone she trusted enough to see her naked or, in our case, examining her post-mortem would find it."

Martinez added, "It's possible that she foresaw something. She might have wanted insurance against something. Could be she was worried about forgetting. But it feels more important than just a reminder."

"The first questions are, what's at those coordinates? And who knew she had that tattoo?" Gaspar thought for a moment. "We need to find this specific location. And then move on to her contacts, the last people she spoke to. See where that takes us."

Martinez swiped a palm over her sleek, black hair. "We're trying. You know how heavy our workload is. Budgets being what they are…"

"Yeah. A dead sailor found six months ago isn't a top priority," Gaspar said flatly.

As he prepared to leave, Martinez slid a flash drive across the table. "Here's a complete copy of our working file. We won't give up. We never give up on cold cases. But maybe you can help her now more than we can."

"How about those old contacts you mentioned? The ones Fonda was reaching out to in the weeks before she died. Can I get that list?" Gaspar said.

Martinez nodded toward the flash drive. "We included the intel we have on them for you."

"Thanks," Gaspar said, accepting the flash drive as he turned to leave.

Martinez placed a hand on his arm, "If someone was willing to kill to stop whatever Fonda was involved with, they won't hesitate to kill you, too."

Gaspar cocked his head. "They can try."

Chapter 22

Thursday, June 9
Washington, D.C.

Kim had texted Jake and Vaughan to meet her at the foot of the Washington Monument. They arrived before she did. She spotted them seated on a bench under a spreading oak tree.

A quick scan of the immediate vicinity looked okay. Which didn't mean no one was watching. Only that the watchers were careful.

A steady breeze rustled the leaves on the trees. Groups of tourists flooded the area around the monument and spilled onto the grass. At least two groups of school children were horsing around, squealing, yelling, and playing with video games while the tour guide explained the legacy of America's first president.

Joggers ran past on the sidewalk and traffic noises provided the background noise. The fortunate consequence of the busy location was its relative anonymity.

If they were being watched, isolating their conversation from the crowd wouldn't be easy. With any luck, it could prove impossible in real time. Video recordings would give them a second chance, but that would take a couple of hours, at least.

"Walk with me," Kim said when she approached and strolled past them.

Jake and Vaughan stood on either side of her like a couple of parents with a kid. From a distance, they might have been mistaken for tourists.

"Gaspar found the black sedan," she said without preamble.

Jake's eyebrows shot up. "The one that piece of scum Neske claims he saw near David's hospital?"

Vaughan said, "I figured Neske was lying, just to get Jake off his back. You mean there really was a black sedan that night?"

"Apparently so," Otto nodded. "Gaspar found the plate number first. Turns out the plates were stolen from a Toyota Camry parked in a lot in Colorado Springs. Owner of the Camry says he has no clue who stole them."

Vaughan interjected, "So, a dead end."

"Seems like it," Otto said, "Gaspar also found video showing the black sedan. The car was there, in the vicinity. Doesn't mean the driver went inside the hospital or into David's room or did anything to David if he actually went there."

"Where is the car now?" Jake demanded.

"It was parked in a back lot at a truck stop for a while," Otto replied. "Later towed and impounded. We can't confirm the car is still there. We'll send forensics to take a look if it's there."

Vaughan said, "I can make a call if you think it will help. Send a squad out there to look."

Jake frowned and shook his head. "Should we bring this to Wilson? He has resources we don't."

Vaughan's raised voice cut through the noise of kids playing frisbee. "Senator Wilson? You think he'd care?"

"He might," Jake said, "If we frame it right."

Kim said, "Senator Tug Wilson? Why would he get involved in any of this?"

"I thought his first name was Tim," Vaughan said.

"They call him Tug Wilson," Kim replied. "It's a nickname from his time in the Navy. There's a story behind it, probably."

"You've met him?" Jake asked.

"Back when he was working in the White House a few years ago," Kim nodded. "He's okay. I don't know that he's got any real clout here, though. Why'd you bring him up?"

Jake gave Kim a quick summary of what happened with Senator Wilson in the restaurant and afterward.

The story made Kim's stomach churn. She slipped an antacid from her pocket into her mouth. "Any idea who the gunmen were?"

Vaughan shook her head. "They wore ski masks over their heads. No identifying marks of any kind. Except for their boss, who was careful to cover all exposed skin *except* his head. Thought that was odd."

"Could mean they have recognizable gang tattoos and wanted to keep them covered," Kim said.

"They're definitely a bunch of thugs," Jake said. "The leader said his name was Captain."

Kim used her phone to enter the alias into the database. The search returned four hits.

"Recognize any of these photos?" she asked as she showed them to Jake and Vaughan.

Jake pointed to the third mug shot. Vaughan nodded. "That's him. Who is he?"

Kim punched a few more keys on her phone and pulled up a list. "Joey 'Captain' Perch. Heads up a crew of Piranhas operating on the East Coast. Long list of priors and most of them violent felonies."

"What are Piranhas? Besides a man-eating fish, I mean?" Vaughan asked.

"They're somewhat new on the scene, from what this says," Kim replied, summarizing the report she'd pulled up and careful not to reveal the classified intel she'd reviewed back in Detroit. "Piranhas are a criminal cartel operating inside and outside the US. Involved in drugs, weapons, money laundering. Possibly worse things."

"What worse things?" Vaughan asked.

Kim said nothing.

"How is it these guys are still walking around?" Jake asked.

"They've got friends in high places." Kim shared a photo from the Piranhas' known associates list. It showed Senator Wilson at a charity function with Captain.

"It's been a while since I've walked a tightrope." Vaughan said, "These Piranhas weren't fooling around. We got away, but only because they let us go."

"What reason did Captain give for releasing you?" Kim asked, practically feeling the wheels turning in her head.

The classified intel she'd reviewed said the Piranhas were connected to the Hornet murders.

Which meant the Piranhas, the Hornet murders, and David Vaughan were all connected.

Somehow.

"Captain wants us to find the others who know about the war crimes he claims David committed in Iraq," Vaughan replied.

Kim narrowed her gaze. "He tell you who these people are or what war crimes he's talking about?"

"It's all bullshit." Vaughan shook her head firmly. "David was a decent, honest, caring human being. He'd never do anything like that. Never."

Jake's gaze met Kim's. He said, "It's what they do. Plant ideas like that to manipulate us. Just means we push back harder."

Chapter 23

Thursday, June 9
Washington, D.C.

They walked along in silence for a bit when Kim leaned in. "I've got a meeting set up at the Christopher Hotel in Colorado. Someone has intel on one of the victims on a case I'm working. We can travel together to Colorado Springs later tonight."

"What kind of case?" Jake asked.

Kim shook her head. "It's not something I can talk about just yet."

Vaughan stopped walking and placed a hand on Kim's arm. "Wait. You don't think the case you're investigating is related to David's murder, do you?"

"That's one of the things we need to find out," Kim's tone was measured. "If there's a link, it could help us discover who's behind this and why."

"You think the Piranhas killed them all?" Jake asked.

Kim shrugged. Gaspar's all-purpose gesture. It could mean anything. Right now, she meant she'd revealed everything she could.

Jake said, "Then we need to find the connection if there is one. Any idea who the witness you're meeting at the Christopher Hotel is?"

Kim shook her head. "Anonymous tip. Said they had valuable information on one of the victims and wanted to meet. It could be a trap. But that's a risk I need to take."

Vaughan gave them both a steady, intense gaze. "I'm in. I want to know what happened to my husband. I need to know."

Kim was reassuring. "I thought you might say that."

Jake gave a curt nod. "On to the Christopher Hotel, then. We could be walking into the lion's den. Everyone needs to understand that going in."

Kim considered his point and made a decision. They were willing to risk their lives. The least she owed them was honesty. About the parts of her case that were not classified, anyway.

"There are four victims in my case," Kim began quietly. "All women, all with military backgrounds. Three were killed by an air embolus—directly injected into their jugular veins. We're waiting for confirmation on the fourth."

Vaughan gasped. "Are you saying there's a chance David was killed in the same way?"

Kim hesitated, weighing her words. "It's a possibility we should rule out."

Jake asked Vaughan, "Did the autopsy report mention any puncture wounds on David?"

"Well, sure. I mean, he'd been in the hospital for years. He'd been poked in lots of places." Vaughan shook her head slowly. "About what you'd expect, under the circumstances."

"It's easy to miss a puncture wound like that, especially if the pathologist wasn't specifically looking for it," Kim pointed out.

Jake replied, "Then we need to speak to the pathologist. Double-check everything."

Vaughan's mouth formed a grim, straight line. "I'll arrange a meeting."

Jake looked back and forth to the two women. "So we all have a reason to head to Colorado. Three heads are better than two. We'll go to the Christopher Hotel tonight and then to the pathologist."

"I'm in," Vaughan said.

"I've got a lot to do between now and then. Our flight leaves from Dulles. I'll text you the details," Kim offered a firm nod as she peeled off, her phone vibrating inside her pocket.

She glanced at the caller ID. She picked up the call. "Agent Otto."

"Agent Phillips," he said. "We finished the interview with your witness, Billy Boy. Thought you might like to stop in and hear about it. Are you anywhere nearby?"

She'd left Phillips in Detroit with the potential witness from the Lydia Harmon crime scene. He must still be there.

BET ON JACK | 155

"Sorry. Can't. Is there a video recording?" she replied, slowing her pace to linger at the back of a large group of Asian tourists all using cell phones for one thing or another.

With so much communications traffic in DC, keeping short conversations under the radar was possible. The downside was ears on absolutely all communications within the city's systems. Which meant that if someone was looking hard enough, they could always find more than Kim wanted them to know.

"Yeah. I'll send it to you," Phillips said. "After he showered, we gave him clean clothes and a hot meal. His mental capacity is diminished."

"Which means you'll need corroboration for whatever he knows," Kim replied. "What did he say about Buster?"

"Not much. But two leads. We got a sketch that Billy says is fairly accurate. Just texted it to you," Phillips said. "He said Buster came around with Harmon quite a bit."

"So some of the others at the crime scene might recognize him," Kim said as she accessed the sketch. Wide face, dark hair, pockmarked complexion, eyes blue or gray. "Billy say anything else useful?"

"Buster is tall. Talks fast. Wearing jeans, brown boots, black leather jacket last time Billy saw him," Phillips relayed from memory. "And Billy said he was a big Tigers baseball fan. Wore a Navy Tiger cap with the white Old English D on the front all the time."

Billy's description didn't fit anyone she'd associated with the case so far. "Did you run the sketch through the system?"

Phillips cleared his throat. "Yeah. That's why I'm calling. The sketch matches Reginald Hodak, a/k/a Buster Hodak. Arrested several times on various drug charges. I'd guess he was Harmon's supplier."

Kim resumed walking away from the park. "Anything else jump out at you?"

"He's a vet," Phillips said. "Army. Iraq. Now employed by one of those paramilitary organizations. We're following up."

"Keep me posted," Kim replied as she disconnected the call.

Chapter 24

Thursday, June 9
Washington, D.C.

The weak afternoon light filtered through the heavy curtains in Maureen Tolliver's home office.

Tolliver had been around the block more than once. She'd spent years in government service, mingling with the rich and powerful, hard scrabbling up the ladder until she'd become one of them. Which meant she'd learned her life lessons the hard way.

Absolutely no one could be trusted. She must take care of herself.

Her world was divided into those few things she handled personally and the rest she could outsource to expendable assets.

All assets eventually became expendable.

Like Willard. He was still useful now. He wouldn't last forever.

She glanced at the grandfather clock. Time to go.

She slipped into casual jeans, stuffed her hair into a black baseball cap, and filled her pockets with a burner phone, cash, and surgical gloves. She slipped her earpiece over and into her ear, making sure it was functioning with the burner.

Within ten minutes, she was out the door.

Willard waited in a black sedan with darkly tinted windows parked two houses down, away from the streetlights. The car was a Toyota Camry, one of the most popular cars in America. She'd chosen it specifically because it would blend into any street or neighborhood.

As she approached, Willard didn't look up.

"Drive," she commanded once she slid into the passenger seat.

"Where to?" Willard asked, a hint of weariness in his voice.

"Safe haven three."

She scanned the streets and sidewalks, always vigilant. The streetlights cast eerie shadows that danced alongside the poles, but she saw nothing worrisome along the way.

Willard broke the silence. "We got the intel you were looking for. But it wasn't easy."

She raised an eyebrow, waiting for him to continue.

"Our insider with the Piranhas went underground."

"What does that mean?" she demanded.

"Buster Hodak disappeared." Willard shrugged. "We're looking for him, but he could be dead."

Tolliver's annoyance moved into the red zone. "You have no intel on what happened to him?"

"Not yet. Still checking," Willard said, casting a quick glance across the console as if to measure the level of her volatility.

They reached a small block building in an industrial district outside of Baltimore. The place looked abandoned, which was the reason she'd chosen it for one of her safe havens.

Willard drove around back and parked the Camry in the shadows behind the building. They left the car and approached the keypad fixed on the doorjamb.

Tolliver placed her palm carefully on the access control pad, allowing the Presentation Attack Detection system to engage. The system used a combination of hardware and software to avoid spoofs, which were presentation attacks used to subvert security.

This PAD system had been designed to Tolliver's exact specifications. Which meant the PAD didn't use the most common, cheaper facial recognition to confirm identity.

The PAD recognized Tolliver and the door unlocked and simultaneously eliminated her palm print from the reader.

She stepped aside to allow Willard to open the door. He drew his weapon, grabbed the doorknob, and pushed the door hard and fast into the darkened warehouse.

Tolliver waited outside while Willard checked the space for intruders.

"Clear," he said, securing his weapon again when he returned.

Tolliver gloved up and led the way to her private interior clean room. Willard handed her a tiny flash drive.

"What's on this?"

"Files," Willard said. "Everything about the FBI's Hornet investigation. The players involved, plans, and more importantly, secrets."

She nodded. "What about Skinner. Has she been added to the Hornet's victim list?"

"Not yet. But they'll get there. Agent Johnson, out of Albany, is leading the Hornet task force. She's not an idiot," Willard said.

"That's unfortunate," Tolliver replied flatly. "And what about Captain?"

Willard hesitated. "Still working on locating him."

Tolliver fixed him with a penetrating gaze. "Find him. Before they do."

"Like I said, I'm working on it. It's not like he's wearing a tracking beacon," Willard replied, just as annoyed with Captain's disappearance as she was.

Tolliver ignored his excuses. "How close is the task force to solving the Hornet murders?"

"Closer than they were before Skinner's body was found. Now they have a fresh corpse to analyze. They've brought in a pathologist who specializes in unusual murders. He's working on the body now," Willard said. "We don't expect them to find anything problematic."

"You have someone on the inside of the investigation?" Tolliver asked to confirm.

"Of course we do," he snapped.

Tolliver smirked. Willard's patience was growing thin, she could tell. Which was fine. He wasn't running this show and the sooner he figured that out, the better.

She held the flash drive up. "You're sure this data is reliable?"

"It's as reliable as anything that comes out of the FBI these days."

"Which is to say reliability is uneven," Tolliver replied.

Willard gave a short nod in response.

"Go make coffee," she said as she examined the flash drive.

The tiny piece of hardware could destroy everything she'd worked for all these years. Not that she'd let that happen. But still, this wasn't something she'd expected to be dealing with.

After Willard stomped out of the clean room, Tolliver moved to the specialty computer built specifically for offline decryption and security. She set it to scan for viruses and malware and inserted the flash drive.

The security scan was completed quickly. The program offered the option to continue or abort. Tolliver chose to continue.

Half a moment later, a series of codes and commands and lists popped up on the screen containing the individual file names.

As the information was processed, Tolliver's gaze never strayed from the display.

Profiles of agents, maps of suspected Hornet operation zones, crime scene photos, and autopsy reports. The FBI had made significant progress in a short time. The agent driving the case knew what she was doing.

Agent Genevieve Johnson was leading the task force. Tolliver clicked on her profile.

She noted Johnson's background, psychological profile, and known associates. Johnson was well trained and sharp, but every agent had weaknesses that could be exploited when necessary. Tolliver scanned for those next.

Then she located the profile the FBI was building on the killer. Assuming they could confirm Skinner, they'd located four Hornet victims now. The lead agent believed more unidentified victims were out there.

All four identified victims were females. Which led the profilers to conclude the killer was male, white, mid-thirties. Same profile they always started with, knowing it was all too often accurate.

Known associates for each of the four victims had been identified. Many had been interviewed already, but not all. None of the interviews had turned up a viable suspect thus far.

Most serial murders had a sexual motive, the profiler said. In these four cases, they'd found evidence of sexual activity on the bodies, but no evidence of sexual assault. Even so, in the absence of evidence pointing to a different motive, the profiler defaulted to sexual aggression as the working theory.

"We need to find Captain," Tolliver reiterated when Willard returned with the coffee.

"Like I said, we're on it," Willard retorted with annoyance.

Tolliver's patience with him was wearing thin. He was too often long on excuses and short on results recently.

The data she'd reviewed on the flash drive raised her personal risk assessment on the Hornet cases. Until the FBI found a suspect, they'd keep digging. Sooner or later, they'd find something. Unless they gave up.

How could she neutralize Agent Johnson's task force while keeping her fingerprints off the effort?

Tolliver took a deep breath to steady her nerves. She had a lot of ground to cover, and she couldn't assign the work to Willard. This job required her personal attention.

She pulled up the crime scene photos again, looking for something she might be able to use.

Bull Gator's was a popular bar. Customers wandered in and out through the back door all night long, every night. The killer could easily have been seen and identified.

Hornet was getting sloppy.

Chapter 25

Thursday, June 9
The Christopher Hotel, CO

"This is some place," Cliff said as he pulled the SUV into the long driveway approaching the historic colonial revival-style Christopher Hotel. He followed the line of traffic turtling to the front entrance.

The hotel was ablaze with lights. Four stories high, painted white with red shingle roofs and dozens of windows, the place seemed inviting if not exactly cozy.

Approaching vehicles moved slowly but steadily, as if they'd been paced by a stopwatch. As each reached the designated spot, one vehicle at a time, elegantly dressed men and women emerged to stand and be photographed at the foot of the stairs.

Each pair climbed a red carpet to the front entrance where uniformed doormen held the double doors wide open.

"Good thing we changed into these fancy duds," Jake said, straightening his tuxedo and giving the women an appreciative nod.

Kim gave him a sour look. Cooper had stashed two evening gowns and one tux in the SUV. They'd changed on the way.

"As long as we don't run into trouble," Kim replied. "There's no way I can run in these heels."

Inside their SUV, still four vehicles back from the entrance, Vaughan cautioned, "The photographer is taking glamour shots at the entrance. He's positioned on the right side of the stairs."

"Seems rude to me," Jake grinned. "I could just grab the camera and punch him out. Works for celebrities."

"Too obvious. Besides, he might punch you back," Kim replied as the SUV rolled closer. "Do something simple. Raise your hand to cover your face or look away until we get up the stairs."

Ten minutes later, their SUV was directed to stop.

"I'll wait for you here," Cliff said. "Call me if your plans change."

"Thanks, Cliff," Kim nodded as they exited the SUV.

"How are we going to find our contact in this crowd?" Vaughan asked as they climbed the stairs, avoiding the photographer and waiting to be admitted.

"What does your witness look like?" Jake asked.

"Dunno."

"Male or female?"

Kim shrugged.

When they crossed the threshold to join the crowd, Kim scanned one of the most opulent settings she'd ever seen. Granite floors sparkled across the open expanse.

Tuxedoed waitstaff mingled among the guests offering champagne flutes and collecting empty glasses. The beautiful people gathered in small groups, chatting, laughing, enjoying themselves.

The air pulsed like a living thing as the exclusive Angel Ball event was underway.

Guests, dressed in evening attire, mingled in the grand ballroom beneath the sparkling chandeliers that cast a soft, golden glow over the exquisite decor. Amid the atmosphere of sophistication and elegance, guests engrossed in lively conversations and clinking glasses seemed civilized and festive.

Kim stood near the entrance scanning the scene. Glistening chandeliers, ornate tapestries, well-dressed men and women mingling. She took stock of her makeshift team.

Jake Reacher exuded a quiet confidence that seemed to come naturally to him but was probably enhanced by his military training. His size alone was an asset Kim appreciated at the moment.

Samantha Vaughan seemed comfortable and nervous at the same time. She was a cop, and a damned good one. Which was what Kim counted on to justify bringing her along.

"Let's split up. Mingle. Let this contact find me," Kim reminded them of the plans they'd made.

Jake peeled off to the left and Vaughan moved to the right. Soon they were absorbed by the crowd and Kim couldn't see them.

Her phone vibrated discreetly. She glanced at the message sent from the same number as the earlier messages from the witness she'd come here to meet.

"I'm in the kitchen near the back entrance," it said.

She slid the phone into her pocket and flagged a passing waiter. "Which way to the kitchen?"

Half an instant later a massive explosion rocked the entrance to the ballroom.

Glass shattered, sending shards glinting like stars against the opulent backdrop. People hit the floor, pulling their screaming companions down with them.

The room filled with disorienting smoke and an acrid burning smell. Panic erupted. The elegant ambiance quickly devolved into chaos.

Through the smoke, Kim saw the first tendrils of flames licking the walls, turning the dreamlike setting into a nightmarish inferno. Amid the clamor, she scanned the room seeking Jake and Vaughan.

Guests screamed and rushed toward the door, only to be met with a wall of fire that had engulfed the main entrance. Panic was palpable now. Desperate attendees turned to face the encroaching flames, trapped in the growing inferno.

Kim's eyes met Vaughan's across the room. She found Jake next and gestured Vaughan toward Jake's position.

The rapidly spreading blaze filled the high ceilings with toxic smoke first. But the smoke was stacking relentlessly. Soon it would extinguish all breathable air from the room.

They had to get out. Now.

Jake assessed the situation and shouted over the roar of the fire. "The front entrance is completely blocked. People are jumping through the windows. We need to find another way out."

"I've been here before. There's a kitchen in the back." Vaughan pointed toward an archway on the left in the back of the ballroom. "There should be service corridors that lead from here to the back of the building. That might be our best chance."

"Let's move," Kim agreed. "Take as many people with us as we can. Remind them to stay low to avoid the smoke and cover their mouths with anything they can find to filter the air."

They gathered a group of disoriented and terrified guests and moved them toward the kitchen.

Smoke had filled the upper reaches of the ballroom and descended to hang thick in the air. Kim took short, shallow breaths, herding guests toward the kitchen. Glass crunched beneath their shoes as they navigated through.

The heat was suffocating, and the heavy plaster ceiling above creaked ominously. The old rafters were ablaze. The entire roof might collapse at any minute.

Kim's phone buzzed again, but she ignored it. Getting these people to safety was her number one priority at the moment.

Twice, Jake persuaded men to help him move heavy fallen beams from their path. Flames licked the walls and joined with the fire and smoke from the ceiling.

Kim pulled a fire extinguisher off the wall and blasted it in bursts to create pockets of breathable air through the choking smoke. The smoke stung her eyes, causing them to water uncontrollably. She blinked to clear her vision.

As the group approached the kitchen and the back exit, gunshots sounded from the ballroom. The group halted, babbling in panic.

Three figures wearing powered air-purifying masks and respirators and armed with guns burst through the smoky chaos. They advanced while firing shots that echoed like thunder amid the already deafening fire.

Kim shouted to the others to take cover. Weapons drawn, Kim, Vaughan, and Jake returned fire from behind whatever protection they could find.

Bullets ripped through walls and shattered crystal fixtures.

"Cover me," Kim shouted to Vaughan as she moved to a new strategic position.

Jake's voice was a calm presence amid the firestorm. "Two o'clock, move left."

Kim fired twice more and hit the lead gunman. He fell and she hit another with her next round. Jake and Vaughan took out two more.

With the shooters momentarily suppressed, the group of frightened guests pressed forward toward the kitchen and outside to fresh air. They fought their way through smoke and suffocating heat, hoping the gunmen didn't have backup in place on the lawn.

As they navigated through the labyrinth, a woman became trapped, cornered by flames, frozen in place when she saw another gunman.

Vaughan locked onto the desperate woman. She fired, forcing the gunman to take cover. Jake moved swiftly to rescue the trapped guest and herd her toward the others.

The frightened group finally reached the back entrance that led to an open courtyard. As they emerged into the cool night air, gasping for breath, Vaughan counted to be sure they'd left no one behind. The bedraggled guests stood staring, mouths agape, as the once-grand hotel was consumed by flames.

Chapter 26

Thursday, June 9
The Christopher Hotel, CO

Kim was the last to leave after she'd ushered the others outside. Coughing, head down, she pushed through the smoke and fire to join the others standing upwind of the blaze. Taking great gulps of air, she stared into the chaos, her eyes stinging.

An imposing man stood off in the shadows. Another gunman?

Kim couldn't see him well. She wiped her eyes and raised her weapon to fire.

Wait.

He directed the survivors away from danger, leading them toward safety.

Was that Jack Reacher? She squeezed her eyes shut for a brief moment to clear her vision for a better look. When she opened them again, the man had moved deeper into the trees out of her sight range.

She shook the fanciful image from her head.

As the flames raged and the night grew darker, a distant explosion rocked the hotel's foundation. The ground trembled beneath their feet, and a shockwave swept through the courtyard, throwing everyone off-balance. The group panicked again, a mix of confusion and fear.

From the billowing smoke following the explosion, a group of armed figures clad in black tactical gear emerged. They moved with precision, faces obscured by powered air-purifying masks and respirators, like the others.

The small band of survivors scattered into the dark woods while Kim, Jake, and Vaughan formed a defensive circle, weapons drawn and ready.

The leader stepped forward. "Hand it over or face the consequences."

Kim Otto's jaw tightened. "We're not handing over anything. Who are you? What do you want?"

The leader glared while brandishing the weapon. "Hand it over and you can walk away. Otherwise…"

Jake Reacher's grip on his gun tightened. "We're not here to negotiate."

With no further comment, the leader raised his weapon in a signal to his squad.

They launched the assault. Bullets whizzed through the air, tearing through the remnants of the elegant hotel. Survivors scattered.

Kim, Jake, and Vaughan returned fire. The scent of gunpowder mingled with the smoky air.

Kim took aim and fired at a silhouette darting for cover behind a tree. Her bullet hit the tree, sending wood splinters into the air.

A momentary pause hung in the air, as if the small squad was shocked to face armed resistance. The respite lasted less than a full minute before they returned fire.

Kim ran for cover, firing into the group with precision required by her limited ammunition. Jake and Vaughan followed suit, experienced hands maneuvering with skill, firing to hold the armed attackers at bay.

Vaughan's voice broke through the gunfire. "We need to move! We're sitting ducks here!"

"Agreed!" Kim shouted back, feeling the sweat trickle down her temples.

They moved in unison, backing away from their original position, moving deeper into the woods, constantly scanning, always vigilant.

Kim caught sight of an abandoned truck half-hidden by the foliage. "There! We can use that for cover."

They reached the vehicle, crouching behind its rusted frame. Kim scanned the perimeter, her ears attuned to the slightest sound.

Vaughan was the first to spot the leader, lurking in the shadows. He stood stock still, as if contemplating his next move.

Jake followed Vaughan's gaze and muttered, "Looks like he's still interested in whatever he thinks we have."

Kim eyed the leader cautiously. "We can't let him leave. He'll come back with reinforcements."

With a nod, Vaughan aimed, but before she could take the shot, a bullet ricocheted off the truck's frame, narrowly missing them.

"Sniper!" Jake barked, pinpointing the direction of the incoming fire.

Kim broke away from their makeshift cover, sprinting zigzag to make herself a harder target. The sniper adjusted, trying to foresee her path. When he sent off another round, he was too late. She rolled into a ditch, momentarily disappearing from the sniper's night vision.

Jake fired several shots toward the sniper's suspected location. The incoming sniper fire ceased.

Vaughan used the distraction to focus on the leader. He sensed her stare and turned to look directly at her. He gave an unsettling laugh and raised his weapon. Vaughan got her shot off first. Her bullet soared through the air and grazed her target. He screamed into the night like a wounded hyena, even though she hadn't managed a solid hit.

Jake and Kim fired several times. The armed resistance was more than the attackers had expected. Apparently unprepared to kill, the leader whistled, and his team vanished into the night swallowed by darkness.

"They'll be back," Kim's gaze scanned for further dangers. "They were surprised. Maybe they know who we are and weren't prepared to kill a soldier, a cop, and a federal agent."

Jake shook his head. "They were well equipped and well trained. They won't stop until they get what they want. We need to find out what they're after and why."

Vaughan nodded agreement, eyes focused and determined. "And we need answers."

Flames continued to consume the hotel and jumped to the nearby outbuildings on the property, casting eerie shadows against the night sky. Helicopters were approaching and Kim heard sirens in the distance. Time was short.

Kim felt a hand clap onto her shoulder. She whipped around, ready to fight.

One of the women Kim had rescued stood behind her, hand extended, offering a partially burned blueprint.

"I saw this on the floor near the kitchen and picked it up. I think one of the gunmen dropped it. Maybe it will help," the woman said, handing it to Kim before she hurried away.

Kim examined the intricate designs, turning the charred paper trying to make sense of it.

"What is it?" Jake asked.

"Looks like there may be a secure vault beneath the hotel," Kim said. "Maybe that's what the gunmen were after."

Vaughan's curiosity was piqued. "What could be valuable enough to orchestrate all this destruction? Why not just sneak in and steal it?"

Jake replied, "Value is in the eyes of the beholder. These guys are paramilitary. You don't send them into combat unless the target is worthy."

"So they lured us here, targeted the event, created a diversion with the fire. All to access the vault beneath the hotel," Kim said thoughtfully. "Whatever is in there is undoubtedly a high-stakes target. We need to find it before they come back."

"The entrance to the vault is through a passageway in the housekeeper's office near the kitchen," Jake said, examining the paper over her shoulder.

Vaughan said, "No way we can go back in there. The fire's too hot and the structure's unsafe."

Jake frowned, "We'll never be allowed back in there after the fire is contained."

"The vault is below ground. Dirt doesn't burn. If we can get into the vault, we should be protected from fire," Kim said, studying the design on the charred paper.

"All we need is a way to get into it," Vaughan said.

"This hotel was built in the early 1900s. Vaults were fairly common among the wealthy. But they'd want easy access to their valuables. Like an entrance inside the master suite of rooms, as an example," Kim said, thinking things through. "Given the positioning of this vault, it might have been originally constructed for another purpose and converted later."

"Like what kind of purpose?" Jake asked.

Kim shrugged. "Root cellar? Food storage? Ice house?

"How does that change the picture?" Jake wanted to know.

"Well, if the space was originally intended for supplies, there may have been an outside entrance. The space could be filled from outdoors and accessed as needed through the kitchen," Kim explained.

"Which means we can get inside if we can find the outdoor access," Vaughan said.

"Exactly," Kim nodded. "This drawing doesn't have any directional markings on it. But the kitchen ran across the back of the building."

Kim looked up at the flames consuming the upper floors of the hotel. If the firefighters didn't arrive soon, the entire structure would collapse. It might already be too late to save it.

Then she scanned the back garden. In the bright firelight, she spotted a brick storage building in the shadows off the southwest corner of the hotel.

Jake followed her gaze. "You think the entrance to the vault could be in there? How do we know they didn't just close it up at some point?"

Kim folded the paper and stuffed it into her pocket. "We don't. If either of you have a better idea, let's hear it."

Vaughan set off toward the storage building. Kim followed. Jake brought up the rear.

The double wood door was locked together in the center by a padlock shackle secured through a hasp. Kim raised her pistol and fired at the wood around the hasp until it was loose enough to kick free.

Kim pushed the doors open.

Vaughan flipped the light switch a few times. The fire had put the electricity out in the hotel and everywhere else on the property.

"No harm in trying," Kim said when the lights didn't turn on. There were three windows, and she pushed the doors open wide as well. The raging fire's light brightened the interior of the shed. "That's as good as it's going to get."

Kim went inside. The building was neatly organized. Benches and cabinets lined three walls. A large riding lawn tractor filled one back corner. The floor was poured concrete in places and heavy wood in others.

She made two assumptions. First, that the entrance to the original space had not been very far from the house. Second, the shed had been built on top of the entrance to provide shelter from the elements. She reasoned that the door would have been oversized. Maybe even two doors that met in the middle.

Kim moved to the corner closest to the hotel kitchen, peering at the floor in the flickering firelight. She ran her shoe over the wood floor seeking uneven places that could be some sort of doorway.

Nine feet from the back wall, she found it. Recessed iron handles. Two of them, one on either side of the joint between the two wood panels.

She knelt and grabbed the right handle and gave it a firm yank. The big door lifted easily enough on well-oiled hinges. She peered into the hole beneath the door, which smelled dank and seemed to go all the way to the bowels of the earth.

"Vaughan! Jake!" she yelled to be heard over the still deafening noise of the fire. When they hurried over, she said, "There must be a flashlight or a lantern or something in this shed. See if you can find it."

Vaughan located a battery-operated floodlight on one of the benches near the lawn tractor. She flipped it on. Using the beam for guidance, she joined Kim in the dark corner of the shed.

"Shine the light down these stairs," Kim said, pulling her weapon for insurance. "Tell Jake to cover us and come with me."

"Copy that," Vaughan replied. She hurried to give instructions to Jake and returned quickly.

"I haven't heard any movements down there, but be careful," Kim said when Vaughan returned.

She pointed the flashlight down the stairs and, testing each tread before she placed her weight on it, Kim moved slowly down into the damp, dark pit. When she reached the base of the stairs, she swept the flashlight in a wide arc.

"Okay for me to follow?" Vaughan called down.

"Stay there," Kim called back. "Let me look around first. This could be a wild goose chase and there's no point in both of us being stuck down here."

Chapter 27

Kim moved deeper into the earth where the air grew cooler, and the faint scent of damp ground mingled with lingering whiffs of acrid smoke above.

As Kim's soles touched the ground of the root cellar, a sense of isolation enveloped her. Dark and dank, the walls were rough-hewn and coated with moisture. The air was heavy with the weight of history, as if the space held the echoes of long-forgotten secrets.

She swept the flashlight's beam across the chamber, revealing ancient wooden shelves that once held provisions. Cobwebs clung to corners and ceiling, and the faint drip of water echoed in the distance.

The old root cellar was a stark contrast to the grandeur of the hotel, a hidden world frozen in time.

Amid the relics and half-buried beneath a pile of debris, she spied an old iron door. Unused or forgotten by those who accessed the underground halls from inside the hotel, probably.

She cleared the debris, revealing the iron door's surface. The metal was cold to the touch. Her fingers fumbled for a moment before finding a sturdy handle.

She braced her feet and tried to pull the heavy door open. It probably weighed more than she did. It wouldn't budge.

Kim retraced her path to the stairs. "Vaughan," she called out.

"Yeah?" Vaughan came into view.

"I need some muscle to open an old door. Send Jake down, will you?"

"Hang on," Vaughan said before she disappeared.

The strapless gown Kim was wearing wasn't nearly warm enough down here. Her teeth began to chatter a while ago. She clamped them shut.

"I'm on my way," Jake called out. His footsteps pounded on the old wooden stairs as he hurried down. He glanced around and captured the feel of the place quickly. "Where's this door?"

"Over there," Kim said, sweeping the flashlight along the dirt floor.

"Man, this place is creepy," Jake said as he swiped cobwebs away from his face.

Kim pointed the light. "Let's see what's behind there."

"Shine that light around the edges. It looks like iron. Which means it's probably rusted shut." Jake moved to examine the door's handle and hinges while Kim provided the spotlight.

He stepped back. "Is there a crowbar or something heavy lying around? If I can knock this rust away from the hinges, I might be able to heave this slab open."

Kim found an old hammer on one of the shelves and handed it to him. "This is the best I can find. Will it work?"

"Maybe," he replied as he hefted the hammer in his big paw. He gave the hinges a few solid whacks with the hammer and rust flaked off onto the floor. "We could use some lubricant. There could be some in the shed."

Kim set the flashlight down and felt her way back along the dark corridor. The walls were damp and disgusting. But they only had one flashlight.

When she reached the stairs, she hurried up and out onto the concrete floor of the shed. Vaughan was standing watch at the entrance.

"What do you need?" she asked when she saw Kim emerge.

"An oil can. Spray lubricant. Anything like that," Kim replied, scanning the neatly organized shelves near the lawn tractor. "What's going on outside?"

"The fire's worse. Helos and sirens are closer. We need to collect whatever you can find and get out while we still can." Vaughan switched her weapon to her left hand and stretched to relieve the cramp of holding it steady. "The bad news is our driver can't get here.

They've closed off the roads leading into the hotel. The only way we're leaving here tonight is by air."

"Copy that." Kim found a half full can of WD-40 and grabbed it off the shelf.

She hurried back down the stairs. When she reached the cold dirt floor, she gave her eyes a moment to adjust and moved toward Jake.

He reached for the can and sprayed a steady stream on the rusted hinges. "Let's give that a minute to do its magic. What's going on up there?"

"Nothing good. We're blocked in. Our driver's stuck on the other side of the barricades." Kim pulled Gaspar's burner from her pocket.

The signal was weak. She hit the redial anyway and crossed her fingers, hoping for a connection.

Gaspar picked up. Why did she ever worry that he wouldn't? "What's up, Suzy Wong? What did your mysterious witness say?"

The connection was weak, and his words cut out. She couldn't have a full conversation about anything right now.

"I need an extraction. For three," she said, hoping he could hear.

"Isn't that Cooper's job?" Gaspar replied sourly.

Gaspar didn't approve of Cooper, mainly because he viewed the Boss as unreliable where Kim was concerned. It was a point she couldn't argue, so she said nothing.

After a brief moment, Gaspar said, "On the way. Thirty minutes. But there's a huge fire out there. Looks like it started at the Christopher Hotel. With the wind gusts, the fire is spreading fast. The pilot will swing around to the east. Maybe a mile from your present location there's an open field. Can you get there?"

"You bet. Thanks, Chico. Send me a bill. I'll put it on my expense report," she teased.

"Yeah, you do that. It'll give Cooper a heart attack and we'll be done with him," he replied with a smile in his voice. "Thirty minutes. The pilot can't wait. Too dangerous."

"Copy that," she said before she disconnected just as Jake grabbed the handle on the iron door.

He braced his feet and heaved with all his strength. After what seemed way too long, the door began to move. Only a few inches at first.

Jake continued to pull and shifted to a different position.

He put his back against the wall and used both hands to push the heavy door open.

When he'd moved it wide enough, Kim said, "I can slip through there."

"I don't like you going back there alone," Jake said when he paused to catch his breath, face red with exertion.

"Yeah, the idea doesn't thrill me, either."

"Let me try one more time. It's moving now. I could get lucky."

But he didn't. The heavy iron door was stuck again. He gave up.

"Wait here. I'll hurry," Kim said as she turned sideways and slipped through into the other side. She reached back through the narrow opening. "Hand me the flashlight."

As she moved deeper into the corridor, the air grew colder, and the dampness seeped deeper into her bones. She was cold and shivering and wet. Her breath was visible in the inky darkness.

Kim's sense of direction suggested she was nearing the space under the kitchen that she'd seen in the drawing. The passage widened and there were small alcoves carved into the stone walls.

Her fingers touched the rough surface as she passed, her internal radar alert to every shift in the air and every slight noise.

Suddenly the narrow passage opened into a larger chamber.

Here, the walls and floor were tiled with marble.

On the right was another door. This one newer.

She approached, grabbed the knob, and turned. She pushed the door open and stepped inside.

Kim was astonished when the flashlight beam illuminated a modern situation room setup. Computers hummed, screens flickered with data, and a large conference table occupied the center of the room.

The space was abandoned, an eerie stillness hanging in the air.

"What the hell...?" Kim's words trailed off, her flashlight's beam dancing over the electronic equipment that continued to run.

Which meant this stuff was being powered by battery backups or maybe a generator. Otherwise, the power would have cut everything off like it had upstairs in the hotel.

She flipped the light switch and the overheads flickered on.

Kim cautiously approached the conference table.

The screens displayed data, graphs, and charts. Unoccupied chairs were placed haphazardly around the conference table.

The atmosphere felt charged, as if the room had been quickly abandoned. But who had been here, and for what purpose?

Her gaze landed on a stack of files neatly arranged in the corner.

"Old school," she murmured as she reached for a folder bound by a sturdy binder clip. She opened the file, revealing a collection of papers.

She scanned the contents—detailed reports, photographs, and intricate schematics that suggested a deep-level operation, meticulously planned and executed. But what was it?

She could figure this out if she had a few hours to spend, but there wasn't time. The helo would be landing soon, and it was their only chance to get out of here without being discovered.

Kim disconnected one of the laptops and grabbed several files. She used her phone to make a video of everything she saw.

"Maybe this stuff will still be here after the dust settles."

The room's electronic hum seemed a subtle reminder of whatever plans had once coursed through the space.

She left the light on, snagged the flashlight, and turned to head back.

Before she could leave the room, a quick shudder coursed through the floor, reverberating beneath her feet. Electronic equipment flickered and a sense of urgency gripped her.

Something was happening.

Hands full, she hurried toward the door.

She glanced over her shoulder. The screens on the walls erupted into a frenzy of activity, displaying cryptic symbols and rapidly scrolling data. The room seemed to pulse with energy directed from a remote location.

Kim ran from the room, along the alcoves, through the damp corridors. When she reached Jake, she handed the laptop to him.

"What's this?" he asked.

"I don't know. Come on, we've got to get out of here," she said, not stopping to discuss anything.

Jake followed her to the steps and up into the brick shed where Vaughan was waiting.

"A helo will pick us up. Follow me," she said as she ran outside.

"What about the witness? Shouldn't we take him with us?" Jake asked following close behind.

"He didn't show," Kim replied.

The fire had consumed more than half the old hotel building now. They were surrounded on all sides by fire and ashes.

The inexplicable room she had discovered in the underground felt like a puzzle piece in a sinister scheme she couldn't figure out.

They heard several helos landing. Firefighters jumped out to battle the blaze. Sirens had finally reached the front of the hotel. First responders piled out of vehicles like ants.

Kim ran toward the pickup point. Jake and Vaughan followed.

The helo set down in the open field. Rotors spinning like a house fan kept the smoke away temporarily.

They sprinted the last hundred feet and scrambled aboard the bird.

Kim took the co-pilot's seat and worked on her harness, gesturing upward with her thumb. "Go go go!" she shouted to the pilot.

Jake and Vaughan buckled into the backseats. Kim settled her headset and turned it on. "Everybody okay?"

"We're good," Jake said.

"Yeah, let's get out of here," Vaughan urged.

As the helo rose, the hotel fire and the chaos surrounding it was laid out beneath them. Guests were being led from the trees to waiting ambulances. Some were coming out strapped to gurneys. Six fire trucks had arrived, and firefighters were hard at work dousing the blaze.

"Where to?" the pilot asked.

Kim supplied the address without taking her eyes off the horrifying bedlam below.

Chapter 28

Friday, June 10
Washington, D.C.

Willard had dropped Tolliver off two blocks away
and she'd waited amid the shadows. She was careful not
to be seen. Too many high-ranking officials lived in
this neighborhood. Which meant the area was heavily
monitored by cameras and patrols and home security
systems.

When Willard was safely out of sight range, Tolliver
moved from cover to cover until she reached a busy
intersection three blocks away.

She used the specialized app on her phone to unlock
a small Honda sedan. She was inside and driving away
within thirty seconds.

The Skinner homicide was her first priority. She'd been in Bull Gator's the night Skinner was killed. The last thing Tolliver and Willard needed was to be involved in a homicide investigation. The damned cops would be hounding her soon enough. She was more than a little surprised that they hadn't been around already.

The police files contained DNA samples taken from Skinner's body. Matching the samples to the killer would shut the investigation down. Unfortunately, the most significant sample failed to return a match from CODIS, the acronym for "combined DNA index system."

CODIS was the computer software that operated federal, state, and local DNA databases. The system was limited because it only contained DNA profiles from convicted offenders, missing persons, and crime scenes.

CODIS was a powerful tool, but it wasn't all-inclusive, and it didn't solve every crime.

Simply put, there were millions of people inside the US who had no DNA profile in the CODIS system at all. And millions more outside the US who were invisible to CODIS.

Which meant if one of those millions without DNA profiles in CODIS had killed Skinner, the DNA samples collected from Skinner's body would not be matched.

The FBI would move on to other databases where the DNA might match, such as military files or commercial ancestry sites. Sometimes, those databases worked to identify leads.

But the truth was that in the real world, a killer could remain unknown forever. Plenty of cold cases around the country were more than ten years old.

As long as the DNA couldn't be matched, the Skinner investigation would remain open.

To shut down the investigation, the FBI team needed a solid suspect. When they found a DNA match belonging to the suspect, they would stop looking and charge the guy.

But who had killed Skinner?

The FBI files contained a name and address for Skinner's ex-lover. Statistically, lovers made the most likely killers. Second most likely killers were ex-lovers.

Which meant Skinner's ex was probably guilty and even if he wasn't, he'd be a perfect patsy. All she had to do was make it possible for the investigative team to find him.

Tolliver parked the Honda several blocks away from his residence address. The night air was cold; she could see her own breath as she exhaled. The wind carried the smell of rain.

She wore fresh surgical gloves. In her pocket, Skinner's burner phone.

Tolliver had picked the phone up from the ground outside Bull Gator's that night. She'd thought the phone was hers. Only later did she realize it was actually Skinner's when she found her own cell phone in her car.

Skinner's phone had been used to exchange several angry text messages with her ex. The call log registered a number of phone calls between them as well. Exactly the kind of situation that too often escalated to murder.

Tolliver's senses were on high alert as she neared his building. She glanced around, noting the positions of the streetlights, the cars parked along the street, the faint sounds of a television from an open window where the owner was sleeping.

She noticed the details: a stray cat dashing across the road, a blinking light from a distant plane in the sky.

If the FBI had found this guy already, they'd be sitting in an unmarked vehicle outside the house watching him. They weren't there. Not yet.

What they needed was enough probable cause for a warrant or an arrest.

She moved with purpose. Swiftly, she used the burner phone to send one last incriminating text. A message that would place Skinner's ex at Bull Gator's the night of the murder. With enough motive and opportunity to kill.

She pulled the pre-addressed bubble mailer from her pocket and slipped the phone inside. She dropped the envelope into a postal box close to his home. When the box was emptied in a few hours, the carrier would collect the phone and arrange delivery to the FBI task force before noon.

As she moved away from the drop box, she saw movement in her periphery. She froze.

It was him, carrying a bag of groceries, puffing on a cigarette held between his lips. He paused on the front stoop, as if sensing something amiss.

Tolliver stood in the shadows, out of sight. She had two choices: leave now and risk detection or wait.

Her hand withdrew the knife from her pocket and held it by her side out of sight.

He glanced both ways and turned around to look behind. After another moment, he took a long drag from the cigarette and tossed the butt into the bushes. Then he opened his front door and stepped into the apartment.

With cat-like reflexes, Tolliver made her choice. She'd come too far to leave this job to chance.

Crouched low amid the shadows, she darted into the bushes, collected his cigarette, and dropped it into an evidence bag she withdrew from her pocket.

She sealed the bag and stuffed it into her pocket again.

Insurance.

Minutes later, she was safely settled again in her car. Her gloved hands gripped the wheel, veins pulsing with adrenaline.

She drove the Honda to an all-night adult theater in a dodgy section of town. She parked the Honda and locked it behind her as she hurried away on foot.

Along the way, she tossed the knife into a trash can, still wearing the gloves, which she dropped into separate trash bins later.

It was very late when she finally returned home. She let herself in through the back door.

Her ears caught the reassuring hum of the refrigerator from the kitchen as she closed the door softly behind her, locked up, and set the alarms. The faint scent of last night's pizza greeted her, mingling with the musty aroma of old books.

Tolliver placed the bag holding the cigarette butt in her safe. Tomorrow, she'd submit it to "Find Your Family," a consumer DNA business she'd used before.

Submitting his DNA on the cigarette butt to the free ancestry DNA sites online should take care of making him visible, if the burner phone wasn't enough on its own to get the cops moving.

Since the infamous BTK serial killer had been discovered using familial DNA, law enforcement units had been routinely checking those sources in tough cases. No doubt, the FBI would do that in Skinner's case, after a nudge in the right direction.

The "Find Your Family" advertising promised short turnaround times for DC customers.

Which meant his DNA should be in their system within a few hours after the sample was received and processed.

The company didn't advertise that it had a contract with the FBI.

The fine print in the consent form advised that all fees were waived, and DNA testing was free. But results would be shared with law enforcement.

After a long, hot shower, Tolliver fell into bed, satisfied that Skinner's lover would be arrested very soon, one way or the other. And the FBI would move on from the patrons at Bull Gator's.

Chapter 29

After his third cup of Cuban coffee, Gaspar entered the coordinates from Fonda's tattoo into his systems, seeking answers. He'd been a soldier not a sailor. His knowledge of all things nautical was limited at best.

But he was well aware of military concerns over the South China Sea.

Within moments, the system pulled up the exact location. Not an island, but a point underwater. He spent an hour sifting through submarine routes, naval exercises, and underwater anomalies worthy of further exploration.

Fonda's coordinates didn't match any key strategic sites he could identify.

He dialed Detective Martinez. She picked up right away.

"It's Gaspar. I've been looking into those coordinates you found on Fonda's body."

"Do you know what time it is?" she replied.

"Sorry. I thought you'd be up. You work the day shift, right?" Gaspar said.

"I am up. I'm in my car on the way to work. But that doesn't mean I want to talk to anybody at this hour," she groused. "We've got people working on the Fonda case. It's not just me."

"Roger that," Gaspar said lightly.

Martinez paused a minute before she gave in. "Okay. What did you find?"

"Not much. The location is deep underwater. A trench or seamount, most likely," Gaspar said.

"What's a seamount?"

He recited the definition he'd found online. "An underwater mountain with steep sides rising up from the sea floor."

Martinez replied, "Yeah, okay. Well, we've found tales of sunken ships and treasures in the area, but Fonda wouldn't have bought into them. Based on what we know, she was methodical, not fanciful."

"Exactly," Gaspar said. "And recently, they've picked up anomalous sonar readings near those coordinates. Unexplained sounds, patterns not consistent with marine life."

"Yeah. We found that, too. Could be someone using the underwater location as a secret base or research facility, we think."

"It's plausible." Gaspar swiped a palm across his face as he weighed his words. "The deep ocean is vast and underexplored. Which makes it an ideal spot to conduct discreet operations without attracting attention."

"Yeah. We know."

"So what have you done about it?"

Martinez paused and then spoke slowly. "If Fonda knew about an unauthorized facility, especially in the sensitive region of the South China Sea, this whole thing could be a matter of national security. We pushed it to the feds late last night."

"Who'd you hand the case off to? FBI?" Gaspar asked.

"Yeah. Local office to start, but they kicked it upstairs already."

"Upstairs to whom?"

"All the way up. Charles Cooper himself," Martinez replied.

Gaspar made no comment.

"If Fonda was aware of concealed operations in the South China Sea, she didn't discover it on her own. But that knowledge could be what got her killed," Martinez said.

"She wasn't in intelligence," Gaspar pointed out. "Her security clearance was good, but not that good."

"Meaning?"

"She wouldn't have stumbled across something like that. Someone had to feed her that information."

"We've been told to stand down on the coordinates. Give the feds a chance to figure that aspect out. And I've gotta go." Martinez sounded a bit distracted now. Before she rang off, she said, "We'll keep working the murder. See where it leads."

Gaspar wandered into the kitchen for a couple of pastries and another big mug of sweet Cuban coffee. He crossed his ankles and leaned against the counter waiting for the espresso to steam and thinking about Charles Cooper. What would he do with the intel?

Cooper couldn't be trusted. No question about that. And he'd sent Otto off on this particular goose chase, which meant he knew something more than he was sharing.

Did Cooper know about Fonda's coordinates already?

Gaspar shrugged. Speculation was getting him nowhere. Regardless of everything else, the tattoo had changed the Fonda case.

Was she a homeless, drug addicted veteran at all?

Or was that a cover she used to keep questions at bay while she engaged in something else entirely?

Had Fonda been a covert operative? Working for whom? Cooper?

What about the other Hornet victims? Were they all operatives for Cooper and his cronies?

Entirely possible.

Cooper's fingerprints were all over these cases.

What the hell was he up to?

And what did Jack Reacher have to do with it all?

Gaspar was a man who lived with his feet firmly planted in the present. He didn't waste his limited time spinning fiction and inventing theories to explain away the obvious.

Emma Fonda was murdered six months ago and her body was dumped in that Miami warehouse. Those were the facts.

What he didn't know was who killed her and why.

The fresh tattoo and the coordinates opened a wider pool of suspects and exponentially more potential motives, for sure.

Gaspar shrugged. Now that Detective Martinez had turned all of that over to Cooper, he would let it go. If Cooper wanted Otto to do more with the Fonda situation, he wouldn't be shy about saying so.

Gaspar could wait for Cooper's next move. He had another approach in mind.

"Let's press the reset button on this one," Gaspar said aloud as he poured the sweetened hot milk into the espresso and headed back to his den.

He pulled up commercial airline schedules. With a few quick keystrokes, he found a nonstop to Albany and booked one seat. A quick up and back.

He glanced at the clock. He needed to bring Otto up to speed.

But it was still the middle of the night in Colorado.

He sent a text asking her to call.

Chapter 30

Friday, June 10
Colorado Springs, CO

Kim's body fairly thrummed with tension as the helicopter's blades sliced through the night air, lifting them away from the blazing hotel fire. The pilot and three passengers didn't try to talk over the helo's noise. Everything Kim wanted to discuss was too complicated to handle over their headsets, anyway. Which meant she'd had a bit of time to think for a change.

Colorado Springs gradually materialized below them, a sprawl of lights in the surrounding darkness. Kim glanced at Jake and Vaughan. Their faces were stoic but lined with exhaustion.

The pilot approached and set the helo down smoothly at a private airstrip on the outskirts of town. The black

SUV that had dropped them off at the Christopher Hotel was waiting.

Cooper must have sent it. Which meant she'd soon have normal clothes to wear again and, with any luck, a place to get a few hours' sleep.

When the rotors slowed Kim thanked the pilot, and they climbed out of the helo's cabin. She retrieved the laptop and files she'd stolen from the situation room back in the underground tunnel and followed Jake and Vaughan away from the cold wind whipped up by the rotor wash.

"This way," Kim shouted to be heard above the noise. She led the way to the SUV.

"Good to see you, Cliff," she said as she tossed the laptop and files into the footwell. The helo was already lifting off the pavement, headed out.

Kim climbed into the passenger seat while Jake and Vaughan settled into the backseats and closed the doors. The interior of the SUV was as quiet as a tomb.

"Everybody ready?" Cliff asked and, hearing no objections, rolled toward the exit. "Sorry I couldn't pick you up at the hotel. All traffic was blocked because of the fire."

"No worries. We made it out," Kim replied. "We need a place to shower and change and get some sleep. Anybody familiar with this area?"

Vaughan said, "Somewhat. I've been here a few times. Worked a couple of cases with the local PD. But I've never stayed in a hotel here."

Cliff glanced across the console. His gaze met Kim's. "We have a confirmed location. I was directed to take you there and stay with you as long as you need me."

"Where is it?" Kim asked.

"Away from town." Cliff tapped the navigation system and the display screen lit up. "The Way Inn Motel."

The blue dot showed the SUV's current location. A red flag showed their destination in a sparsely populated area twenty miles away.

"Wi-Fi will be spotty out there. Cell service, too," Vaughan said when she leaned over to look at the screen.

"Perfect," Kim said as she flipped on her heated seat. Exhaustion, lack of food, slowing adrenaline, and the cold night air had combined to make her shiver.

"Still got your bags in the back. Want me to stop so you can change into something warmer?" Cliff offered as he followed the nav system's twists and turns.

"Let's just get there first. A hot shower and a gallon of coffee will fix me up," Kim replied.

They traveled the rest of the route in silence until Cliff pulled into the Way Inn Motel parking lot. He turned off the ignition and the SUV fell eerily silent again.

"Here we are," Cliff said, looking at Kim.

Kim's eyes scanned the motel. Single-story, isolated, no cars in the lot. Her gut clenched.

"Let's check in," she said, still feeling the edge of her nerves.

They grabbed their bags and walked to the front office. A woman sat behind the counter, half-glued to her paperback. The title was *Nothing to Lose* by a bestselling author Kim recognized.

"That book any good?" Kim asked the desk clerk.

"Why? You want to borrow it when I'm done?" The woman's customer service was too surly for Kim's taste, so she got straight to the point.

"We need three rooms," Kim said, placing three one-hundred-dollar bills on the counter.

The woman plopped her open paperback onto the counter, glanced at the cash, then at each of them in turn.

"You're in luck. Got exactly three rooms left." She handed over the keys and pushed the three hundred into her pocket. "Rooms 8, 9, and 10."

"Got any coffee?" Kim asked.

"There's a pot in each room." She picked up her book as if she were eager to finish the story when Jake and Vaughan left the office.

Kim held back a second. "Is this place usually so deserted?"

The woman shrugged, lifting her gaze from the paperback. "Hit or miss. Quiet lately. You got the whole place to yourselves right now. Can't say how it'll be tomorrow."

Their rooms were next to each other in a line along the back of the motel. Doors faced a dark stretch of woods. Kim looked at Jake and Vaughan.

"Get some sleep," she said, unlocking her door. "We've got a lot to talk about in the morning."

She waited until Jake and Vaughan went inside and both locks clicked into place.

Kim went into her room, flipped on the heat, and set the laptop and files on the table. She surveyed the room. It was clean but dated. Probably last decorated about 1980, judging from the colors and the sagging mattress.

She stripped off the filthy ball gown and dropped it in a heap on the floor as she headed for the shower. The hot water felt like Heaven. She stayed under the spray until her teeth finally stopped chattering.

When she stepped out of the shower wrapped in a skimpy towel, she found a text from Vaughan on her phone.

"Check your room for bugs."

Kim frowned. Bed bugs were a common thing even in good hotels these days. But Vaughan's warning wasn't about creepy crawlers.

Kim pulled a small electronic scanner from her bag and began sweeping. A red light blinked when she reached the underside of the parson's table across from the bed, but nowhere else.

"Got one," she texted back.

"Same. Jake, too," Vaughan replied.

Kim removed the listening device and crushed it under her boot and dropped it into the toilet. She had no idea who planted the bugs or why.

She found a pair of red silk pajamas in her bag and got dressed for bed. The silk wasn't warm enough for early spring in the mountains, but there was nothing she could do about that now. She sat on the bed and dried her hair with a blow dryer.

It had been a long night. She needed sleep. But the listening devices worried her.

Her phone buzzed again, this time with a text from Cliff.

"I'll be in the car. Need anything, call me."

Kim moved her phones and her pistol into easy reach before she climbed into bed, switched off the lights, and closed her eyes.

In what felt like a few moments later, a heavy fist pounded on her door.

"Open up!"

How long had he been out there? She grabbed her gun, slipped her feet into her shoes, and moved silently to the window adjacent to the door.

She peeked around the curtain. It was daylight already. And Cliff stood on the left side of the door. Broad-shouldered, serious face. He glanced at his wristwatch impatiently.

Kim relaxed a fraction, tucked her pistol into the back of her waistband, and opened the door.

Cliff stayed on the sidewalk holding out a satellite phone. "Cooper wants to talk to you. You've got no cell service in here, he says."

Chapter 31

"Otto," she said. "What's up?"

Cliff pulled the door closed and waited outside.

"Update on Suanne Skinner, the most recent victim. Locals have arrested her ex-lover. They've got a witness who puts him at Bull Gator's an hour before she died. Still unconfirmed, but we expect the DNA they found on her body is his," Cooper said. "They finished the specialized autopsy. No air embolus detected. Looks like cause of death was blunt force trauma. She hit her head on a corner of the pavement, probably when he knocked her down. He's been arrested."

Kim blinked, still waking up, not sure she heard correctly. "Skinner was not a Hornet victim?"

"Unlikely. Looks like a separate homicide," Cooper replied. "Locals jumped the gun. They put her on the list when she shouldn't have been added."

"You think Reacher was involved with Skinner somehow?"

Cooper said, "Doesn't look like it from where I'm sitting. Unless you know something about the situation that I don't."

"Unfortunately not."

Cooper's attention was already diverted by something on his end. "Keep the satellite phone so you can reach me if you need to. Dispose of it when you're finished."

"What about Cliff? He's a competent agent, I assume. And I could use an extra pair of hands," Kim said.

"You can keep the SUV." Cooper paused briefly. "Cliff's got other things to do. Drop him off somewhere. He's resourceful. He'll find his own way."

Kim considered telling him about the listening devices in their rooms and the situation room she'd found in the labyrinth below the Christopher Hotel. Before she had a chance to make up her mind, he'd already disconnected.

She returned to peek through the curtains. Cliff was no longer standing by the door.

It was almost six o'clock. The sun was well up in the sky. No point in trying to sleep.

Since there was no cell service in her room, she couldn't call Gaspar unless she used the sat phone, which was the same as inviting Cooper to the conversation.

"Nope," she said. "Not doing that."

The laptop and files from the situation room were right there on the floor near her bag. She slipped into her jeans and boots, pulled on a sweater, and started a pot of coffee.

While it brewed, she turned on the laptop. As it loaded up, she sorted quickly through the hard copy files she'd stolen. Everything was encrypted and coded. She didn't have time to figure them out and no way to transfer the files.

Thirty minutes later, she'd drained the coffee pot and packed everything up. She heard a light tap on the door. Kim peeked through the curtains again. This time, Vaughan was standing there.

"Jake's taken our bags to the SUV. Are you ready? Don't want to be late for the appointment with the pathologist," Vaughan said.

"Right," Kim said, gathering her bag, the laptop, and the files, and following Vaughan.

She glanced briefly over her shoulder at The Way Inn as she made her way to the SUV. It looked even more decrepit in the daylight.

Jake stood at the open cargo door. "Did you sleep at all?"

"That your way of telling me I look like hell?" she grinned as she lifted everything into the SUV.

Cliff pushed a button to lower the cargo door while Jake, Vaughan, and Kim repositioned themselves in the same seats as last night.

"Where to?" Cliff asked.

"El Paso County Coroner's office," Vaughan said, giving him the address.

He punched the address into the navigation system, which gave him three routes to choose from. "We're passing near Colorado Springs Airport. You can drop me off there."

Kim nodded. "Roger that."

Thirty minutes later, Cliff handed off the wheel to Jake and walked into the terminal at the departure gate entrance.

"Where's he going?" Jake asked.

"Wherever he's told. That's how this gig works, as you'll soon find out," Kim replied.

Jake followed the nav system, which led them along surface streets traveling west toward the coroner's office.

"It's a one-story building off Las Vegas Street," Vaughan said. "Near the jail. The sheriff's office and the police impound lot are nearby. Easier to transport the bodies."

"Have you been to the coroner's office before?" Kim asked.

"Couple of times. Always for professional reasons. Since David died, I've talked to the pathologist who performed his autopsy once," Vaughan said.

"What can you tell us about him?" Jake asked.

"Name's Merlin Thacker. Nice enough guy. Competent. Testifies well, my boss says," Vaughan replied. "He's fifty, I'd guess. Give or take. He's been around the block."

Jake took the last turn into the complex. He drove past the jail and found a space big enough for the SUV in the visitor's lot close enough to the morgue building.

Vaughan led the way. Kim and Jake followed along the sidewalk to the front entrance. Vaughan showed her badge to the duty officer. He pushed the door release to the interior of the building and waved them through.

They walked along a narrow corridor and made a couple of right turns until Vaughan stopped to rap her knuckles on a wooden door. She pushed it open into a cramped office.

Behind the desk piled high with papers was a middle-aged man with graying hair wearing a white lab coat. He was reading one of the files, deep in concentration. He didn't seem to notice them.

"Dr. Thacker," Vaughan said to catch his attention.

"Yes?" He looked up over the reading glasses perched on the end of his nose, as if he had no idea why they were standing in his doorway.

"I'm Officer Samantha Vaughan. We've met before. These are my colleagues Jake Reacher and Kim Otto. We had an appointment," Vaughan said by way of reminder.

"Yes, yes, yes. Come in. Sorry I don't have chairs for you. As you can imagine, I don't get many visitors," he said, not getting up. "Standing room only, I'm afraid."

"No problem. We won't be long," Vaughan replied.

The three moved into the room and closed the door.

"Officer Vaughan, after you called, I reviewed the autopsy report and the photographs we took of your husband's body," Dr. Thacker said pointing, as if giving a lecture to medical students. He turned the screen around to display it.

Kim said, "You did the autopsy on David Vaughan yourself, Dr. Thacker?"

"Yes, that's right." He nodded as if she were a particularly apt pupil. "I recall it well and I've reviewed the reports, as I said. What would you like to know?"

"We're investigating another homicide. The killer used an unusual murder weapon," Vaughan said, finally catching Dr. Thacker's interest. "He gets close enough to inject an air embolus into the jugular vein."

"So the victim knows the killer, or the killer incapacitates the victim in some way first," he said. "Couldn't pull that off if the victim resisted in any way."

"Yeah, that's what we're thinking," Vaughan nodded. "We're investigating whether David might have been killed in a similar way?"

Dr. Thacker squirmed, looking a bit uncomfortable. "I didn't specifically check. Having gone to that much trouble to conceal the crime, he'd have made a tiny puncture. Hard to find, even if we were looking for it. Which we weren't."

"Can we see the photographs you took of the body before the autopsy?" Kim asked.

He hesitated, then clicked his mouse a few times, sorting through his computer files. After a couple of seconds, a series of gruesome images appeared on the screen.

Vaughan barely flinched when he enlarged four photos of David's neck. Dr. Thacker peered at the screen, and they all leaned in to see as well as they could.

"Anything?" Kim asked.

He shook his head. "I can't confirm it."

Kim stifled a surge of frustration. "Can you take another look? We need to rule this out, if we can."

"The body was cremated, wasn't it?" Dr. Thacker said with a regretful glance toward David's widow.

"So, you can't verify that a puncture wound to David's jugular did or did not happen," Vaughan stated flatly.

"Not from the autopsy or these photographs. I'm sorry, Mrs. Vaughan," he replied.

"What do you believe caused David Vaughan's sudden cardiac arrest?" Kim asked.

Dr. Thacker shook his head. "In this case, it's impossible to say. We didn't suspect foul play at the time. There was no reason to believe his death wasn't natural causes."

"He was a young man, physically healthy back when he received the head injury in Iraq. What would cause his heart to stop like that?" Jake asked, as if he was a little worried about the answer because healthy young men should be invincible.

"It happens. Athletes can die from cardiac arrest. Being young and physically fit is no guarantee against mortality," Dr. Thacker replied.

"But an air embolus can cause sudden cardiac death, as we know," Kim said.

"It can." Dr. Thacker nodded. "But the most common cause is an irregular heart rhythm called ventricular fibrillation. Other causes are things like drug overdoses, heart attacks, blood loss, electrocution."

"And did you rule all of those out in David's case?" Vaughan asked.

Dr. Thacker removed his reading glasses and offered her a sorrowful look. "Mrs. Vaughan, our autopsy findings were consistent with natural causes. We saw nothing that would lead us to believe otherwise."

"But you didn't look for puncture wounds to his jugular veins. So you can't say that didn't happen, can you?" Vaughan pushed.

Dr. Thacker shook his head. "That's right. I can't say it didn't happen. But I can't confirm that it did, either."

Vaughan cocked her head. "If you were me, and we were talking about the love of your life, would you just let this go?"

Dr. Thacker blinked slowly like a frog. He seemed to be considering her question. He turned his attention to the computer screen and scrolled through to another file.

"What are you looking for?" Vaughan asked.

He didn't look away from scrolling the screen to answer her question. "There are other ways to introduce a fatal air embolus into the body. I'm just reviewing the nurse's notes."

"Find something?" Kim asked as the scrolling slowed.

"I was checking to see what IVs David was getting before he died. Patients who are bedridden for long periods of time can have a special kind of line inserted in the chest called a PIC line," Dr. Thacker said. "Did David have a PIC line, Mrs. Vaughan."

She nodded. "He did. He'd become so frail. They had trouble using other methods."

"Why is that important here, Dr. Thacker?" Kim asked.

"Well, it would be easy to deliver a fatal air embolus through a PIC line. No reason to inject the jugular when you've got a direct line in place," Dr. Thacker replied.

Vaughan gasped.

"So you're saying David could have been murdered," Jake said.

"I'm still saying that we can't make that determination now. The cause of death was sudden cardiac arrest. But yes, a large air embolus could have stopped his heart," Dr. Thacker explained. "I couldn't testify to that, you understand. It's nothing more than supposition."

"But it is possible that David Vaughan was murdered," Jake insisted.

Dr. Thacker shrugged. He'd said as much as he was prepared to say. And there was no body to exhume for further testing. So they'd never know for sure.

Vaughan looked pale and shaken. Jake escorted her out of the office.

"We need to get going," Kim said as she moved away from the screen.

"I'm really sorry I can't do more," Dr. Thacker said.

"Thank you for your time, Dr. Thacker. We appreciate the help," Kim said, offering her business card. "If you think of anything else, please call me."

He did the slow blinking thing again as he studied the card. "Of course."

Kim thanked him again and left the office. Jake and Vaughan were waiting outside. As they returned to the SUV, the weight of missed opportunities hung in the air.

Vaughan seemed preoccupied, Jake frustrated, and Kim knew they were running out of time.

Jake reversed out of the parking space and rolled to the exit. "Where to?"

"I need to eat and to make a few calls," Kim replied. "Vaughan? Any ideas?"

Vaughan remained quiet. Kim pulled out her phone and searched for diners nearby.

"Let's try Daisy's Diner. Says here it's known for strong coffee and hearty breakfasts. I saw the strip center earlier. It's not far," Kim said, pointing east.

"Roger that," Jake said, hitting the reverse route button on the navigation. "Daisy's Diner it is."

Chapter 32

Friday, June 10
Colorado Springs, CO

Vaughan slid into the turquoise vinyl booth at Daisy's Diner. Jake filled the bench across from her. The air felt heavy with the smell of frying bacon and the murmurs of other diners.

Kim's stomach growled with hunger as soon as the aromas hit her. "Order coffee and pancakes for me, please. I've got to make a call."

Kim's fingers tightened around her phone as she stepped outside. The neon "Open" sign cast a red glow on the sidewalk, doing little to warm the chill that had settled over her.

She fished Gaspar's burner phone from her pocket as she walked toward a bench located in a quiet section of the parking lot. She checked the signal strength and hit the redial.

It was two hours earlier in Miami, but Gaspar would be awake.

"Good morning, Sunshine. How are things out there in the Wild West?" he teased.

"Lots of questions. Very few solid answers," she replied. "You?"

"Same."

Wiping a palm across her face, she said, "Tell me about Emma Fonda."

"Curious case. Miami coroner found a tattoo under her left breast during the second autopsy—coordinates. They point to a spot in the South China Sea."

"That's more than a little crazy, isn't it?"

"Yeah, and here's the kicker: there's nothing out there. Nothing I could find in any database. No islands or land of any kind. No submarines resting on the ocean floor, even. Didn't find so much as a hungry school of fish," Gaspar said. "If there's anything down there underwater, it's completely buried by more than just the ocean."

Kim's mind raced. "That's bizarre. Could we be on the wrong track here? Maybe the tattoo isn't coordinates at all?"

"Possibly not, but don't get your hopes up. Chances are slim. Still checking," Gaspar replied. "What about you? Any updates?"

Kim filled him in. "The Christopher Hotel burned to the ground last night. Probably arson."

"Did the mystery witness contact you before that happened?" Gaspar asked.

"No. I still have no idea who the witness was or what they wanted," Kim said.

"Sounds like he wanted you dead," Gaspar replied angrily.

"Possibly," Kim admitted. "But here's the crazy thing. I found an underground situation room at the hotel."

"That's not just crazy, it's insane. Who would need a hidden situation room under a resort hotel?"

"Dunno. Possibly the Piranhas. They might have been directing operations from there, whatever the operations were. Or are," Kim replied.

"The Piranhas? The criminal organization? What could they be involved in that would require a situation room?"

"You keep asking questions to which I have no answers," Kim said.

"Right. Sorry," Gaspar said. "I can think of a few options. The call from the witness luring you out there could have been genuine. Maybe he got spooked. Or his motives could have been sinister. He might have intended to lure you to the fire. Or the situation room."

"Yeah, well, any of those guesses are as good as the others at the moment."

"Or it could be something else entirely," Gaspar reminded her.

"We need more intel. I grabbed a laptop and files before I had to run. Everything's encrypted. I need you to crack the laptop and analyze its contents," Kim said. "Maybe you'll find something useful."

"Roger that. What else?"

"I swiped a few hard copy files filled with coded communications. We need those unlocked, too," Kim said. "I'll have everything delivered to you as soon as I can."

"I'll get right on it," Gaspar promised. "What about David Vaughan? Any progress there?"

"I talked to the pathologist who did Vaughan's autopsy, Dr. Thacker," Kim paused and lowered her voice. "It's possible David was murdered, as his wife suspects. Pathologist can't prove it because the body's been cremated. But he can't rule it out either."

"So the only way Samantha Vaughan will ever know for sure is if you catch the killer and make him confess," Gaspar said. "Tall order."

"Hey, if this job was easy, anyone could do it," Kim replied with a smirk Gaspar couldn't see. "And Cooper called. He says the latest body, Suanne Skinner, isn't a Hornet victim after all."

"And how did they figure that out?" Gaspar asked slowly.

"The usual. Good police work and DNA." Quickly, she brought him up to speed on the arrest of Skinner's ex. "So Hornet didn't kill her. No reason to suspect the Piranhas either."

Gaspar's protective instincts were working overtime. His response was swift and hard. "Cooper was wrong. Reacher's not involved in any of this. You're wasting your time and sticking your neck out for no good reason."

"Possibly. But not likely, is it?" Kim replied. "Cooper's never been wrong about Reacher before. His intel is often incomplete, but every time Cooper says Reacher's connected, he was connected. He'll be connected here, too. I just don't know how yet."

Gaspar was quiet for a good long time.

"What's bothering you, Chico?" Kim finally asked.

"You're working on the Hornet murders. The David Vaughan case. The Piranhas. And hunting Reacher," Gaspar said. "Are they *all* connected to Cooper or Reacher?"

"That's what I've been pondering. They're loosely connected, but not related, I think," Kim replied. "I think there's actually four *different* things going on."

"What does that mean?"

"There's the David Vaughan murder. Because I now believe he was killed, even if Dr. Thacker can't prove it," Kim frowned. "It is what it is. Sooner or later, we'll catch the killer."

"Because he pulled this one off so easily, you mean? I agree. And he'll kill again if we don't figure out why and stop him," Gaspar replied. "But unless the crime connects to Reacher, you can move the David Vaughan murder down your priority list or hand it off."

"And there's something else and then another something else," Kim said slowly, mentally counting on her fingers. "And then Reacher."

"You're losing me, Suzie Wong."

Which she knew was not true. He just wanted her to spell it all out for him.

"David Vaughan, we've already covered," Kim said. "The Piranhas. Where do they fit in? Why did they need a situation room, assuming the one I found was theirs? Are they connected to Fonda's tattoo somehow?"

"Dunno." Gaspar said, and Kim could almost see him shrug while he said it.

"The third thing is the Hornet murders. Looks like there may only be two or three of them now that Skinner has been ruled out."

"That we know of," Gaspar said.

"Yes. That we've found so far. There could be more, and Agent Johnson's team will keep working on that."

"You don't think the Hornet murders are related to David Vaughan's murder or the Piranhas?"

"Nothing we've found so far to suggest it," Kim said with a frown. She thought she could hear announcements from a loudspeaker in the background.

"Except Cooper told you so," Gaspar replied flatly.

"Right." Kim paused. "And the fourth thing is Reacher. All of it involves Reacher. Or did. Or will."

"You're making me tired," Gaspar said with a sigh. "What do you want me to do now?"

"Wish I knew. If anything brilliant pops into your head, shout it out. Meanwhile, I've got to get back inside." She paused to be sure he was listening. "We're driving one of Cooper's vehicles, which means I can't talk openly while I'm in the SUV unless I want him to know every thought in my head. Which I don't. So I'll call you again when I can."

"Okay," Gaspar said.

She heard the disembodied loudspeaker again. "Where are you, anyway?"

"Albany Airport. On my way to the WarDel Motel," he replied a little breathlessly, as if he were walking faster than he could comfortably move.

"The dumpy place where they found Melody Bennett's body months ago?" Kim asked. "What do you expect to find there?"

"I don't know. But something's nagging me. Skinner's murderer turned out to be her ex. It's possible the task force is on the wrong track with Fonda. We don't know much about Harmon, but the task force is all over that one." He seemed to stop walking and she heard the sound of a vehicle door opening and closing and a moment later, the engine started. "So now I'm wondering what the FBI task force might have left out of the briefing packets on the Bennett murder."

"Okay. Let me know what happens," Kim said as she hung up and returned to the diner where her coffee was cold, and her pancakes congealed on the plate.

The waitress came over with a fresh cup of coffee and removed the untouched pancakes. "Let me get you another order. You two want anything else?"

Jake said, "Hot coffee would be great."

Vaughan said nothing. Her eyes were wide, and she kept her head facing forward. She looked almost catatonic.

Jake touched her arm, startling her. She blinked rapidly and glanced toward the waitress. "I'm fine, thanks. Nothing more for me."

The waitress smiled and nodded and scurried away.

When she was out of hearing range, Vaughan said, "I've remembered something about David. Could be important. Or not."

Kim nodded encouragement. "What is it?"

"During his second tour, he was approached about future employment with a contract security firm called the Boxer Group," Vaughan said. "Have you ever heard of them?"

Jake shook his head.

"There're quite a few of those companies out there. They hire ex-military personnel, usually. Lot of places in the world will pay good money for US military trained soldiers. Blackwater was one of the better-known ones," Kim said.

Jake asked, "Did David take the job?"

"He wanted to. The money was good. Some of the guys from his squad had already signed up. He thought it would be a good fit after he finished his second tour," Vaughan explained. "But that…didn't happen."

Kim waited a minute before she asked, "What made you think about the Boxer Group right now?"

"One of the reasons David thought the job might be good for him. I was working in Hope, Colorado. Still am. And the Boxer Group was based in Colorado," Vaughan said quietly, eyes glassy with tears. "We'd been separated too much and too long. That's why he was interested in the offer. He wanted us to be together."

Kim asked, "Where was the Boxer Group's home base? Denver?"

Vaughan shrugged. "If David ever told me, I don't remember now."

"Should be easy enough to find out," Jake said.

Chapter 33

Tolliver stepped under shelter away from the gusty wind, folded her oversized umbrella, and pushed open the aquarium's heavy glass doors. She pulled the ticket stub from her pocket and scanned it for the exhibit's location.

Children's laughter and ethereal background music created a surreal contrast to the weight of her purpose here. She had very little time to spare before she'd be missed.

Navigating quickly through the corridors, she spied him. "The Abyss" was a special exhibit envisioning a futuristic underwater base of operations where humans could live and work.

The exhibit buzzed with an array of LED lights mimicking bioluminescent sea creatures. The creatures glowed in the dark, illuminating glass cases filled with submersed displays. Farms, homes, workplaces.

The designer's vision depicted harmony between technological ingenuity and the ocean's hidden world.

The fanciful exhibit was science fiction now, but it wouldn't be fiction forever.

Willard stood near a large digital screen that cycled through blueprints of the imaginary base. His trench coat and old-fashioned wide-brimmed fedora were dripping rainwater on the tile floor.

"A fascinating vision of what could be," Willard said, continuing to gaze at the screen as Tolliver approached.

"Not in our lifetime," Tolliver replied, standing beside him while also keeping her focus on the exhibit.

"You say that, but we know our enemies are developing these projects as we speak," Willard insisted. "With so many minds working on the problems, they'll be solved sooner than you believe."

Tolliver shrugged. She hadn't come here to listen to his propaganda. "The Christopher Hotel. Status?"

Willard gazed at the exhibit as if it were nirvana. To him, it probably was. "The hotel and the situation room beneath it was destroyed, as planned."

"And the secondary targets?"

"All three remain unaccounted for," Willard said plainly. "For the moment."

"You lost them?" Tolliver willfully suppressed her anger. "That's the definition of failure. You understand the repercussions."

He nodded solemnly. "We're still the best and only option you have at this point. Replacing us isn't feasible. We all know that. So let's move forward, shall we?"

"The Boxer Group remains a contentious choice. Many were not satisfied when that decision was made. There's plenty of time to make a change," Tolliver said, pretending to be engrossed in the futuristic undersea base. "The Christopher Hotel failure could tip the scales in the wrong direction. How do you plan to handle it?"

"We'll locate the targets and revisit our security measures for the future," Willard assured her. "You can't make an omelet without breaking a few eggs."

Tolliver weighed her options. He was right. Replacing the Boxer Group wasn't possible. They couldn't turn back time and start over.

She said, "You have forty-eight hours to find and deal with them. Otherwise, I'll have to bring this issue to the attention of the others."

"We'll get it done," he responded. "Thurman is on it. He's smarter than his old man was."

"You'd better hope so. Because if you don't get it done…" Her gaze met his as she allowed her words to drop off instead of completing the threat.

He already knew the depth of the consequences. She had no need to repeat them.

"Duly noted." He gave a curt nod. After a brief pause, he said, "I hear the Skinner case was closed. Good news."

"For both of us." Tolliver stared down his implied threat. "Don't overestimate your worth, Willard. You're not too big to fail."

"No one is, it turns out. We've seen too many of the rich and powerful drop to hold onto that fantasy," Willard replied. "I'll let you know when the three secondary targets are eliminated. We know where they are. Shouldn't take long."

The aquarium's halls reverberated with ear piercing squeals and laughter. Which only slightly less irritating than Willard's entitled attitude.

He wasn't wrong, though.

The Boxer Group was not just another contractor.

They were an integral cog in a complex machine that had been assembled over several years.

A machine designed for high-level covert operations.

No one involved would come out unscathed if Willard couldn't be controlled.

"See that the job gets done. Very soon. We can't move forward while those three are still out there stirring things up."

She turned and began navigating her way through the throng of school children like a fish swimming upstream.

As she left the building, she opened her umbrella and turned her collar up against the pounding rain. She flagged a taxi at the curb and climbed into the backseat, a pool of water under her feet.

"Pentagon, please," she said to the driver.

The taxi moved slowly in the afternoon traffic.

Tolliver's phone buzzed. A live news update flashed on her screen. The National Aquarium—at "The Abyss" exhibit where she had just met with Willard—was swarming with hazmat teams and emergency personnel.

The news ticker scrolled with alarming words: "Chemical Leak at National Aquarium, Possible Sabotage."

Her first instinct was to order the driver to turn around, but her presence at the scene would raise questions.

Instead, she sent a quick message on a secure line. "Confirm you're clear and update developments."

Seconds felt like minutes until her phone buzzed with Willard's reply: "I'm clear. Wasn't us."

Tolliver felt the weight settle squarely on her shoulders. If she had been compromised, the entire operation was at risk.

Her phone buzzed again. Another message from Willard's secure line: "Targets to be eliminated shortly."

She breathed a bit easier. Willard's crew was set to handle Otto, Reacher, and Vaughan, as promised.

But the sabotage at the Aquarium complicated matters. Had it been a warning? A distraction? A message?

Tolliver considered her options as the taxi driver battled downtown traffic.

Willard and the Boxer Group had a short window to course correct. If they didn't get things back on track, her options were limited.

But she did have options.

Even her enemies agreed she was a brilliant tactician.

Regardless of where things were now, the end game was rushing up fast.

Time, as ever, was of the essence.

Chapter 34

Friday, June 10
Colorado Springs, CO

Kim took a slow sip of her fresh coffee, absorbing the significance of Vaughan's revelations about her husband's job offers from the Boxer Group and similar security firms.

"Since the Boxer Group was based in Colorado and that was part of the appeal, did David ever meet with them or mention any specifics? What type of operations they were involved in?" Kim asked.

"I don't know if he met with them or not. He never said." Vaughan stared into the distance, dredging up old memories. "He talked about the job, but it was vague—something about 'special assignments' that required 'a certain skill set.' He said there would be travel involved, but he'd be home a lot more."

"Special assignments can mean a lot of things in a military context." Jake was skeptical. "Did he give any other details?"

"No." Vaughan shook her head. "David was always tight-lipped about work. And then, of course, he never got the chance to find out more."

Kim nodded. "If the Boxer Group is based in Colorado, it's worth looking into while we're here."

"Or they could be completely unrelated to David and whatever the rest of all this is," Jake pointed out reasonably.

The bells above the entrance to the diner jingled as a group of road bikers walked in, diverting Kim's attention for a moment. They horsed around like high school kids from the front entrance to two tables in the back, making conversation impossible.

When the noise subsided and she had Kim's full attention, Vaughan said, "Do you think the job offer is connected somehow? To David's death, I mean."

"Possibly. We don't know enough yet," Kim replied. "But the more pieces we have, the easier it will be to see the bigger picture. I'll add the Boxer Group to the list of leads."

The waitress returned with a plate of fresh pancakes for Kim and more coffee all around. "Anything else?"

"We're good, thanks," Kim said, handing her cash for the check and a generous tip.

The waitress beamed, "You folks have a nice day!"

They finished eating and left the diner. The smell of bacon and coffee lingered in Kim's nose as she stepped out into the cool morning air. The magnificent Rockies were visible in the distance.

Outside on the sidewalk, Vaughan picked up the conversation again.

"It's just that… If David were considering joining a security firm like the Boxer Group, maybe that's the connection to the situation room you found," she suggested. "Maybe it's all part of some underground military operation we can't even fathom."

"That's a compelling possibility. Something like a situation room doesn't just pop up overnight. Implies long-term planning, resources, and serious backing," Kim said. "If The Boxer Group is involved somehow, we're entering a whole new level of difficulty."

Jake nodded. "We have to consider that David might have been working on something without Samantha's knowledge. Something that eventually led to his murder."

Vaughan's response was swift and strong. "I need to know the truth."

Kim put a reassuring hand on her shoulder. "First things first. Let's find out why David was killed. If we can do that, we'll be a lot closer to finding his killer."

"I've read through David's diary three times. He never mentioned the Boxer Group even once," Vaughan said as she climbed into the backseat of the SUV. "But I know it was on his mind because we talked about him coming home and getting a job and we'd settle down. We talked about that a lot."

"But there was nothing about the job offer in his diary. What that tells us is that David had at least one secret he was unwilling to put on paper." Jake settled behind the steering wheel.

Kim nodded. "I'll look into it. What we have at the moment is plenty of questions. We need some answers."

She didn't say that David Vaughan likely had more secrets his wife didn't know about. She didn't need to mention it because Cooper was monitoring all communications inside the SUV and his mind would go in the same direction.

She was sure Cooper was already on it.

Kim's mind ran through the list of issues quickly. Emma Fonda's tattoo. David Vaughan's secrets. The situation room and the destruction of the Christopher Hotel. The Piranhas and now the Boxer Group.

And Reacher. Always Reacher. Looming over everything like a dark storm cloud.

Cooper believed Reacher was the common thread and Cooper was usually right.

"Samantha," Kim said to catch her attention. She half-turned in her seat to face Vaughan. "Tell me about your experience with Jack Reacher. You knew him. Were you lovers?"

Vaughan's eyes widened as big as espresso cups. "Why does that matter?"

"It might not. But I still need to know."

Vaughan said nothing.

"Jealousy is a powerful motive for murder," Kim said, repeating Cooper's words.

"Reacher wouldn't be jealous of David," Vaughan declared firmly. "He was passing through Hope. We had a very short affair. Not even that, really. Reacher wasn't in love with me, and I certainly wasn't in love with him. We were both in trouble and we helped each other out. That's all. Regardless, he didn't kill David."

"Okay."

Privately, Kim agreed. Reacher wouldn't be jealous of another man, even a husband. Kim had met plenty of Reacher's women in the past eight months. None of them considered Reacher the love of their lives. But she didn't say so.

What she said was, "I don't mean to pry. I really don't. But this could be important."

Vaughan's gaze was steady and strong. "What's your question?"

"David was gone a long time. Was Reacher the only one?"

Vaughan said nothing, but her face had flushed crimson and her nostrils flared.

"Is there anyone else who might have been jealous of David?" Kim asked more pointedly.

"You mean was I having sex with every man who came through town? While my husband was putting his life on the line during a war? Or maybe when he came back all broken and twisted and barely clinging to life?" Vaughan's white-hot rage bubbled over. "Is that what you think? I was going out every night finding men in bars? Maybe I encouraged some hot-headed lover to fix my life? Get rid of my ball and chain, is that it?"

Jake glanced in the rearview mirror to see her.

Vaughan turned her gaze on his. "I suppose that's what you think, too?"

Jake said, "No, of course not."

Silence filled the cabin and Jake kept his eyes on the road.

Kim waited a few miles until Vaughan's anger had a chance to burn itself out before she spoke again.

"Samantha, you're a cop. You're well aware that murder victims are too often killed by someone they know," Kim said calmly, one colleague to another.

Vaughan's anger flared again. "So now you're accusing *me*, is that it?"

"I'm not accusing anyone. But we won't find David's killer and figure out what's going on here by ignoring everything we know about murder, killers, and victims."

Kim paused a couple of beats, watching Vaughan's breathing. She was still fuming.

"You want to know what I think? I'll tell you," Kim said reasonably.

"Okay. You do that," Vaughan snapped.

"You came looking for Reacher because you wanted him to destroy David's killer."

"Yeah?"

"You're an officer of the law and you take the oath seriously. You wouldn't hunt the guy down and kill him yourself. But you've got good reason to believe that Reacher would be willing to do it for you," Kim said, laying things out in stark terms.

"Why would Reacher do that?" Jake asked.

Chapter 35

Friday, June 10
Colorado Springs, CO

Vaughan didn't answer Jake's question.

"Because Reacher would consider removing David's killer from the planet a public service homicide," Kim said. "Am I wrong?"

Vaughan cocked her head and stared, her mouth a straight, hard line.

Kim continued, "If I'm right, then you have some idea who's responsible for your husband's death. You might even know where to find him."

Vaughan said nothing.

"We're here. We're ready and willing to help you get David's killer." Kim paused a moment. "So just tell me what you know. We'll make faster progress if I don't have to reinvent the wheel."

Jake gave Vaughan another glance in the rearview mirror before he piled on. "I'm running out of time, Sam. If we don't figure this out soon, I'll be forced to give up. And I hate giving up. You must know that much about me by now."

Vaughan's gaze wavered, but she'd made a decision. Her jaw was clamped tighter than a Rottweiler on a thief's ankle. "I don't know who killed David. If I did, I wouldn't be sitting here with you."

"Okay," Kim nodded. "But you have something you were planning to share with Reacher. And you have a good reason for thinking he'd be willing to help you. He's not here and we can't read your mind. So now's your chance."

Another few miles passed in silence before Vaughan relented. "How do I know I can trust you?"

Valid question, under the circumstances. Although Vaughan couldn't possibly know that everything she said inside the SUV was feeding straight into Cooper's ear.

"You don't. We're willing. But it's up to you," Jake replied before Kim was forced to lie. "You could find Reacher on your own, like you planned. But if you knew where he was, you'd have gone there before reaching out to me. At this point, we're the only option you've got. And you won't have us much longer."

Vaughan stared at them both, her gaze finally settling on Kim. She sighed, a deep, weary exhale as though letting go of a heavy burden she'd been carrying for a long time.

"Fine. I was going to take this to Reacher because—yes—you're right. He would take action, no questions asked."

"I can't promise to do the same," Kim said. "But I'll do what I can."

Before Vaughan could say more, the SUV jerked violently to the right, tires screeching as though they'd hit an oil slick at full speed.

"What the hell?" Kim grabbed the safety handle and whipped her head around to stare out of the front windshield.

She saw nothing at all on the road. No oncoming traffic, even. They were on a stretch of almost deserted road.

Jake fought with the steering wheel, trying to regain control, but the vehicle had a will of its own. As soon as he righted the SUV on the road, it swerved and veered like a wild bronco.

After five minutes of struggle, Jake lost the fight.

The SUV careened off the road and slammed head on into a concrete pole.

The collision jerked the body of the vehicle and set off a symphony of crunching metal and shattered glass and sparks from the downed electric wires.

Kim was slammed back against the seat and then blacked out.

When she regained consciousness inside the damaged vehicle, the first thing she noticed was the hissing sound of the airbags deflating.

She glanced across the cabin. Jake's airbag had deflated and covered the steering wheel. He was slumped forward, blood trickling down his forehead.

She turned to check on Vaughan. Which was when she saw the back passenger door hung open like a broken wing.

Vaughan was no longer in the SUV.

Groggy and dizzy, Kim reached for her phone—only it wasn't there. The collision must have knocked it to the floor.

Through her fuzzy thinking, Kim was sure Jake's sudden loss of control over the SUV was no accident.

Had the vehicle been hacked? Sabotaged?

To prevent Vaughan from revealing what she knew?

Or was it Vaughan herself who couldn't be trusted?

Before Kim could wrap her mind around the situation, another sound pierced the air. Something between a hum and a buzz, growing louder by the second.

She looked through the damaged windshield and saw it.

A drone, hovering about thirty feet above, its undercarriage glowing with a soft, ominous light.

Kim knew instantly what it was.

Jake opened his eyes and saw the drone. He seemed stuck in momentary paralysis.

She reached over to get him moving with a hard push.

"It's a bomb," Jake whispered, his voice tinged with both disbelief and a kind of terrible clarity.

"Get out! Now!" Kim yelled, unbuckling her seatbelt. She gave Jake another shove and lunged for the door. "Run!"

They tumbled out and sprinted fast. They were only a few feet away when a deafening explosion erupted.

The force of the blast hurled them forward like ragdolls.

They landed on the grass. Kim's ears were ringing. The smell of burnt upholstery and scorched metal filled the air.

The explosion reverberated through her body as she coughed and tried to blink away the stinging smoke. The SUV was a flaming carcass.

Jake sat up.

"Still alive?" Kim asked.

He nodded. "Yeah. You?"

Kim swiveled her head, scanning the charred remains of the SUV. The backseat where Vaughan had been sitting was a mangled, unrecognizable mess.

The laptop and the files from the Christopher Hotel and any evidence, leads, and secrets it might have contained were all reduced to smoldering ash.

It felt like some kind of reset button had been pushed. By whom? And whatever for?

For half a second, Kim considered Cooper. He could have destroyed the SUV at any time. Out here in the middle of nowhere was a great place to do it.

But why would Cooper want to kill them and destroy all the evidence?

And if Cooper didn't do this, who did?

Jake stood and offered her a hand up.

As he pulled her to her feet, he said, "Where's Vaughan?"

Chapter 36

Friday, June 10
Colorado Springs, CO

The acrid smell of burning metal and melted plastic assaulted Kim's nostrils as she and Jake staggered away from the SUV's fiery remains. The stench of it filled her lungs, settling in her stomach like a leaden weight.

"Jake, are you really okay?" she rasped, her voice muffled by a weird sensation of sharp glass in her throat. "You get yourself killed and it'll be my ass."

Jake coughed heavily before he replied, "Yeah, I'm good. But what about Vaughan?"

"I don't know. I don't see her." Kim's gaze darted around, squinting through the trees into dark shadows. "You said you heard her yell something?"

Jake's eyes were bloodshot, and blood oozed from the gash on his forehead. "I couldn't make out the words. It was right before everything went to hell."

Kim's mouth was parched. There was nowhere to get water. "Just before the explosion, I noticed the back door was open. She must've jumped out after the crash."

They both scanned the hillside. Kim's eyes strained to see into the surrounding trees. The uneven terrain was marred with stones and clumps of dry grass. She couldn't distinguish anything clearly.

Finally, she spied a cluster of rocks halfway down the slope large enough to shield Vaughan.

"She might be there," Kim pointed. Her ears were still ringing from the aftereffects of the blast, so she didn't try to call out.

Together, they scrambled down, feet slipping on loose stones and twigs.

As they neared the rocky outcrop, Jake's boot landed on something solid and metallic, causing his body to lurch forward.

"Dammit!" He managed to right himself before he hit the ground.

"What is it?"

Jake bent to pick up a pistol. "Looks like it could be Vaughan's sidearm."

He shoved the weapon into his belt, and they kept moving. When they reached the rock cluster, Kim saw Vaughan lying on her side.

Relief flooded Kim's senses so swiftly it almost knocked her off-balance. She dropped to her knees beside Vaughan. "You jumped out before the crash? While the SUV was still moving?"

Vaughan's lips were bloody, but her eyes were alert. "Yeah, I tumbled out, hit the ground rolling. Stumbled to get behind these rocks for cover. Twisted my ankle."

"Let's get you out of here." Jake scanned the landscape as though he were expecting another attack at any moment.

Vaughan wiped the blood from her mouth. "There's a trail. Leads into the woods. We can regroup there."

Kim locked eyes with Vaughan, who gave a sharp nod of reassurance as if to say she was fit enough to keep up.

"Let's do it," Jake said.

Vaughan struggled to stand. Jake threw her arm over his shoulder and helped her limp forward as Kim led the way deeper into the trees. The scent of damp soil and decaying leaves was a reprieve from the harsh odors of the blast site. Branches underfoot snapped like dry bones, and the leaves rustled softly overhead like whispering secrets in the wind.

Kim saw an abandoned cabin ahead. "Let's check that out," she said, leading the way.

When they reached the cabin, it looked like something out of a horror film—old, decrepit, windows dark like a vacant stare. Kim pushed the door slightly. It gave way with a mournful creak.

The cabin door creaked all the way open, and they stepped inside. The air was stale, the scent of mildew and rot strong enough to taste. A mouse skittered across the floor and disappeared into a hole in the far corner.

Kim shivered in the musty cold. It was clear no humans had lived here for years.

Vaughan's ankle was swollen and obviously painful. She was pale and clammy. Jake helped her sit on a dusty bench just inside the door.

"Let's not get too comfortable," Kim said, her voice echoing in the empty space. "Jake, how's that gash on your forehead? Looks like it might need stitches. We need to deal with that before you die of sepsis or something."

Jake felt the wound with the back of his hand, wincing as he pulled away, sticking slightly to the drying blood. "Should be okay for a while."

Kim scanned the cabin, taking in the nasty furniture and peeling wallpaper reflecting years of neglect. They couldn't stay here. They needed a plan. She was about to ask for suggestions when a low hum reached her ears.

"Do you hear that?" Jake cocked his head as if that might improve his hearing.

The hum grew louder until Kim recognized it. "Someone's coming. Vaughan, can you handle your weapon?"

"Yeah." Vaughan clamped her jaw and held her palm out.

"I can take care of myself." Jake gave her the gun and moved to one side of the door, positioning himself to look through the grimy window.

Tension spiked as if the air itself had thickened. Kim's fingers closed around the grip of her Glock as she took cover behind an old armoire.

Kim regulated her breath, ears straining to hear when the vehicle's engine stopped. Three doors slammed. She heard boots crunch on the ground and the murmur of low voices approaching.

Three heavily armed men came through the trees outside.

Jake saw them first and warned the others. "That's Captain. The other two work for him. Looks like the same two guys we dealt with back in DC."

Vaughan gasped.

Kim raised her weapon and aimed half a moment before Captain shoved the door open.

"Stay where you are," she demanded.

Captain's gaze locked onto hers, and for a moment, everything else faded away. The cabin, the explosion, Vaughan's ankle, Jake's drying blood—none of it mattered.

"Captain." Kim's gaze was icy, aim unwavering. "Drop your weapon."

"You hear that, Choker? Tramp?" Captain chuckled, unfazed.

Choker and Tramp offered sneers and smirks along with their nods of agreement.

Captain said, "You thought you'd just waltz into my backyard and steal what belongs to me and I wouldn't know about it?"

Kim's heart pounded hard enough to break through her chest. "We're full of surprises."

"So am I," Captain shot back.

Choker, standing on Captain's right, pulled out a device and pressed a button.

Kim had been focused on Captain. When Choker moved, she saw the taser, but her reaction was half a moment too slow.

A sharp electric shock raced through her when the two taser probes hit. Every inch of her body experienced excruciating pain all at once. She lost the grip on her weapon and collapsed to the floor.

As the first wave of pain subsided, she was attacked by a swarm of bees crawling under her skin.

Her vision blurred, a fuzz of shapes and colors swimming before her eyes. Her body was sprawled on the ground, muscles twitching involuntarily, the residual hum of electricity buzzing through her veins.

Her senses were painfully acute. The cold damp wood of the cabin walls, the caustic burn of ozone left by the Taser, the bitter taste of defeat in her mouth.

The taser probes were pointed to penetrate clothing and barbed to prevent removal. He could shock her over and over again unless he was stopped.

But Kim had no muscle control at all. There was nothing she could do.

Chapter 37

When Otto went down, Choker was still holding the taser, still smirking. After that, everything seemed to happen all at once.

Jake sprang forward across the floor like an enraged bull.

Choker saw the lunge and tried desperately to get out of Jake's path.

Choker bobbed and weaved, wiry and fast, and wildly overconfident. But he was half a beat too late, and the cabin was too small. There was nowhere for the guy to go.

Jake's shoulder rammed into Choker's midsection with the force of a freight train, and they both went crashing into the wall. The taser clattered out of Choker's hand and skidded across the floor, coming to rest near the worn-out hearth.

The other guy, Tramp, leveled his gun at Jake, but before he could shoot, Vaughan aimed and fired. Her bullet missed Tramp's shoulder, embedding itself in the wooden wall, as she'd planned.

The warning was enough to distract him, but not enough to stop him.

Tramp whipped around and raised his weapon in Vaughan's direction.

Captain's head swiveled to scan and evaluate, calculating, as if he were a human computer processing variables at an incredible speed.

Jake twisted Choker's arm and jerked it up high enough to dislocate his shoulder. He pinned the guy's face to the wall with his forearm pressed against his neck to hold him there.

"I would think twice," Jake growled close to his ear.

Otto began to stir, her eyelids flickering as she regained muscle control. She spied her Glock within reach and lunged for it. Her fingers closed around the grip.

Before Tramp could fire at Vaughan, Otto aimed and fired in a single, fluid motion.

The shot hit Tramp exactly as she'd placed it. He screamed and dropped his gun, clutching his bleeding right leg. The bullet shattered his femur. He collapsed on the plank floor, writhing and spewing a stream of curses.

Captain, outraged, shouted, "Enough of this!"

He raised his gun and pointed at Vaughan. The cabin was small, the air thick with tension and the sharp tang of gunpowder.

Jake yanked Choker's body away from the wall. Holding Choker in front to block Captain's aim, Jake shoved Choker forward, throwing him into Captain. The two men collided in a tangle of limbs and hit the floor.

Captain's gun went off in the scuffle. The bullet lodged in the ceiling. Plaster and dust rained down as Jake wrested the gun from Captain's hand and tossed it across the room. It slid under a rickety table, far from reach.

Vaughan limped forward, aiming her pistol at Captain's enraged face. "Relax. Stay down. It's over," she said with grim satisfaction.

From his pocket, Captain produced a switchblade and flicked it open. He jumped up from the floor, knocking Vaughan back, and lunged at Jake.

Jake dodged the blade, grabbing Captain's wrist and twisting it hard until it snapped. He dropped the knife. It clanged on the floor.

Still twisting the wrist, Jake delivered a hard punch to Captain's face. Jake heard a satisfying crunch when his fist made contact with Captain's nose.

He staggered back, blood covering his mouth and chin and streaming from his nose like a river.

Otto had climbed to her feet and removed the taser barbs. She trained her weapon on Tramp still whimpering and holding his ruined shoulder. She showed him the taser wires. "Move one more inch and I'll be glad to show you how this feels."

Jake looked around the room. Vaughan was breathing hard, but otherwise, she looked okay. Otto was standing over Tramp, the temporary paralysis from the taser shot resolved.

Choker and Tramp were incapacitated, moaning on the floor, clutching their injuries. Captain was subdued, a mixture of rage and disbelief contorting his face.

Jake glanced toward Otto and said, "Now what?"

Otto said, "I don't have handcuffs. How about you, Vaughan?"

Vaughan grinned, reaching for her back pocket to pull out a shiny silver pair of cuffs. "Never leave home without them."

Jake said, "I'll be right back. They used plastic ties on us back in DC. They probably have more in their vehicle."

He left the cabin, breathing in the cool mountain air and stretching his limbs after the fight in the cramped cabin. They'd parked out of sight of the cabin, behind a stand of trees. Jake's long strides covered ground to the panel van quickly.

He rummaged around in the cargo space until he found the plastic ties. He collected six ties and headed back.

Otto and Vaughan were still holding the three on the floor. Jake flipped each one on his belly, grabbed arms and jerked wrists together behind their backs. He cinched the plastic ties uncomfortably tight.

Once the three were secured, Jake pulled each onto his feet and shoved him out the door. "Run if you want. I'm more than happy to shoot you in the back."

Jake watched with satisfaction as the three shuffled out, blood still dripping from Captain's nose, Tramp's wrist twisted and hanging at an odd angle, Choker's shoulder poking in the wrong direction.

He glanced toward Otto. "You okay?

She nodded. "I've been tased before. Hurts like hell, but no lasting damage."

"Unless they manage to kill you while you're down for the five-second count," Vaughan said.

Otto didn't prolong that conversation. Instead, she asked, "What kind of vehicle do they have?"

"A white cargo van. Big enough for all six of us, if you want to take them along," Jake said. "But it's totally okay with me if we leave those three here to figure it out on their own. That's what they tried to do to us."

Otto shook her head. "We need a place to sleep, eat, clean up, and figure out what to do next. Vaughan, you're the local among us. Anyplace nearby?"

"We're a couple of hours from my house. We can go there," Vaughan replied. "There's probably a jail we can dump these guys into, if you like."

"You want to arrest them?" Jake asked.

Vaughan shook her head. "I'd rather not. I've got plenty to do already and I'm way outside my jurisdiction here. Let some other cop have the glory."

Otto seemed to give the matter a full minute's thought before she responded. "Okay. Sounds like a plan."

"This way," Jake said as he led the way to the van.

"Nice job, young Reacher." Vaughan gave him a broad grin along with a slap on his broad back. "Tell me again how you're really not much like your uncle."

Chapter 38

Friday, June 10
Albany, NY

After Otto hung up, Gaspar slipped the cell phone into his pocket. He stretched his legs enough to reduce the limping, but the pain was always with him.

At the rental car kiosk, a bored attendant handed him keys to the SUV he'd reserved.

Since he'd retired from the FBI and taken the Scarlett Investigations job, he didn't fly often anymore. He stepped out of the terminal at Albany Airport, glad to have his boots on the ground again.

The chilly spring air was far from Miami's balmy cocoon. He should have brought a coat.

Gaspar hoofed over to the SUV, started the engine and took to the road. The navigation system led him through the city's underbelly. Definitely not the areas Albany's Chamber of Commerce featured on the travel brochures.

The route took him straight to the WarDel Motel. The place where Albany PD had found Melody Bennett's body eighteen months ago.

The pathologist reported the time of death two days before the body was discovered.

The stench of decay must have been overwhelming. Gaspar's nose wrinkled at the mere thought of it. Nothing in the files explained why it took so long to find the body.

The WarDel's sign was mostly peeled paint and faded aspirations. The "Vacancy" neon flickered like a dying star. What a depressing place. Hard to fathom why a woman like Melody Bennett would be caught dead here.

Gaspar parked amid the potholes in the lot. He was careful to lock the SUV and set the alarm. If the SUV was still here when he came back, he'd be lucky.

The motel was L-shaped with the office on one end. Gaspar followed the scent of stale cigarettes to the entrance. Inside, a clerk sat behind a desk with his eyes closed. Yellowed walls and chipped linoleum tiles were as sad and decrepit as the rest of the place.

Gaspar approached the clerk, his gaze steady but not confrontational. "A woman died in one of your rooms eighteen months ago. Melody Bennett. I'm sure you remember."

The clerk's eyes narrowed as if evaluating whether Gaspar's questions were laced with threat or promise. "Yeah, I remember. Terrible thing. Cops all over. Bad for business."

"So you know the case is still open. I'm trying to find some answers for her grieving family." Gaspar leaned closer, lowering his voice to capture the clerk's attention.

"That was a long time ago, man. Cops were around here for days. Came back several times. Something to find, they'd have found it," the clerk said, as if that were the end of the matter.

"I've got a new lead. Something they didn't know back then."

"Yeah? Like what?"

"Some explanation, some solace. Can't bring her back, but we can maybe give them the why," Gaspar said. "I'm looking for any unusual cash transactions around that time."

The clerk hesitated, gaze darting to the entrance door, then back to Gaspar. "What's in it for me?"

"Peace of mind," Gaspar said, reaching into his pocket to hold up a bill. "And fifty dollars right now."

The clerk considered, as if weighing the value against Gaspar's fifty. Finally, he nodded. "Make it a hundred."

Gaspar didn't argue. He added a second fifty, holding both between his fingers.

As if Gaspar might change his mind, the clerk snatched the money from his hand and stuffed it into a pocket. "Fine. Follow me."

The clerk led Gaspar around the desk and through the doorway to the back offices, which turned out to be a maze of cubby holes and small rooms.

Papers were strewn across surfaces like the aftermath of some natural disaster. Fast food containers were everywhere. The trash bins overflowed.

The appalling odor of cigarettes, marijuana, uneaten food, and body odor combined was a wall of stench strong enough to stop a horse.

The clerk kept walking deeper into the bowels of the place until he came to a locked door. He pulled a key on a retractable cord from a stainless-steel holder attached to his belt. He slipped the key into the lock and gave it an easy twist. When he pulled it out again, he let it snap back into its resting position.

The small office was neater than everything else. The walls were lined with shelves. Some were stacked with looseleaf binders.

The clerk scanned the binders and finally, a ledger materialized. He pulled it down from the shelf and skimmed through, his finger tracing the columns until it stopped, hovering over numbers inked in black.

"Here," he said, pointing. "Big cash deposit, week before she was found. Never sat right with me. Don't usually get money like that here."

Gaspar looked at the numbers, then at the annotations. He pulled out his phone and snapped a few pictures of the ledger pages.

"Thanks," Gaspar said. "Any idea what this payment was for?"

The clerk shrugged. "I just work here, man."

Gaspar flipped through a few pages of the book. The clerk was right. The majority of the listed transactions were less than fifty dollars. Except the one deposit he'd flagged.

Gaspar said, "I'd like a look at the room where she was found. Room 237."

The clerk raised an eyebrow, as though the very question was disturbing. "A lot of folks have come and gone since then. Don't know what you're hoping to find."

"Sometimes," Gaspar said, his voice as steady as the unwavering line of his gaze, "the place itself holds memory. Echoes. I'd like to listen."

The clerk gave him a look that suggested Gaspar might just be crazy. But he didn't argue. He led the way as they returned to the front lobby.

He rummaged behind the counter and produced another key. This one was a card with a magnetic stripe. The kind that could be easily replaced or reprogrammed.

"Don't make a mess," he said as he handed it over. "Just leave it in the room when you're done."

Gaspar took the keycard, and left the front office, walking across the cracked asphalt. Room 237 stood in the far end, isolated as if even the other rooms wished to disown it.

He unlocked the door, its hinges squealed as he pushed it open and stepped inside. The curtains were closed, and the lights were off inside. He flipped the switch beside the door and a dim bulb illuminated over the television.

The air was stale, laced with despair and transience. Too many carpet stains reflected the sins of its users. He spied two more wall switches and flipped those lights on, but they didn't illuminate much.

Gaspar stood still to let his eyes adjust and then began his search. He scanned the room, taking in the frayed curtains, scratched tabletops, and tarnished bathroom fixtures. Ordinary scars left by time and neglect.

Seeing the room in three dimensions rather than the flat crime scene photos, he matched the specifics to the images. This wasn't a place where people left things behind, not even by accident.

He almost missed it.

A small difference between reality and the photos captured by Albany PD and confirmed by the FBI.

An off-color speck on the ceiling corner farthest from the door.

Gaspar pushed a chair into the corner and climbed atop it. Reaching up, he touched the spot and felt a hard lump embedded in the ceiling tile.

Had to be a buried camera. He snapped a few photos with his phone before he gouged the camera from the tile. The lens was pointed to cover the breadth of the room.

Gaspar yanked the camera out and pulled the wires with it. The ceiling crumbled, leaving a gaping wound.

Chapter 39

With camera in hand, Gaspar walked briskly back to the lobby. The doorbells chimed the familiar tuneless greeting as he entered. The clerk looked up, eyes betraying a flicker of something—recognition or guilt, it was hard to tell.

"What the hell is this?" Gaspar slammed the camera down on the counter, jolting the clerk out of his stupor.

"I got no idea, man," he stammered, but the pitch of his voice confirmed the deceit.

Gaspar's voice lowered, filled with menace. "Who's been spying? Who put this in Room 237?"

The clerk lunged over the counter, swinging a fist at Gaspar.

Gaspar dodged, grabbed his arm, and twisted it behind his back, forcing the clerk's torso down onto the counter.

"Who put the camera in the room?"

The clerk grunted and squirmed, trying to get away from Gaspar's angry hold. "You got it all wrong. I didn't—"

The front door burst open and a large, burly man wearing a dirty wifebeater T-shirt rushed in, shouting, "Hey! Let him go!"

Gaspar released the clerk instantly, throwing him off-balance. He stumbled and then crumpled onto the floor, clutching his arm.

"You okay, Mike?" The burly guy moved to stand in the gap between Gaspar and the front desk.

"Yeti! He attacked me," the clerk gasped. "Call the cops!"

"Good idea." Gaspar eyed them both, sizing up the situation.

Yeti and Mike exchanged guilty looks. No one moved to call the police.

"This," Gaspar said, showing the camera he'd yanked from the ceiling, "is evidence. If you're smart, you'll tell me what I want to know before the real trouble starts."

Mike and Yeti looked at the camera as if it were a feral animal. A long, fraught pause filled the room as they struggled to breathe evenly.

Then, as if some invisible decision had been made, the burly man lunged forward, fist clenched, aimed at Gaspar's head.

But Gaspar was faster. He sidestepped the swing, grabbed Yeti's extended arm, and used the man's momentum to shove him onto the counter. The thud reverberated through the room when he hit the counter and dropped to the floor.

Snarling, Yeti righted himself and began to launch jabs and hooks.

Gaspar leaned out of arm's reach to avoid the heavy strikes, his gaze steady. Each move he made was calculated, defensive, searching for the weak point in Yeti's human barricade.

Yeti was getting tired. He'd swung and missed several times, putting his full weight behind every punch. He was burning himself out.

A momentary wince as Yeti put his full weight on his left leg. In the next flurry of heavy fists, Gaspar feinted right and then used his left leg to deliver a vicious kick to the side of Yeti's knee on his weakened left leg.

Yeti howled in pain as his knee twisted and folded sideways, definitely not the right direction. Yeti stumbled and Gaspar put all of his weight into landing a hard straight punch to the center of Yeti's face, staggering him back against the wall.

For a moment, the room seemed to hold its breath. The air was thick with the scent of Yeti's sweat and the possibility of more violence.

"Last chance," Gaspar said, holding the camera up and giving it a wiggle.

The two men exchanged glances. The balance of power had shifted irreversibly.

"It's okay, Yeti. I'll take care of it." The clerk stood up, holding his injured arm. "This way."

Yeti's angry red face showed he wasn't thrilled with the turn of events, but his energy was spent. He held his ruined knee, howling when pain shot through the torn muscles and ligaments. Sweat had plastered his hair to his head.

Mike led Gaspar through a narrow door beside the counter, into a room cluttered with a jigsaw of aging electronic equipment. Old monitors hummed softly, and rows of blinking lights cast a sickly glow.

"Sit," the clerk gestured to an unoccupied chair as he navigated through a maze of files on the computer.

He clicked on one labeled with the month and year and a grainy video began to play.

Melody Bennett lying on the bed in the dimly lit room, listless, her eyes closed. She might have been asleep or high or both.

After a moment, the door opened, and a shadowy figure stepped inside. Gaspar narrowed his eyes as if that would improve the bad image quality. It didn't.

The figure was dressed in black, head to toe. Gaspar couldn't tell if it was a man or a woman.

Gloved hands produced a syringe and injected its contents into Bennett's jugular vein. Bennett didn't move during the injection or afterward.

The black-clad figure dropped the syringe into a pocket and waited, checking a watch on its wrist a couple of times. After ten minutes, the gloved hand reached to check for a carotid pulse in Bennett's neck. Bennett's lifeless pulse confirmed her soul's departure.

The black-clad figure retreated into the darkness.

Gaspar felt a cold silence. He moved the clerk out of the way and sent the video to his secure email. Then he grabbed a flash drive from the desk. He downloaded the video from the feed for two weeks before and two weeks after the murder and slipped the flash drive into his pocket.

"You done?" the clerk finally asked, his voice a fragile mask of indifference.

"Not quite," Gaspar replied.

He grabbed the clerk by the collar and pushed him out of the room. Gaspar closed the door. He used the phone on the reception desk to dial 9-1-1. When the dispatcher answered, Gaspar asked to speak to the detective who had handled the Melody Bennett case.

After a few transfers, a gruff voice answered the call. "Detective Ernie Jones, Albany PD Homicide."

"This is the clerk at the WarDel Motel. We've found the CCTV video you guys have been asking about. That woman who died in one of our rooms. Yeah, send a car over. I'll be here."

Gaspar's phone vibrated with a text from the airline. His flight to Miami would depart sooner than planned due to impending weather conditions.

"You're a lucky man," Gaspar said. "Today you get to make a choice most people in your line of work never get. A second chance. Use it."

"What are you talking about?" Mike scowled.

"Detective Jones and the FBI are on the way. Show them your little porn video room," Gaspar said. "You try anything before they get here and you'll both spend the rest of your lives as a guest of the prison system."

Gaspar drove back to the airport, returned the SUV, and dashed to catch his flight, the flash drive nested securely in his pocket.

Chapter 40

Friday, June 10
Colorado

Behind the wheel of the SUV, Jake rolled his shoulders and flexed his neck to work the soreness from his muscles. Events of the past couple of days seemed to be catching up with him.

Vaughan was a police officer, but Colorado Springs was not her jurisdiction. She'd declined Jake's restated invitation to arrest Captain and his two thugs. "No thanks. The governor might give me a medal, but the paperwork alone would keep me occupied for a year."

Otto had made a couple of calls on her satellite phone and worked things out.

First, they'd collected an SUV from a rental lot near the Colorado Springs airport. Inside the SUV they'd found a laptop.

From there, Vaughan drove the SUV and Jake drove the white van. They dropped off the van at the Colorado Springs police station with Captain and the other two still bound and gagged in the back.

"Don't worry about them," Otto had said. "Someone will sort them out."

Jake had moved behind the wheel of the SUV and Vaughan took the passenger seat. Otto had stretched out in the back.

They'd stopped at a strip mall to pick up clothes and toiletries and a few burner phones and sandwiches for the road.

That was a few hours ago and the sun had set a while back. He'd been running on miles of empty highway with nothing but his headlights to illuminate the pavement for the past hour. There wasn't much out here. No gas stations or fast-food joints. Certainly no streetlights.

But they had pulled into Hope, Colorado, twenty minutes ago. From there, Vaughan gave him verbal directions to her home.

"Turn onto Fifth Street, coming up on the left," Vaughan said pointing.

Fifth Street was residential on both sides. Small, neat houses rested quietly in the moonlight. Trees, picket fences, yards, and mailboxes on both sides of the street.

Looked like a nice place to live.

Near the end of the block, there was a mailbox with *Vaughan* written on the side.

266 | DIANE CAPRI

The house itself was a low one-story ranch maybe fifty years old. A single attached garage on one end and a T-shaped bump-out on the other end, probably for bedrooms. There were no lights on inside.

The yard was covered with gravel instead of grass. The driveway was paved with slabs the same color as the gravel. A winding rock walkway led to the front door.

"Just park in the driveway," Vaughan said, gesturing in that direction. "My truck's in the garage."

Vaughan unlocked the front door and turned the lights on inside. Otto followed and Jake brought up the rear.

The interior space was nice. Painted cabinets and a wallpaper border at the top of the walls. The counters were tidy, but the room felt lived in. There was a four-place table with only three chairs.

The room displayed some of Vaughan's personality. Dried flowers, bottles of virgin olive oil, antique spoons, things like that. There was no evidence that a man lived here or any second person at all. The living room had a single armchair, a TV set, and a comfortable looking couch.

"Anybody want coffee?" Vaughan filled the big shiny coffee machine with water and spooned coffee into a gold basket. She hit the switch. She opened a cabinet and took out three white mugs.

"How long have you lived here?" Jake asked, to be polite.

"A few years. We lived in an apartment over on Third Street for a while. But we decided we wanted a ranch when he was home before his second deployment."

Jake understood her point and asked nothing more. She'd moved in while David was in Iraq. Her husband had never lived in this house and now he never would.

Vaughan poured the coffee and set the mugs on the kitchen table, one in front of each of the three chairs.

Otto said, "Do you still have David's diary?"

Jake had wondered that, too. Everything they had with them burned to a crisp in the SUV explosion. But Vaughan had been especially careful with the diary. She might have kept it closer.

Vaughan nodded, reached around and pulled the slim volume from her back pocket. She held it in both hands as if it were precious to her. "It's David's handwriting. I've read it many times. It's all I have left of him now."

"Can I read it?" Otto asked.

Vaughan gave her a long steady stare. Otto didn't ask again. Jake waited to see how it would work out.

After a while, Vaughan pushed the diary across the table. "Please be careful with it."

"I promise," Otto said with just the right amount of reverence.

Otto opened the diary and began to read. Her eyes scanned the text, pausing on certain sentences that seemed innocuous but might have carried more weight. Her eyes narrowed as she read through David's spidery handwriting.

"This mentions David's time in the Army," Otto said. "He talks about his squad, the camaraderie, the hardships, but then…" Her voice trailed off as she pointed to a phrase: "dark secrets were left in that sand."

Jake guessed David had been holding back, unwilling to commit to paper the full scope of what he'd witnessed.

Otto turned another page, skimming over David's handwriting. Then her gaze froze. She showed the page to Jake. A single name: Willard.

"That name appears a few times," Vaughan said. "I assumed he was a fellow soldier, maybe a friend."

Jake said, "Captain wanted us to find people who knew what was going on with David over there. What if this guy Willard is one of those people?"

Otto said, "Jake, check the internet. Can you find a guy named Willard? Was Willard ever accused of war crimes?"

Jake pulled out his phone and started searching. After a few minutes, he looked up.

"There are rumors, allegations that never led to charges. But it seems like controversy followed Willard like a con trail on a jet," Jake said, locking eyes with Otto.

Otto turned her attention back to the diary, flipping through the pages and reading between the lines.

She stopped at a passage where David had described a day that started like any other but ended in horror. He'd written about an IED, an explosion that had wiped out an entire squad. Guys he knew and cared about.

Otto said, "He mentions that the IED was planted on a route that was supposed to be safe, one that they'd received clearance to drive. A route that only a few knew they'd be taking."

Vaughan met her gaze. "What if it wasn't an accident?"

"Exactly," Otto said. "What if someone wanted that squad gone?"

Jake said, "Why? Because they knew too much? Too much about what?"

A heavy silence filled the room. Vaughan's face contorted in anguish and realization. David hadn't just been a casualty of war; he'd been a victim of deliberate sabotage. His death years later could have been a continuation of that crime.

"David's squad," Otto said slowly. "They could have been deliberately eliminated because they'd witnessed something. If they were eliminated…"

"Then it wasn't just about silencing David," Vaughan said. "It was about erasing an entire chapter, a group of men who could've exposed the truth."

The air seemed to grow colder as they considered the implications. Otto closed David's diary gently, her eyes narrowing.

Jake, thumbing the edge of his phone, looked from Otto to Vaughan. "Should we dig deeper into Willard? If he's the common factor here, it would be good to know who he is and how he's involved."

Otto nodded. "You'll only be able to find intel that's publicly available. But if he was charged with anything, someone should have reported it. Tread carefully."

Jake blocked out distractions and searched military records, social media accounts, and obscure forum posts. Names and faces blurred together, forming a mosaic of lives lived in and out of uniform.

Minutes later, he broke the silence. "I found something. A picture of David and Willard, taken during a deployment. They're with a few other guys, looks like members of David's squad."

"Can you show it to me?" Vaughan asked and Jake handed her the phone.

Otto leaned in to look. "Is there any context? Any caption or comments?"

Jake scrolled down. "Someone posted this on a memorial page, remembering 'those who were lost too soon.' But no one mentions how they died, just that they're gone."

Vaughan took a deep breath. "So, if we're reading this right, then what? Are we thinking David, Willard, and the others were involved in something they shouldn't have been? And someone orchestrated their deaths to cover it up?"

"Possibly," Otto confirmed. "Looks like Willard is still alive. That's a start."

Jake felt his phone vibrate in his pocket with a call. He looked at the screen. The caller ID was unknown. Could be his CO wanting to know where the hell he was.

"Reacher," he answered and saw Otto flinch. He flashed an apologetic look in her direction as he walked outside to take the call.

Chapter 41

When Jake went outside to take his call, Kim was alone with Vaughan at her kitchen table. Kim tried to picture Jack Reacher spending time in this cramped space.

Reacher sucked all the oxygen out of every room he entered. It wouldn't have taken him long to do that here.

So why did he hang around? Just to have an affair with Vaughan? Not likely.

"You and Reacher, what was the real story? He doesn't seem like your type to me," Kim said conversationally.

Vaughan took a slow sip from her coffee mug. "Well, let's just say he was different—quiet and observant. He was a one-man tactical team. Kind of like he was always calculating the odds."

"That doesn't surprise me," Kim said. "What else?"

Vaughan paused, considering. "He could sleep anywhere, anytime. Said he learned it in the Army. How'd he put it? 'Eat when you can, sleep when you can.'"

Kim nodded. Gaspar often said that, too. But then, Gaspar's training and Reacher's training had been identical in their early days. "Anything else?"

Vaughan seemed to think about the question, her gaze fixing somewhere beyond the kitchen. "He had an issue with the guy who ran the next town over—Despair. Reacher was pissed off with the guy. Spent most of his time in Hope trying to settle those scores."

"What scores?" Kim leaned in.

Vaughan shrugged. "It was personal. Something about Reacher's freedom and his right to move around as he pleased. There was an edge to it."

The corners of Kim's mouth twitched. "An edge? Reacher's usual demeanor isn't exactly cuddly, is it?"

"True," Vaughan conceded with a smile. "But this was something more. It was like a vendetta. He was focused, almost obsessive, about getting even with that guy."

Kim's thoughts flipped through the many reports she'd gathered on Reacher over the past eight months.

Hot-blooded vendettas weren't his style. He was more like a cold-blooded reptile. Deadly, sure. But always steady and calculated.

Reacher wasn't known to fly off in a rage against anyone or anything.

"He was careful not to say too much," Vaughan said. "I'm a police officer, after all. He was fully aware that anything he told me could be used against him."

"That's surprising," Kim replied.

"Is it? A lot of suspects clam up when we read them their rights, don't they?" Vaughan said.

"Reacher knows his rights. He was a military policeman for thirteen years," Kim replied. "But he does what he wants, when he wants, in whatever way he wants to do it."

"Meaning what?" Vaughan asked.

"Meaning that if he'd wanted you to know what he was involved with over in Despair, he'd have told you," Kim said flatly.

Vaughan gave her a shrewd look. "You really are trying to get into his head, aren't you?"

"It's part of the job," Kim replied. "But it's also more than that. Understanding Reacher will help me find him."

"That's the goal? Finding Reacher?" Vaughan asked, eyes wide.

Kim shrugged. "That's certainly one of them."

Vaughan set her coffee mug down and looked Kim squarely in the eye. "If you're going after Reacher, you'd better be ready. It'll be like poking a wasp's nest."

Kim nodded. "Noted. Anything else I should know?"

Vaughan sighed. "Just that Reacher's the kind of man who finishes what he starts. That business over in Despair? You can bet it didn't end well for the other guy."

The door swung open, and Jake returned just as Kim felt her burner phone vibrate in her pocket. Gaspar.

"My turn," she said with an apologetic smile. She left the kitchen table and walked outside, leaving Jake alone with Vaughan.

"Chico," she said when she picked up. "Good to hear from you."

"Likewise. Look, I'm on my way back from Albany," Gaspar said.

"Albany? Why?"

"Checked out the first victim, Melody Bennett," Gaspar said. "She was military. Marines, not Army. But Reacher was at West Point once upon a time. And it's just a couple of hours' drive from Albany."

"So, you're saying Reacher could've been there at some point. With Bennett," Kim said thoughtfully. "Which could be one of the things Cooper knows and isn't saying."

"I'm with you, though. I never could see Reacher killing Bennett or anyone else with a needle," Gaspar said. "Beyond that, the sleazy motel where Bennett died had a couple of troublesome issues. The place had CCTV running in the rooms whenever they were occupied."

"You're kidding," Kim said flatly. "Why didn't Johnson's task force figure that out?"

"They don't have my charm and persuasive personality?" Jaspar deadpanned.

"I'm sure that's it," Kim smiled, putting the amusement into her voice. "Did the video capture anything useful?"

"Possibly. It's not great quality, but we might have video of the killer. I sent the file to you. You should have it now," Gaspar said. "The one thing I can say for sure is that the image captured on the video is not Reacher."

"You said there were a couple of troublesome issues. What's the second one?"

"The WarDel Motel received a large cash payment not long before Bennett died," Gaspar said.

"Cash? From where?"

"Good question. The clerk claimed he had no idea. Agent Johnson might be able to trace it," Gaspar said.

Kim's mind raced through the implications. "Any idea how Bennett ended up in Albany?"

"No, but it's worth noting that she was last seen leaving a bar alone. One frequented by military personnel," Gaspar said. "You want to send this stuff off to Agent Johnson?"

"Probably. But I'll have to do it. Cooper would have my head if he knew I'd read you in on all of this," Kim said, realizing Cooper might already know what Gaspar had discovered and more.

"He could fix that, and he's chosen not to," Gaspar replied. "Meanwhile, I'll see what I can find out."

"Can you check out something else for me? We're looking for intel on a guy named Willard. Served in Iraq at the same time as David Vaughan."

"That all you know about him? No first name, even?" Gaspar asked.

"Not that we've been able to find with our limited resources so far," Kim said.

"Okay. I'll run the two names through and see what I can dig up." Gaspar paused. "You're done out there, right? Want me to send you a ride?"

Kim considered the question. Was there any reason to stay in Colorado? "I might take you up on that."

"Okay. Let me know."

"Will do."

Kim hung up and returned to the kitchen, where Vaughan and Jake sat in quiet conversation.

"New lead?" Jake asked as Kim took her seat.

"Possibly," Kim said, avoiding his gaze. She told them about Bennett and the potential West Point connection. She didn't mention the video or the cash.

Vaughan looked from one to the other. "So, you're thinking Bennett may have known others from West Point, which might have something to do with her death?"

Kim nodded, realizing how flimsy that sounded. "Bennett was last seen leaving a bar frequented by military personnel. She could have met someone there."

Kim's phone buzzed again. A text message from Gaspar.

"WarDel Motel phone records show contact with a classified DC number."

Kim's eyes narrowed. A classified number in DC could mean a lot of things. But it wasn't a normal contact for a military veteran who ended up dead.

Chapter 42

Friday, June 10
Washington, D.C.

Tolliver's biometric security system chimed to confirm her identity and unlocked the back door. Preoccupied, she walked inside, flipping the lights on as she entered her kitchen. She crossed to the refrigerator to grab a bottled water.

She pushed the door closed with her hip as she twisted the top from the bottle and took a long gulp.

"Hello, Maureen," Charles Cooper's voice startled her from the shadows.

"How did you get in here?" she gasped, spilling water on her shirt, glaring in his direction. "What the hell are you doing in my house?"

"You called me, asking for intel on the Hornet murders, remember?" Cooper said with mock sincerity. "Did you want to meet somewhere we'd be more likely to be discovered?"

"You could have called." Tolliver glared at him.

"True." Cooper smirked, as if he'd received the reaction he wanted.

He wandered into the den where the chairs were more comfortable. Before he sat, he poured two glasses of scotch from the bar cart she kept fully stocked.

Tolliver accepted one of the glasses and they settled in. "I have other things to do tonight."

Cooper gave her a knowing look and sipped his scotch. "We've got a task force working these Hornet murders. We thought there were four victims, but possibly more. Our operating theory was a single killer, although we were open to other possibilities."

"Who were the four victims?"

Cooper cocked his head as if he found the question curious. "Bennett, Fonda, Harmon, and Skinner."

"There was an arrest in the Skinner case. Her ex-boyfriend. You think he killed the others?" Tolliver asked.

"Matter of fact, I don't." Cooper shook his head. "I don't even think he killed Skinner."

Tolliver widened her eyes. "The news is reporting otherwise."

"Sure they are. They're reporting what we told them. Doesn't make it true." Cooper sipped the scotch with exaggerated appreciation. "The real killer is more likely to make a mistake if he feels safe."

"Who is the real killer?" Tolliver held a sip of the warm whiskey on her tongue, forcing herself to wait him out.

She'd known Cooper a long time. He didn't just drop in for a drink. Whatever he really came here for, she'd like him to get to it and get the hell out. She had things to do.

After a while, Cooper said, "I had my suspicions right from the start. But I wanted to be wrong about this."

Tolliver nodded, thinking that no way in hell did he want to be wrong. What he wanted was to be in control. That's what he always wanted. To rule the world and everyone in it.

"When these cases first came up, I actually thought we might be able to let this one go," Cooper said, warming to his subject as the booze seemed to loosen his tongue. "These women were already dead. Nothing we could do to bring them back to life. And there was too much to lose if the truth came out."

"But you changed your mind," Tolliver said. "Why?"

Cooper drained his glass and Tolliver noticed when he slipped it into his pocket. He knew all too well how easily it would be to match his DNA to a saliva sample from the crystal rim.

"My agents turned up two pieces of evidence which make that plan impossible," Cooper said. "A large cash payment was made to the motel where Bennett died. That money is traceable. In fact, I've already done it. Which means someone else can do it, too. And they will."

Tolliver controlled her breathing with force of will, attempting to steady her heartbeat and speak simultaneously. "Where'd the money come from?"

"Joey 'Captain' Perch. Head of a group of east coast Piranhas," Cooper said. "You know Captain?"

Tolliver shook her head, although she did recognize the name.

"One of my agents arrested him a few hours ago. He's in custody and he's lawyered up. But he'll talk if he gets the right deal," Cooper said.

"They always do," Tolliver agreed, her pulse racing. "Why did he send money to the place where Bennett died?"

Cooper shrugged. "My guess, and it's only a guess so far, is to buy something from the motel owner. Time, maybe, to keep the body before it was reported. Perhaps he wanted the staff to look the other way if any unforeseen problems came up."

Tolliver had nothing to say to that, so she drained her glass and waited until she felt compelled to move the conversation along. "You said there were two pieces of evidence. What's the second one?"

Cooper kept his gaze steady on her, waiting for her to slip up, probably. Which meant he had no idea who he was dealing with. That thought cheered her a bit and she felt her lips curve upward slightly.

"The second thing is more troublesome in its own way," Cooper said enigmatically, as if he were trying to torture her.

Tolliver said nothing.

Cooper shifted in his chair. "The motel is a sleezy place. A real dump. Hard to imagine a woman like Bennett hanging out there, let alone, bringing a date."

"A date?" Tolliver asked, unable to help herself.

"A sleezy place like that has to make money somehow. Charging hourly for a hot sheets clientele isn't going to make anybody rich. But blackmail..." Cooper let his voice trail off as he cocked his head again and added a slight nod.

"What are you talking about?" Tolliver was feeling, all of a sudden, like she'd had way more to drink than two fingers of warm scotch. Her body flushed with heat from her chest to the top of her head. Sweat popped out on her upper lip and droplets rolled down from her hairline at her temples.

"The video quality isn't the best. But some tech nerd will work with it a while. The image will become clearer. The killer will be identified," Cooper said flatly.

"What video?" Tolliver asked, sitting straight up in her chair. "They have video of Bennett's killer?"

"Yep. Comes in using a key, so it was someone she knew. Bennett was already passed out on the bed. Drunk or high, or maybe drugged. Hard to say," Cooper explained. "Walks over to the bed, bends over Bennett, and injects her in the neck."

Tolliver stared without blinking.

"Puts the syringe in a pocket and walks out, making sure the door locks afterward," Cooper finished.

"Who was it? Who killed Bennett?" Tolliver asked.

Cooper shrugged again. "We're working on that. But we know the killer was connected to the Piranhas because of the prepayment. Joey Perch will fill in the blanks to keep himself off death row. It's only a matter of time."

Tolliver nodded, unable to come up with a cogent reply. Instead, she asked, "And what about the other victims? Do you have videotape and blackmail money on those murders, too?"

"Not yet. But we will," Cooper said with firm confidence as he stood. "You wanted to know where we are and where we're going on this thing. Pass it along to whoever needs to know."

"Yeah. I'll pass it up the chain of command. The Joint Chiefs will be relieved to know the matter will soon be closed," Tolliver replied.

"I'll show myself out," Cooper said as he made his way to the exit.

Tolliver heard the back door open and close, but she didn't move from her chair.

Chapter 43

Saturday, June 11
Hope, CO

Kim had grabbed a couple hours of fitful sleep before she returned to Vaughan's kitchen table with the laptop Cooper provided. She figured he was monitoring the laptop but at this point, she didn't care.

She brewed more coffee and connected to her secure server to download Cooper's encrypted files, the ones she'd stored there back in Detroit. Felt like two lifetimes ago.

There were too many loose ends and unanswered questions churning in her head. She needed to sort through and make sense of it all.

A giant white board would have been useful, but she didn't have room for that in Vaughan's tiny kitchen.

She created a quick list of the four main issues she'd been chasing. The Hornet murders. David Vaughan's death. The Piranhas. The fourth item on the list was Jack Reacher, although finding him was her number one priority.

She marked the Piranhas with a big green check. After the fight at the cabin in the mountains, her small team had secured the three Piranhas and turned them over to Cooper. They were his problem now.

Which left her with the Hornet murders, David Vaughan, and Jack Reacher.

Early on, she'd considered Vaughan a Hornet victim, too. But at this point, she'd ruled out that theory.

David Vaughan's death didn't fit the pattern. The victimology was all wrong. He wasn't a drug addict. He wasn't homeless. He wasn't alone. He might not even have been killed by an air embolus.

She set David Vaughan aside for now and moved on to the Hornet's victims. At this point, the possible fourth victim, Suanne Skinner, had been eliminated because her ex was charged with her murder.

Which meant three victims had died at Hornet's hand, not four.

Gaspar had taken a deeper look at the first victim, Bennett, and the second, Fonda. Kim had integrated Gaspar's intel and found nothing particularly useful. No need to spend more time digging old ground.

Which left Lydia Harmon, the third and most recent victim. The one found in Detroit.

Her body had been dumped in the alley along the Cass Corridor, not that far from the FBI's Detroit Field Office.

Billy Boy, the witness she'd sent to be interviewed by Agent Phillips, had identified the man who had dumped Harmon's body. Reginald "Buster" Hodak.

Kim pulled up a few headshots from Buster Hodak's public records. Wide face, dark hair, pockmarked complexion. Eyes so pale they seemed to disappear. She shuddered. Not the kind of guy you'd want to meet in a dark alley. Lydia Harmon must have been terrified.

Phillips said Hodak had been arrested several times on various low-level drug charges in Michigan, Florida, and Colorado. Those charges were dropped. He was an Army vet. Served in Iraq. Now employed by the Boxer Group.

At the time, the intel had meant nothing to Kim. But the Boxer Group had also tried to recruit David Vaughan. Which meant now she was intensely interested.

Was there a Boxer Group connection to the Hornet victims as well? Possibly.

Kim stood, stretched, and refilled her coffee mug, draining the pot. She made another. While it brewed, she returned to her work.

Vaughan padded into the kitchen wearing a warm robe and slippers on her feet. She leaned against the counter waiting for the coffee to finish. "You're up early."

Kim replied, "Couldn't sleep. Too much to think about."

"Can I help?" Vaughan said as she filled her mug with coffee strong enough to wake the dead.

"Maybe." Kim leaned back and rubbed fatigue from her eyes. "The three Hornet victims were female veterans. But that's where the similarities ended."

"While they were alive." Vaughan nodded, encouraging Kim to think aloud.

"Right," Kim replied with a weak grin. The classified FBI task force file on Lydia Harmon was thinner than the others, but Kim didn't say so.

"Harmon's military service record is spotless. She joined the Army after a college degree in International Relations from a small liberal arts college."

"What was her specialty?" Vaughan asked.

"Africa."

"She'd never served in Iraq or Afghanistan?"

"No. Harmon was forty years old when she died, the oldest of the Hornet victims. Bennett was thirty-six and Fonda was twenty-nine," Kim said.

Vaughan nodded, testing the temperature of the scalding hot coffee. "So they were adults, close in age, military backgrounds."

"Right. Bennett was killed in that motel room where they found her," Kim said.

Vaughan said, "But Fonda and Harmon were killed elsewhere, and their bodies were dumped."

"Yes. Dumped in locations where the bodies were likely to avoid discovery for several days at least. Maybe longer," Kim replied.

Vaughan sat across the table from Kim and leaned back. "Any indications in the files that any of these women had any contact with the Boxer Group?"

"Not that we've found so far," Kim said. "Which could mean the files are incomplete."

Jake walked into the kitchen pulling his sweater over his head. "You didn't start the party without me, did you?"

Vaughan gave him a smile. "Coffee's ready."

"Smells great," he said as he opened the refrigerator and stared at the empty shelves.

"I don't actually have any food in the house, but there's a good diner in town," Vaughan said.

"Okay. Breakfast at the diner it is. So what have you learned about the Boxer Group?" Jake asked, closing the refrigerator and yawning as he filled his coffee mug.

"Nothing new so far," Kim replied.

Jake flashed Vaughan a meaningful glance and then turned his attention to Kim. "Don't freak out."

Kim stopped staring at the laptop screen and looked up. "What?"

He brought the coffee mug to the table and took the last chair. He looked directly at Vaughan as he spoke. "Reacher called me last night. He heard you were looking for him. He knew about David's death. Didn't say how he'd found out. Said he'd tried to call you and got no answer."

Vaughan lowered her gaze and wiped a tear from the corner of her eye.

"Where is he now?" Kim asked, sitting up straight and leaning in.

"I asked. He didn't say." Jake gave her a lazy smile when she scowled. "He knew Vaughan would be grieving and angry. He figured she'd try to find him and get me instead. Which is exactly what happened. Crazy how he can figure things out like that, isn't it?"

"Guy's a regular Einstein," Kim said sourly.

Jake's grin widened. "So I asked him about the Boxer Group. He said he'd heard things here and there."

"Like what?" Vaughan wanted to know.

"Wouldn't say. Except he told me to be careful and to pass that message along to both of you."

"He said that?" Kim challenged, an edge to her voice.

"Yeah," Jake nodded. "Guess he just figured we were all together here."

Kim shook her head. "Not likely. He's seen us together somewhere. That's the only way that message makes sense."

Vaughan said, "I agree. He could be here in Hope. The town's small enough that he could have seen us drive through. He knows where I live. He could have come around to the house last night, too."

"Why wouldn't he just come to the door then? I went outside to take his call. He could have approached me alone if he'd been watching," Jake said finishing his coffee.

"Because he doesn't want to deal with me," Kim replied flatly. "He's had plenty of chances before and I'm easy to find. If he wanted to talk to me, he would've done that."

"Oh, come on. Reacher's not afraid of you or anyone else," Vaughan replied.

"Agreed. Reacher's not afraid of anything," Kim said, nodding.

"Why is he avoiding you, then?"

Kim shrugged. "Long story."

"Are you planning to arrest him? What for? What did he do?" Vaughan pressed.

"Reacher's being considered for a classified assignment. I've been asked to find him and bring him to my boss. Reacher doesn't want to do that, for reasons of his own. I have no clue what those reasons are," Kim said, an explanation she'd offered many times before.

"You might have told me Reacher wouldn't show up if Otto joined in before you called her, Jake. You knew I wanted him with us." Vaughan cocked her head as if she now had more to consider. "As long as Otto's along, looks like Reacher won't be joining."

"No problem. One Reacher should be enough for any crisis." Jake grinned as he stood and stretched and turned toward the bedroom. "I need a shower before breakfast. Let's get going. I'll tell you the rest while we eat."

Chapter 44

Saturday, June 11
Hope, CO

They piled into the SUV and Jake drove into Hope, following Vaughan's directions. The diner was on Second Street. Jake found a parking place out front, and they walked inside.

Vaughan led the way to a booth in the far corner away from other customers. She sat with her back protected where she could see the whole room at once. Pure habit, Jake figured. He'd seen other lawmen do the same.

The waitress came over with three mugs and a Bunn flask. She didn't ask, just poured the coffee. "The usual for you?" she asked Vaughan.

"Thanks, Rita. That would be great," Vaughan replied.

Jake ordered eggs and pancakes and two rashers of bacon and whole wheat toast. Rita gave him a wide-eyed look.

"I'm a growing boy," he said with a grin, which made her smile.

Otto ordered a waffle. When Rita took her notepad back to the kitchen, Jake said, "Don't like eggs?"

"Not even a little bit," Otto replied. "I'm not all that thrilled with breakfast, actually."

Vaughan grinned. "Okay, Jake. Spill. What did Reacher say when he called last night?"

"It was a short conversation. Mainly, he warned me about the town just west of here, Despair. Which, by the way, is a depressing name for a town, don't you think?" Jake asked.

"It's even worse if you live there," Vaughan said. "There was a large metal recycling plant there, the largest in Colorado. Despair was a company town all the way. Everything owned by one guy, and everyone worked for him. Until he died."

"Definitely sounds depressing to me. What about now that the despot is dead?" Kim asked. "Someone else must have bought the recycling plant, surely."

Vaughan shrugged. "I haven't been over there in a long time. No reason to."

The food arrived and Jake dug in like a man just released from prison. Vaughan and Otto were more civilized about it, but they were obviously hungry, too.

After a few minutes, Otto put her fork down and said, "What else did Reacher say when he called you last night?"

Jake swallowed a big forkful of pancakes and washed them down with the coffee before he answered. "He said to tell Vaughan that Despair has rebuilt. Old man Thurman's kid runs the place now. He said it was still a company town and you'd know what that meant."

Vaughan nodded, still eating, chewing thoughtfully. "Did Reacher say what business Thurman Junior is running over there now?"

"He says it's a training facility. They already had a runway for private planes. They've improved it and made it longer so they can accommodate bigger planes. They've also got a couple of helipads and a mess of shooting ranges," Jake said, finishing up between bites.

Otto cocked her head and asked Vaughan, "Hunters common around here?"

"We don't have the kind of great elk, deer, and pronghorn hunting you'd find in the northeastern part of the state. But, sure. Most folks around here are comfortable with guns, I'd say," Vaughan explained. "The runway has been there a long time. Old man Thurman was an avid pilot. Flew in and out every day."

"Every day? That's a little crazy, isn't it?" Jake said, wiping his face and hands with the paper napkin and tossing it onto his plate.

Vaughan shrugged. "Despair keeps to itself. I thought the town would die when the recycling plant closed. But it didn't."

"Guess this new business must be enough to support the folks who live there," Otto said.

"Reacher says the facility was originally built by the Army, back in the day. It was abandoned and old man Thurman bought it, of course. Whatever the new business is, it's operating out of the old Army buildings," Jake explained.

The waitress brought the check. Otto paid and they walked outside.

After a few seconds standing on the sidewalk staring west, Otto said, "I'd like to take a look at this facility over in Despair."

Vaughan shook her head. "Whatever they're doing, they don't want anybody messing with it. They won't take it well if they think we're sticking our noses into matters that are none of our business."

"There's a highway running straight through the place," Otto said on her way to the SUV. "We'll be passing through. Maybe we'll get lost or take a detour."

"Old man Thurman was a piece of work. But his son is a thousand times worse," Vaughan warned.

"You've met him?" Jake asked.

"A couple of times. Junior was a rowdy kid. He'd come over here and get out of hand. Spent a few nights in our jail for drunk and disorderly before his daddy came and bailed him out," Vaughan said. "There's three of us. Three guns. They've got a whole town over there. Everybody's armed and dangerous and looking to protect what's theirs from the likes of us."

"Copy that. Jake, you can drive." Otto opened the rear passenger door and climbed into the SUV to make a call.

Jake gave Vaughan a steady gaze. "Are you really worried about this?"

Vaughan replied, "Hell, yes. And you'd be worried, too, if you knew anything about Despair. People die over there, Jake. Reacher and I barely made it out alive the last time."

Jake scuffed the toe of his boot on the pavement for a moment. He'd never backed down from a fight in his life. But that was him. Vaughan might feel differently about it.

How could she make an informed decision if she wasn't informed at all?

For her ears only, he said quietly, "Reacher's there. In Despair."

Vaughan whipped her head around. "How do you know?"

"He told me. When he called last night. He says the Boxer Group runs that old facility now," Jake admitted, wondering whether he'd done the right thing.

He could have spilled everything Reacher said, and perhaps he should have. Vaughan and Otto had a right to know what they were getting into.

But Reacher's instructions were to say nothing. Jake had to respect that.

Chapter 45

Saturday, June 11
Miami, FL

Gaspar was seated in his ancient Crown Vic waiting for his kids to pile in when he picked up Otto's call. They had swim lessons that morning and his wife deserved an extra hour's sleep. She'd been up half the night with the baby. The little guy had a set of lungs on him, for sure, Gaspar thought with a grin.

Maria would have walked the girls to the pool, pushing the baby in his stroller. But the baby was sick, and Maria was dead on her feet. Which meant Gaspar's turn was up.

He had the seat pushed all the way back so that he could stretch his right leg. Sitting behind the steering wheel was one of the worst positions for him. He found driving the small vehicles they sold these days close to impossible.

The old Crown Vic was a challenge to keep on the road since production of the sedan had stopped long ago. But as long as he could keep it running, he planned to do it.

The girls came running out, squealing with joy, as usual. They piled into the backseat and buckled up. He backed out into the street and headed west. Just about everything was west of Miami, except the ocean.

They'd just piled out of the car when Otto's burner phone vibrated in his pocket.

"What's up, Suzy Wong?" he asked when he picked up the call, still smiling.

"Morning, Chico. We're headed into some potential trouble. I need current satellite images," Otto said, as if she were looking at a map on her laptop screen which showed very little. "We're in Hope, Colorado, right now. Just finished breakfast. There's only one road from here into Despair. The town is seventeen miles west, but I figure the facility we're looking for is south of town."

"Sounds quiet out there. Are you in a vehicle of some kind?"

"Cooper provided this SUV," she said by way of warning.

Gaspar shook his head as he pulled into traffic. "So, there's two towns. Both in the middle of nowhere, Colorado. One is Hope and the other is Despair? Man, that's nuts."

Otto replied, "Agreed. But I still need those satellite photos. Can you get them or not?"

"Can you wait half an hour?"

"No. We should be there in twenty minutes. Maybe less, depending on how far the facility is from the town," Otto said. "I can't find it on the map, so I'm not sure of the exact location."

"All I can get is public intel. Cooper's got access to government satellites," Gaspar suggested, turning into his driveway. He figured Cooper was listening, so he attempted to cover his ass.

The only way Gaspar could access government satellite images was to hack into the system. Which was about a dozen federal crimes. Otto knew as much, but she didn't reply.

"Give me ten minutes. I'll do what I can." Gaspar hung up, parked the car, and headed inside. He stopped in the kitchen to grab a quick Guava Danish and Cuban coffee on the way to his desk.

He'd been working on Otto's cases for several hours already, but he hadn't focused on Despair, Colorado. He set the cup and plate on the desk and took a seat at the keyboard.

Charles Cooper was a vindictive sonofabitch who had made crystal clear how he felt about Gaspar continuing to work with Otto on Jack Reacher matters. Gaspar was no longer FBI, but he still had his clearances, which he couldn't afford to jeopardize.

Which meant he'd need to avoid triggering any of Cooper's alarms.

In a place as empty as East Colorado, finding a big facility in a lot of empty land shouldn't require proprietary or classified intel.

If he'd been within range, a drone would have been the best option. Drones could fly lower and capture clearer photos. But he didn't have the time to find one and put it into position.

Gaspar pulled up public satellites first.

After less than five minutes of searching, he found the two towns and the road that connected them. One entry said there had been a recycling plant west of downtown Despair, but it had been closed.

He zoomed out for a wider look. There was only one road, a spur off the main drag west of the town, leading to the facility. Which meant no one would have seen the place while driving from Hope to Despair.

Then again, from the look of the poorly maintained road and the empty land surrounding it, Gaspar guessed people rarely traveled from Hope to Despair anyway.

Gaspar located the facility about ten miles south of town, as Otto had guessed.

Abandoned and decommissioned military installations weren't uncommon. This one could have been a Cold War-era radar base. Or maybe a WW II Army base similar to the larger abandoned one at Fort Ord in California before it was repurposed.

The difference was that this place had been updated and modernized. The pavement was new. There were dormitories, a guardhouse, and a stockade. One building looked like a headquarters. The runway was west of the buildings, and it had been extended and repaved.

There were vehicles moving within and around the facility. He identified two helicopters and two jets parked near the hangars. What looked like gun ranges were spaced out on the southeast side.

Gaspar used another computer to search decommissioned military installations. After a few tries, he identified the Despair facility.

Fort Sandy Patch. Apparently named after an underrated Army general who served in both World Wars and for a while afterward. Gaspar had never heard of General Sandy Patch, but he wasn't a student of the history of war.

He sent everything he'd located to Otto's encrypted burner phone. Cooper would intercept, which was okay. Gaspar had included nothing objectionable in the transmission and Cooper needed to know where they were headed with this leg of the investigation.

Gaspar's daughters would ride home after their swim lesson with a classmate's mother and his wife was still sleeping with the baby. So he refilled his sweet coffee and gobbled a couple of Torticas de Morón shortbread cookies Maria had made using the last of the rum yesterday, resisting the urge to lick his fingers while he waited.

Soon, Otto called again. He heard noises in the background. She was on the move.

"Did you get everything?" he asked when he picked up.

"Yeah, thanks. Can you research a guy named Jerry Thurman, Junior? He owns the town of Despair, I'm told, like his father before him," Otto said.

"Okay. Anything specific I'm looking for?"

"Not sure."

"Why do we care about this guy?" Gaspar asked as he settled behind his desk again.

"He's connected to the Boxer Group, somehow. All of the facets of this situation are starting to come together, Chico." She took a big breath before she told him just enough to make him worry. "Looks like Reacher might have killed old man Thurman a few years back."

"Probably not a surprise to Cooper, I'm guessing." Gaspar nodded and washed down the cookies as he swallowed the last of his sweet coffee and went back to work.

This time, he used all of his resources to get everything he could find about the Boxer Group. After an hour of searching, he unearthed the truth.

Fort Sandy Patch had been sold five years ago to a private equity firm. The firm's owners were buried under layers of shell corporations registered offshore.

But a list of holdings had been filed with the State of Colorado.

Among them, the owner of Fort Sandy Patch was listed.

The Boxer Group.

Chapter 46

Saturday, June 11
Despair, CO

Jake drove across a wide bump in the road where a spacer had been placed in the pavement. The spacer had deteriorated over time. On the Hope side of the line, the road was smooth and on the Despair side, it was like riding on a washboard.

The road between the two towns was an east-west two-lane rising gently to the west. Eastern Colorado was mostly flat, like Kansas. The mountains were farther west. The Rockies were massive, and they looked much closer than they actually were. An optical illusion. A trick of light, nothing more.

The first peaks were about two hundred miles away. The earth was hard and crusty and dry. Jake was glad they weren't walking and had a full tank of gas.

At the first rise in the road, he glanced into the rearview mirror. The town of Hope was visible in the distance. Maybe ten blocks by six blocks with some outlying buildings on the periphery. Ahead, were miles of flat land with only the town of Despair to break the monotony.

Or so it seemed. Which was another trick of perspective. Although he couldn't see it from his current vantage point, Fort Sandy Patch was southwest of Despair.

"Despair straight ahead," he said, in case Otto wasn't looking.

With no traffic on the road, Jake saw the town was larger than Hope. The shape was sort of teardrop instead of square. Ten minutes later, they reached an old gas station. Then sidewalks and a street sign that claimed the road was now called Main Street.

Jake saw about twelve brick buildings, square and solid, mostly on the south side of Main Street. The place was dowdy and gloomy and so were the few citizens he saw walking the sidewalks and driving the old trucks and SUVs and sedans.

Otto spoke up from the backseat. "Turn left at the next intersection. Fort Sandy Patch is about ten miles south on Thurman Street."

"Roger that," Jake replied as he slowed the SUV to make the turn.

They passed a grocery store, a bar, a barber shop, a rooming house, an old hotel, and a restaurant. None of them seemed to be brimming with customers. The restaurant seemed busier than the others.

"You think Junior is hanging around here somewhere?" Jake asked.

Vaughan shook her head. "Probably not. We can't stop and ask. We don't want him to know we're coming for him. Assuming that's what we're doing."

"Would you know him if you saw him?" Otto asked. "We haven't found any photos of the guy anywhere."

"Possibly. It's been several years, and he was a kid back then. But he was the spitting image of his old man. Pink, plump, and prosperous. Last time I saw him, he had dark hair. It's probably white by now," Vaughan said, straightening in her seat. "Old man Thurman had white hair. The style was something to see. Teased and coiffed like a televangelist or something."

Jake kept his eyes on the road. "The fort is coming up. There will be a guard shack and we'll be asked for our purpose. What should we say?"

"Say we have a meeting with Thurman. Say we were told to meet him here. Ask if he's arrived yet," Otto said. "Maybe Vaughan can flash her badge if we get any guff."

"My badge means nothing over here. You should show yours," Vaughan replied. "The FBI has jurisdiction everywhere."

Otto cocked her head. "Showing my badge tends to cause more problems than it solves. I'd like to get inside and look around before the trouble starts."

Jake gripped the steering wheel as they approached the entrance. A large sign identified the old fort's new name. "The Boxer Group." He felt like fist pumping the air, but he didn't. Instead, he exchanged glances with Vaughan and Otto and flashed a thumbs-up.

A shack was posted just ahead, a mix of weathered wood and reinforced concrete built during the last century and restored.

A skinny uniformed guard sporting aviator sunglasses leaned lazily against the door frame. He straightened up as they approached, strolling to the middle of the road. He raised his hand signaling stop.

Jake buzzed his window down.

The guard leaned in, gaze sweeping over each of them. "Purpose of your visit?"

"We're meeting with Jerry Thurman," Jake said, keeping his voice friendly. "Is he here yet?"

The guard arched an eyebrow as he looked at Vaughan, then Otto, and back to Jake. He didn't toss them off the property or request ID, which was more than odd.

"Drive straight up, then take the first left," he gestured as he talked. "You'll find visitor parking. I'll call ahead. One of our guys will come out to meet you."

Jake nodded and buzzed the window up as they rolled past. "That was easier than I thought."

"Don't jinx it," Vaughan warned from the back seat. "We're not inside yet."

"Do you think he recognized you?" Otto asked.

Vaughan shrugged. "Possibly. I've never been here before. Didn't even know this place existed. But maybe Thurman has passed our photos around or something in case they came into Hope. We sure arrested him enough times."

Jake took the left turn and entered a lot filled with surplus military vehicles and a smattering of civilian cars. He parked in a vacant spot, and they got out to stretch.

As they approached the main building, a stout man in civilian clothes walked up. His face was ruddy under the weight of a sloppy beard. He gave Jake an odd stare before he said, "You're here to see Mr. Thurman?"

"Yes," Jake replied, "that's correct."

"I'm Ben, Mr. Thurman's right-hand man," he said and gestured toward the sidewalk and led the way. "You look like a guy I met over in the restaurant in Despair last night."

"Wasn't me. I just got here." Jake shook his head while thinking that Reacher should be more careful.

"He was older than you. But same size, same build, same coloring. Sure you aren't related? Brothers or something?" Ben asked.

"Sorry." Jake shook his head again, willing the guy to drop it. "I'm an only child."

They followed Ben through a maze of hallways. The walls were decorated with historical memorabilia including photographs depicting military exercises and deployments. *It was like visiting a movie set or a theme park*, Jake thought. Nothing like the two Army bases where he had served during his short military career.

They reached a closed door and Ben knocked twice before waving them through. Inside, the room was spare but functional. A stack of papers and a vintage-looking landline phone were perched on the old metal desktop.

A name plate on the desk identified the man behind it as Jerry Thurman, Jr. As Vaughan had guessed, Thurman's hair was no longer dark, but it wasn't completely white yet, either.

He looked up and smiled. "Welcome. Have a seat."

Jake, Vaughan, and Otto took the chairs opposite him. Thurman leaned back, steepling his fingers. "I presume you're not here for a social call, Officer Vaughan. But before we get to that, I heard about your husband. I'm sorry for your loss."

Jake exchanged glances with Vaughan and Otto before Vaughan took the lead.

"Thank you," Vaughan replied, managing not to tear up. "We won't take up your time. I'll get straight to the point."

"Always best." Thurman's gaze didn't waver. "Ben, would you get our guests something to drink? Water, coffee?"

"No need," Jake interrupted, "we won't be staying long."

"Suit yourself." Thurman shrugged and looked at Ben. "Make sure the preparations for the demonstration continue on schedule."

Ben nodded and left the room, closing the door softly behind him.

With Ben out of the way, Vaughan asked, "What kind of demonstration are you planning?"

Thurman replied conversationally, as if he were making a presentation to the Rotary Club. "We're in the middle of some big moves here at Fort Sandy Patch. A demonstration for potential clients. They're expecting a show, so everything must be perfect. It's like preparing for the president himself."

"The president of what? The Boxer Group?" Jake said to get the ball moving in the right direction.

Thurman indulged him with a slight smile, but he didn't reply.

"That's a good question," Vaughan said. "How long has this place been up and running? I don't remember seeing it before."

"The facility has been here for decades. We never found a use for it until after you and Jack Reacher decided to destroy our recycling operations," Thurman said with a steely stare. "For a long time, we thought Despair might never recover. But, as you can see, we're up and running now. The people of Despair have jobs again. Everything worked out okay in the end."

"Right," Vaughan said as if she were agreeing with him. "You mentioned my husband. David was being recruited by the Boxer Group. Was that your doing?"

Thurman's eyes widened and he shook his head. "Not at all. We'd have been happy to have him on the payroll. By all accounts, David Vaughan was a fine soldier. But I thought he was, er, disabled and not working. I guess my information was wrong."

Vaughan blinked and looked down at the floor as if she needed time to compose herself.

"How many people do you have working here?" Otto asked.

Thurman gave her a hard look. "And you are?"

"FBI Special Agent Kim Otto," she replied in her official tone.

Thurman nodded, but he didn't seem bothered. Which was odd. The FBI usually made people nervous, whether they should be nervous or not.

And what was that crack about Jack Reacher destroying the old recycling plant?

Jake wondered what the hell was going on with this guy. He came across as one weird dude, for sure.

"What does the Boxer Group do, exactly?" Jake asked. "I'm active Army now, but I'll be looking for a job soon enough."

"You let us know when that time comes, and we'll talk." Thurman stood, his hand extended for a quick, professional shake. "I'm expected elsewhere, I'm afraid. We've got a lot to do here today. You're free to look around, within reason, of course. Might help you make up your mind about joining the Boxer Group one day."

Jake kept his eyes on Thurman. "Thanks. We'll take you up on that."

Thurman left, leaving the door open. Jake exchanged looks with Vaughan and Otto. "Since we're here, let's take that look."

As they traveled through the corridors of the building, Jake noted the atmosphere was bustling but disciplined. Some personnel wore civilian clothes, but others were dressed in combat fatigues.

Everyone moved with purpose, polishing floors, aligning chairs, setting up equipment. The vibe reminded Jake of pre-game jitters back when he played football in college. Routines and purposeful activity were ways to manage the stress.

"So, a big demonstration," Vaughan said as she walked about the place like a health inspector or something. "Wonder what they're planning to show off."

"Must be significant," Jake replied. "All this polishing. It's like they're hosting a world summit."

They passed through a corridor lined with doors on both sides. All the doors had frosted windows and nondescript nameplates. Jake felt like they'd wandered into a stringent and heavily guarded installation.

Unlike the others, one room was cordoned off with the sort of yellow ribbon used by law enforcement, although it didn't actually say the words "crime scene" on it. Amid the bustle, no one seemed to notice when Otto stopped walking.

"Wait a second," she said, veering off toward the room. "I want to check this out."

Jake and Vaughan paused while Otto gingerly lifted the yellow plastic and pushed the door open.

The room seemed musty and unused. No desks, no computers. Metal cabinets lined the walls, and a cluttered large steel table filled the center.

Otto sifted through the files on the table quickly but carefully while Jake stood lookout. At the bottom of the pile, she found a file labeled "Harmon, Lydia."

Vaughan's eyes widened. "Lydia Harmon? The woman found dead in Detroit?"

"Exactly," Otto said, flipping the file open. Among the reports and documents was a surveillance photo. Lydia Harmon entering a building here at Fort Sandy Patch.

"Looks like Harmon might have visited Thurman before she ended up dead in Detroit," Otto said.

Jake surveyed the room. "We need to wrap this up. If they find us here, who knows what Thurman's reaction might be."

Otto slipped the Harmon file under her jacket and scanned the room one last time. "Let's go."

Jake replaced the yellow ribbon carefully and they rejoined the flow of workers, melting into the disciplined chaos.

Chapter 47

Kim climbed into the back of the SUV where she'd have room to spread out. She'd read a novel about a lawyer who worked from the back of a Lincoln SUV. The idea had seemed crazy to her at the time, but there was more room in here than some of the cubicles she'd worked from.

Jake drove the SUV from Fort Sandy Patch north into town and turned east heading out of Despair. Vaughan was in the passenger seat, flipping through a manila folder she'd picked up on a table near the exit filled with promotional material about the Boxer Group.

Kim had questions for Vaughan and decided to raise them while she had a captive audience. Cooper would hear, which wasn't great. But she had the sense that time was running short and almost everyone knew more about Despair than she did.

"What did Thurman mean when he said you and Reacher destroyed his family's recycling business, Vaughan?" Kim asked as she opened the Lydia Harmon folder she'd stolen off that table.

"It's a long story for another time," Vaughan replied, as if Kim might let it go.

"Thurman sounded certain when he made the accusation. And he's got a whole arsenal back there. If we're compromised here because of something Reacher did back then, don't you think we should know about it?" Kim asked.

"It's not relevant," Vaughan replied.

"Thurman thinks it is. What he said sounded like a threat to me," Kim said.

Vaughan sighed. "Reacher was pissed. He and Thurman played a game of chicken and Reacher won. That's it," Vaughan replied.

"So Reacher took a sledgehammer to a mosquito," Kim said.

Vaughan shrugged. "Believe me, old man Thurman deserved everything he got."

"Sounds like there was significant collateral damage," Kim said, but Vaughan didn't offer anything more.

Watching the empty road ahead, Jake interjected, "Fonda, Harmon, David—all seem to lead back to the Boxer Group."

"Bennett, the first victim, wasn't connected to Despair or the Boxer Group," Vaughan said, grabbing the chance to change the subject from Reacher.

"Possibly. Or we haven't found the link yet," Kim added, her eyes flicking to the rearview mirror when she heard a faint thumping noise in the distance gradually getting louder.

"Is that a helicopter?" Vaughan asked, swiveling her head to peer through the windows in search of the source.

A shiny black Chevy Suburban with an even shinier chrome push bar across the front rocketed into view from behind.

"Brace for impact!" Jake yelled as he pushed the accelerator to the floor.

The SUV jumped forward, barely widening the gap between the two vehicles for a couple of seconds.

The Suburban closed the gap and kept gaining. Jake gave the SUV everything it had, but the Suburban kept coming.

Kim had placed her alligator clamp at the seatbelt retractor to avoid being decapitated in a crash. She yanked the clamp off the belt and jerked the harness tight against her body, bracing her head against the back of the seat.

A second later, the Suburban's cattle bar smashed into the rear of the SUV with a violent crunch.

The speed and weight of the heavier vehicle shoved the SUV forward.

Jake wrestled with the steering wheel as it skidded forward. He managed to stabilize the vehicle after a long, precarious skid off the pavement and onto the hard, dry ground. The SUV finally stopped.

Vaughan's view of the Suburban was skewed in the side mirror, but she recognized the driver. "That's Thurman," she growled, reaching for her weapon.

Kim already had her gun in hand. "Looks like we're popular today."

The Suburban pulled up in front of the SUV, blocking all possible paths. The front door swung open, and Jerry Thurman stepped out. His flushed face was a hard mask of rage.

Vaughan released her seatbelt and stepped out of the SUV. "Stand down, Thurman."

"Too late for that. You wanted to avoid me, you should have stayed in your own town," he snarled, eyes narrowed and fierce like smoldering coals.

Kim stepped out on the opposite side of the SUV, dividing Thurman's ability to target them both with one aim. "FBI, Thurman. You're right that Vaughan doesn't have jurisdiction here. But I do. You've attacked a federal officer. You're under arrest."

Thurman's face displayed anger, bitterness, and a deeply etched hatred that twisted his features into something almost unrecognizable. He was beyond listening. Beyond reason.

Vaughan's boots made a soft crunching sound on the gravel. Her gaze was locked on Thurman, unyielding. "Get the hell out of here, Thurman. Before you make a mistake you can't take back."

"The mistakes were all yours, Vaughan." Thurman barked a harsh guttural noise tinged with madness. "You and Reacher destroyed us. Obliterated everything we had in Despair. Turned our home into a living hell."

Thurman's movements were fluid, as though he'd long practiced, preparing himself for the moment when he'd exact revenge on Vaughan and Reacher, too.

Without another word, Thurman raised the gun and fired. The shot echoed like a drumbeat through the open landscape.

Kim's focus narrowed the world to her weapon and Thurman. She aimed and fired before the echo of Thurman's attack faded from the air.

Her bullet slammed into Thurman's chest.

He staggered back as his shirt displayed the spreading red bloom.

Disbelief swept his features, erasing the contorted hatred, if only for an instant.

His eyes met Kim's, wide with realization. He staggered forward toward Vaughan, attempting to shoot again.

Jake had jumped out of the SUV. He lowered his head and tackled Thurman from his blindside, knocking him to the ground and landing on top of him.

And then Thurman stopped moving.

Jake climbed off the ground and dusted himself off.

Kim hustled over to Thurman. She kicked his pistol away from the body and bent to check for signs of life. She found none.

For a moment, the world was silent except for the low whine of the SUV's engine.

Vaughan's gaze moved from Thurman's body to Kim, a mixture of relief and grim acknowledgment flashing in her eyes. Her gaze lingered on Thurman for a moment longer, as if committing the details of the scene to memory. Which she probably was.

Vaughan said, "It was him or us."

"We need to move, now," Kim said. "Thurman controls the law in Despair. Let's not hang around to find out how good his goons are."

Which was when she heard the unmistakable whap-whap-whap of helicopter blades.

Kim searched the skies until the helo came into view.

"Friend or enemy?" Jake asked.

"Doesn't matter. We'll sort it out when we're aboard. Unless you want to walk all the way to Hope and pray there aren't more of Thurman's thugs on the way," Kim said.

Neither Jake nor Vaughan argued the point.

"Grab your stuff and let's go," Kim yelled as she rushed back to collect the Harmon file, the laptop, and her bag.

The helo landed and they rushed to climb into the cabin.

Kim took the co-pilot's seat and donned her headset.

"Good to see you again, Agent Otto," the pilot's voice said into her ear.

Relief flooded her body, leaving her legs feeling like overcooked spaghetti.

"Good to see you, too," she replied, unable to recall his name in the moment.

She'd been far from certain that Cooper would deploy the extraction. The helo could just as easily have been one of Thurman's.

The pilot lifted off, helo blades slicing through the air and raising a blinding dust storm on the ground.

The landscape receded below. She saw Despair, the road through, and Thurman's body beside the two demolished vehicles. To the south, four white Chevy Tahoes with the word "security" stenciled on the sides, rushed toward the scene.

At five thousand feet, she could see Fort Sandy Patch to the south. The installation was bigger and spread out more than she'd realized. The Boxer Group had to be very well funded indeed.

Briefly, she wondered if Thurman's crew would try to take the helo down before the pilot reached safe air space. With all that equipment out there at Sandy Patch, the thought wasn't as crazy as it first seemed.

Bringing down a helo wasn't particularly difficult. Which was one of the reasons she hated flying in the whirlybirds.

She was certain that Thurman would have done something as insane as blowing up Kim's helo. But Thurman was dead.

Which led to a second worry.

Now that Thurman was out of the picture, who was in charge out there?

She glanced back toward the crash site. Her gaze locked onto the terrain below as the helicopter cut through the sky. The rotor blades drummed a ceaseless, rhythmic beat.

The two big vehicles below rested like tiny metal toys on the sprawling ground.

The racing Tahoes were almost there. Maybe two miles out.

She wondered what the Tahoes would do when they reached the scene.

Cooper's SUV was equipped with all sorts of advanced technology and surveillance equipment. If they inspected it well, they'd find things no production vehicle would possess.

Cooper wouldn't be thrilled about that at all.

Before she finished the thought, a brilliant flare of orange and red burst from Cooper's SUV.

Kim gasped and she heard Vaughan's gasp through the headset, followed by a whispered, "Reacher."

"What the hell was that?" Jake wanted to know.

Vaughan replied, "Remote detonator. I've seen it before."

Jake's incredulity was palpable. "You've seen Reacher use a remote detonator to blow things up?"

Perhaps realizing she'd said too much, Vaughan didn't reply.

The explosion swallowed Cooper's SUV whole, shooting plumes of thick, black smoke into the air.

Moments later, what would have been the overwhelming blast noise on the ground reached the helo. Kim heard a muted thud, and the compression wave shook the helo slightly, even from such a distance.

The monstrous explosion had blasted Cooper's SUV off the ground. A blooming cloud of fire shot up from the interior of the vehicle, burning everything inside almost instantly.

The fire spread to the ground around the SUV and burned toward Thurman's body and the Suburban beyond it. Seconds later, the flames caught the combustible interior of the Suburban, too.

From her vantage point high in the air, Kim watched without fear even as she understood that Cooper must have detonated the bomb remotely. He intentionally destroyed the asset.

She'd ask him to confirm when she had the chance. He'd deny it. Which wouldn't shake her conviction at all.

But now that she knew he had both the capability and the willingness to use it, she vowed she'd never get into one of the vehicles Cooper provided ever again.

Unless Vaughan was right, and Reacher had been the one to detonate the explosion.

Which would open a whole new level of problems.

It would mean that Reacher proactively planted an explosive in Kim's transportation.

Cooper and Reacher. Locked in some sort of ruthless dispute, were willing to blow her up, on the ground or in the air.

The insidious idea crept inside her head and sparked a series of shudders and shivers that Kim seemed powerless to control.

She spoke into her headset to the pilot. "We need to set down. Now."

Chapter 48

Saturday, June 11
Despair, CO

Kim Otto's gaze shifted from the helo's instrument panel to the landscape below. Fields intermingled with patches of trees like a ragged quilt. They were flying over Despair, and every foot closer to the ground made the tension in the air thicker.

"You can set down in that vacant lot on the Eastern edge of town. We can walk from there," she said, pointing.

"Are you sure?" the pilot asked.

"Definitely," Kim replied. The sooner she had her feet on the ground, the better she'd like it. Even if she was landing in unfriendly territory.

Her gaze stayed locked onto the town of Despair below. Next to the abandoned lot was the old motor court. Next to that, the old gas station. A hundred yards farther west the sidewalks sprang up on Main Street.

Despair was plain and severe and unadorned and out of date. Kim shuddered to think they'd be there soon. Having made the decision, she stuck with it.

She was counting on the primal instinct of self-preservation. Not only her own, but the townspeople of Despair, too.

Kim figured they wouldn't want to blow up their own nest. If the helo was remotely detonated by someone in Despair, shrapnel, fallout, and casualties would be inevitable.

Same result if Cooper or Reacher pressed the button.

She had to hope that none of them wanted that kind of destruction.

As the helo came closer to the ground, she scanned for abnormal movements or anything else out of place. Despair was the same eerily creepy place it had always been.

The pilot glanced across the cockpit toward her. Their eyes briefly met in silent understanding. Kim sensed that he was aware of the seriousness of their situation. He gave her a brief nod as he lowered the helicopter's nose and maneuvered to descend in a controlled landing.

The town approached rapidly, and Otto scrutinized the areas they passed over. There were rooftops with missing shingles, open fields with overgrown grass and weeds, abandoned cars left to rust. This was a town that had surrendered to its gradual decline into disorder and decay.

She considered the people who still lived here and carried on with their lives. Were they unaware of Sandy Patch and what was going on out there? Or had they simply accepted fate and harbored the secrets?

Kim took a quick look in the back seats. Jake's gaze also swept over the landscape. Jake took in details like a sponge—every potential exit, every sightline. His mind would be cataloguing and running two steps ahead of every situation. She'd seen Gaspar do the same thing many times. Jake shared the habit, which she had mentally assigned to Reacher, too.

Vaughan, on the other hand, clutched her service weapon in her lap. She'd been through Hell and back these past few weeks. Vaughan was a strong woman, well trained, reliable, and trustworthy. The burden of her late husband's situation weighed her down, but she refused to quit. Kim had to admire her determination.

Kim caught Vaughan's gaze for a moment. Vaughan offered a quick nod in reply, as if to affirm Kim's decision to land and take their chances on the ground.

The helicopter began its final descent onto the vacant lot, churning the dust on the asphalt like a whirling dervish. The lot was empty, save for a single pickup truck parked in the far corner.

Kim narrowed her eyes to peer at the vehicle. As the helo came closer, she saw the truck's paint was faded and the bed was filled with junk. It had probably stopped running and been abandoned. Not a threat.

The helo touched down softly, making minimal contact with the asphalt like a cat testing uncertain ground. Kim felt the subtle jolt of the landing travel up her spine. This was it. They were down.

As the rotors began to slow and the whump-whump faded, Otto removed her headset and unlatched her harness.

Jake pulled the door open with a smooth motion. He stepped out first, landing solidly on the crumbling asphalt, scanning the perimeter. Kim followed, feeling more secure as her boots made contact with the ground.

Vaughan came out last. She'd holstered her gun, but it was still within easy reach. Kim noticed something else in Vaughan's demeanor. She seemed furious. Good. Whatever kept her going was fine with Kim.

They moved away from the helo and Kim gave a thumbs-up to the pilot. He returned the gesture.

The helicopter's rotors roared again, and the machine lifted off. Kim watched as it climbed higher into the sky before veering westward and disappearing from sight.

She felt a momentary sense of vulnerability as the helo vanished, sailing away, leaving them in hostile territory. They were on their own. Seventeen miles from Hope. Long way to walk.

"All right, let's move," Kim sliced through the heavy silence. "Vaughan, you're somewhat familiar with this place. Where can we go to blend in until we figure things out?"

Vaughan replied, "The restaurant is probably the best place. This way."

They followed Vaughan's lead deeper into the town of Despair, which seemed more defeated and decrepit with every step Kim took. They walked a dozen blocks and passed a grocery store and a bar and a faded old hotel. Traffic was light and they passed few pedestrians on the sidewalks.

When they arrived at the restaurant, it looked like it had seen better decades. A doorbell chimed as they entered, presumably to alert the hostess. A high ceiling and plate glass windows were the first things Kim noticed. The floor was tiled, and the furniture was worn brown wood polished to a dull sheen by years of wear.

A dozen people were seated in groups of two to five at tables scattered around the room. When they walked in, all talking and movement ceased. The room was silent.

Kim scanned the restaurant quickly. "You know any of these folks?" she asked Vaughan.

"Those two guys at the back table?" Jake said. "The snively one's name's Neske. Works at the hospital where David died.

Vaughan looked straight at Neske's companion, willing him to notice her. Which, after half a second, he did. His eyes rounded and his mouth fell open.

The guy seated across from Neske craned his neck in Vaughan's direction. Kim saw a brief flicker of recognition in his eyes.

Chapter 49

Saturday, June 11
Despair, CO

Vaughan said quietly. "I saw his picture in David's things. He's the only one in the photo I couldn't identify."

"Could it be Jeffrey Willard?" Kim asked.

"One way to find out," Jake murmured as he moved toward Neske's table. In a voice loud enough to be easily heard, he called out like he would have to a friend, "Willard! Is that you?"

Willard said something to Neske before he stood and walked toward the back as if he might avoid them altogether.

Jake trailed Willard. Vaughan and Kim followed close behind.

The door opened into a damp corridor. Like a maze, it was a dimly lit snarl of turns caused by years of sloppy construction and neglect. Stale beer and old cigarette smoke and the odor of boiled vegetables permeated the air.

Willard stopped when he reached a dead end. A blank wall covered with peeling paint and mold. Felt like no living human had been back here for years.

Kim sensed he'd chosen this place intentionally. A confined area. Only limited movement allowed. His back was against the wall as he waited for Jake to catch up.

"Jeffrey Willard," Jake said flatly.

"Jake Reacher," Willard replied in the same tone. "What do you want?"

"Answers," Vaughan said in response, stepping forward to allow Willard to see her. "Why did you kill my husband?"

An innocent man might have protested the accusation.

Willard smirked and moved first.

He lunged forward, his fist targeted at Jake's jaw, a quick strike, with all of his weight behind the punch.

But Jake was faster than he looked. He dodged Willard's fist and threw up his forearm to deflect. The hit looked hard enough to send shock waves up both their arms.

Jake pivoted in the narrow space and jabbed an elbow into Willard's abdomen.

Willard doubled over, but it was a feint. He shot up, his elbow swinging wide to catch Jake in the side of the head.

Jake stumbled but didn't fall. His eyes never left Willard's.

"Come on," Willard sneered, his voice a ragged whisper. "Is that all you've got?"

Jake's response was a flurry of moves, a sequence of punches and blocks that forced Willard back against the wall time and time again.

They were equally matched in strength, but Willard had an edge, like any feral animal trapped and unable to escape.

Jake was younger and absolutely livid. He fought as if Willard were the devil himself.

Willard tired. His counterattack grew sluggish. A sheen of sweat coated his forehead. The man was running on adrenaline and desperation, dangerous and unsustainable fuel.

Willard threw a haymaker that Jake easily dodged.

Seizing the chance, Jake grabbed Willard's extended arm. Using his momentum against him, Jake twisted the arm rapidly, up and back, high and hard.

Willard cried out in pain and staggered, colliding with the wall.

Jake could have delivered a final, fatal blow. He didn't. They needed answers, not another dead body.

Instead, he stepped back. His gaze locked onto Willard's.

A brief pause.

A silent question.

Willard's bravado crumbled. He was beaten, and he knew it.

Quickly, Jake swept Willard's legs out from under him. Willard crashed to the ground, his breath coming out in ragged gasps. Jake stood over him, every muscle poised for the next move, should it come.

But Willard was defeated.

Vaughan stepped forward, her service weapon aimed squarely at Willard's chest. Her hands were steady, but her eyes were infernos of pent-up rage and unshed tears.

Willard coughed, spitting out the last remnants of his dignity along with a streak of blood.

"You're crazy." He glared at Jake as a small, defiant chuckle escaped his iron control.

"You think this is a joke?" Vaughan interjected. Her eyes were pools of barely restrained anger, challenging him to lie again.

"It's over, Willard," Kim leaned in closer, her voice so low that only he could hear. She let each syllable hang in the air for a heartbeat longer. "It was over the moment you killed David Vaughan."

Willard's eyes shifted between Otto and Vaughan as if he were startled and surprised by the accusation. His face settled into a chilling smirk that seemed to crawl from the depths of some hideous place inside him.

"David Vaughan died in Iraq when an IED hit his Humvee," he sneered, locking eyes with Vaughan as he said it. "Too bad his wife couldn't accept that. Would have been easier for all of us."

Vaughan's cataclysmic collision of grief, rage, and realization broke all at once. Her grip tightened on her weapon, turning her knuckles white.

Willard's instincts recognized the danger instead of the victory he'd expected when Vaughan simply crumpled in response to his cruelty.

Sensing the shift and without warning, he lunged forward. His one good arm reached out to take her down.

Perhaps he thought he could use Vaughan's momentary emotional vulnerability as an opportunity.

Perhaps he was simply reckless.

But he'd misjudged Vaughan and the situation.

Her grip tightened on the pistol. From this distance, she couldn't miss.

The gunshot and the acrid smell of gunpowder and the deafening noise seemed to happen all at once, magnifying and reverberating as if it were a nuclear blast inside the confined space.

Willard's body jolted from the impact.

He collapsed onto the cold, unforgiving floor.

His eyes remained open, staring into an eternal void. His face froze in disbelief and resignation.

Whatever moves he'd calculated, they ended here, in this squalid corridor along with his secrets and grudges.

Vaughan's hand trembled as she slowly lowered her weapon. Her eyes, filled with unspeakable emotions, met Kim's. Then, almost robotically, Vaughan holstered her pistol. The gun settled into place, as if marking a full stop.

A moment later, Kim heard the unmistakable sounds of a struggle in the restaurant. Shouts, curses, and the dull thud of fists landing.

Kim exchanged glances with Reacher and Vaughan. No words were necessary. All three pivoted, boots pounding as they raced back.

Jake burst through the back door into the restaurant first. Kim and Vaughan followed. No one noticed their sudden entrance given the uproar that filled the big room.

A crowd had gathered, forming a ring of spectators around the source of the commotion. Kim couldn't see who was involved, but the elevated timbre of the shouts gave her a clue.

Jake moved first, plowing through the throng with the unstoppable momentum of a freight train.

Kim and Vaughan followed close, weapons drawn but held low.

They reached the inner circle just in time to see two men—Captain and Butch, unmistakable in their Piranhas attire—locked in a savage melee with a third man whose back was to them.

The man was holding his own, fists flying in hand-to-hand combat. He bobbed and weaved, ducking Captain's wild punches and landing a solid blow on Butch's jaw, sending him staggering backward.

Jake's gaze met Kim's. She gave a slight nod, and like synchronized swimmers in a pool of chaos, they moved.

Chapter 50

Saturday, June 11
Despair, CO

Jake went for Captain, his hand closing around the man's wrist, twisting it. The movement was so swift, so precise, Captain barely had time to register what was happening before his wrist was shattered, and his knife clattered to the ground.

Simultaneously, Kim went after Butch. She kicked the inside of his knee, buckling it. He went down like a sapling hit by a bulldozer. She lunged and her weapon connected solidly with the side of his head. Butch crumpled, out cold before he hit the floor.

The unknown man took advantage of the momentary distraction, landing a brutal punch to Captain's solar plexus that bent him double. He joined his companion on the ground, incapacitated and gasping for air.

The room fell silent, the tension dissipating like steam from a ruptured pipe. The crowd parted, and the unknown man turned to face Kim.

It was Ben, the guy they'd met at Sandy Patch.

His gaze was hard, unreadable.

"You have no idea what you've just walked into," Ben said, his voice tinged with a grim finality that sent shivers down Kim's spine.

Kim's senses were razor-sharp, still humming from the adrenalized encounters. But the moment Ben uttered those words, a chilling premonition gripped her. She exchanged glances with Jake and Vaughan and tilted her head toward the door.

Just then, the front door of the restaurant burst open. A group of men stormed in, weapons drawn, faces obscured by the grim intent that comes from following orders you don't question. They wore no uniforms, their attire a patchwork of rugged practicality and militant anonymity.

Ben grabbed a chair, hurling it into the closest pair, disrupting their approach. It bought them mere seconds, but seconds counted.

"Go!" Jake bellowed.

Kim didn't hesitate. She grabbed Vaughan by the arm, and the two bolted toward the kitchen, Jake right on their heels. The crowded restaurant erupted with shouts and gunfire. A bullet zinged past, embedding itself in the wall just inches from Vaughan's head.

They burst through the kitchen doors, dodging startled cooks and servers.

Kim spied the fire exit sign. Her legs pumped harder.

Jake slammed through the door first, holding it open as Kim and Vaughan dashed through.

The door clanged shut, and they were out, sprinting through a narrow alley cluttered with full dumpsters and discarded crates.

They reached the street, their eyes scanning for a way out. A beat-up truck sat parked a few yards away, keys recklessly left in the ignition by a too trusting driver. Vaughan sprinted forward, her hand already reaching for the door.

Jake hopped into the passenger seat as Kim took the wheel. The engine roared to life on the first try—luck or fate or a guardian angel, there was no time to ponder.

Kim slammed the truck into drive and floored the accelerator. They squealed onto the main road and kept going, leaving Despair and its secrets in a cloud of dust.

The road ahead was dark, flanked by towering trees and looming shadows. There were no streetlights. No moon. No stars. Kim's knuckles whitened on the steering wheel. Every few moments, her gaze flicked to the rearview mirror.

"Where are we going?" Vaughan finally broke the silence, her voice strained.

"Hope," Kim replied, staring at the road ahead. "It's the closest place. You have friends there. Cops who aren't bent."

The truck sped on, crossing the boundary that separated Despair from the surrounding world.

Kim's gaze met Vaughan's.

As they drove on, the distance growing between them and all they'd left behind, Kim felt the first tendrils of real civilization lightening the horizon, casting long shadows across the road to Hope.

And then the truck sputtered and began to slow.

Kim glanced quickly at the dashboard to confirm what she'd already guessed. The truck was out of gas, running on fumes.

Hope seemed suddenly very far away.

She gripped the wheel tighter, willing the vehicle to keep going.

She wanted to believe the old engine really did try. Momentum carried them a few feet farther before the truck rolled to a stop.

Kim looked at Jake and Vaughan. Then, she looked in the rearview mirror again. A vehicle was following from Despair, headlights growing larger as it closed the distance.

The truck was silent, not even the wheezing of the engine to fill the air. Kim was about to speak when the glow behind them became larger, brighter. She gripped her weapon.

A white Tahoe, the word "Security" painted in green on its sides, pulled over a few yards ahead of their stalled truck. The door opened, and a man they all knew stepped out.

"We have to get you out of Despair," Ben announced without preamble. "Five more miles east, and you'll be in Hope."

Options were in short supply. Staying here like sitting ducks was out of the question.

"Thanks, Ben. We'd appreciate a ride," she said, while keeping her weapon within easy reach.

Jake seemed to sense her wariness, as he climbed into the backseat of the Tahoe. Vaughan took the front passenger seat.

All three remained alert and wary. But what choice did they have? As Mrs. Otto often said, when there's only one choice, it's the right choice.

Ben drove and Otto kept her weapon ready. Every mile seemed to stretch on indefinitely, each passing tree and brush adding to the tension.

Jake sat behind Ben, coiled, ready to spring.

Vaughan stared out the window, her eyes unreadable but her posture taut.

Finally, they reached the gap in the pavement marking the transition between Despair and Hope. Ben brought the vehicle to a stop and turned off the engine.

"This is as far as I go," Ben said.

"I'll call for a ride," Vaughan said, stepping out of the Tahoe.

Kim and Jake stepped out, carefully watching Ben. Questions piled one on top of the other. Who was this guy? Why had he helped them? What did he know?

"Just helping out a friend," Ben said with a smile. "He said to warn you not to come back to Despair."

"And what friend is that?" Kim asked.

"He said you're all too young to die," Ben replied before he turned the Tahoe around and headed back toward Despair.

They watched him go.

"Guess we'll have to walk." Vaughan pocketed her phone. "No signal."

Kim took a few steps into the dark while she reached into her pocket to retrieve Cooper's satellite phone. "Try this."

Vaughan dialed, walking a few feet behind for privacy. Moments stretched until she finished and waited for Kim and Jake to catch up. "Hope PD will send a car. A guy I work with. He'll be here soon enough."

They walked shoulder to shoulder in the dark, taking up most of the two-lane. Jake located the flashlight on his phone and used it to illuminate the asphalt.

After a while, Jake said, "So who do you think sent Ben to give us a ride? We certainly didn't make any friends back there."

"I suppose you think it was Reacher," Kim suggested.

Truth was, she'd been wondering that very thing herself. Could have been Cooper, but somehow, Reacher made more sense to her, too. If Reacher had rescued her and Jake and Vaughan once again, he'd taken his own sweet time about it.

"Can't think of any other possibilities. Can you?" Jake asked. "We know he likes me. He and Vaughan have history."

"You're saying he doesn't like me?" Kim teased, because the truth was that she had no idea what Reacher thought of her. She wasn't sure what she thought of him these days, either.

And then, headlights—distant but fast-approaching.

"That'll be Craig, probably," Vaughan muttered, squinting into the darkness.

A few minutes later, the police cruiser rolled to a stop in front of them. The door swung open and a solidly built man in a Hope PD uniform stepped out.

"Vaughan!" he called, clearly relieved. "You okay?"

Vaughan nodded, though her gaze never fully left Otto and Jake. "We're fine, Craig. Thanks for coming. Can we—"

"Get in before someone from Despair changes their mind and comes after you," Craig interrupted, his eyes narrowing as he scanned the roadside.

They climbed into the cruiser. Craig revved the engine and sped away.

As Craig put distance behind them, he said, "Care to fill me in? This is weird, even for you."

Vaughan glanced at Kim before answering. "I'll tell you about it. But let's just get into town first."

Craig pulled into the parking lot outside the Hope PD station. He shut off the engine and turned to face them. "You'll be secure here."

"I know," Vaughan nodded, exiting the cruiser. Kim and Jake followed suit, still wary.

Vaughan started toward the station, but Kim held back. "Something on your mind?" Craig asked, catching her hesitation.

"I need to make a couple of calls," Kim replied, her eyes meeting Jake's. "Any place in town sell burner phones?"

Chapter 51

Sunday, June 12
Washington, D.C.

Maureen Tolliver observed Charles Cooper, who had settled comfortably into one of her leather chairs. He held the glass of scotch in his right hand. He looked calm and relaxed, which he probably was.

The ambient lighting cast a dim glow over the room, highlighting the rigid lines of his face. He sipped the scotch and held it on his tongue appreciatively for a couple of seconds before he swallowed.

Then he said, "You killed Melody Bennett."

Tolliver met his stare with a steely gaze, her spine as straight as a rod. She refused to admit or deny the accusation. No reason to. He wasn't here to arrest her.

"You were seen."

"What do you mean?" She held her breath, replaying the scene in her head.

No way could anyone identify her, even if she'd been seen. She was sure. One thousand percent sure.

"There were cameras in the room at the motel where Bennett died."

Her heartbeat thumped hard and rapidly in her chest. Tolliver said nothing. The best defense is always silence. Second best is denial.

"We both know why you did it. You viewed her as a threat to your advancement," Cooper said thoughtfully. "Ambition is like electricity. Helpful when properly harnessed, but deadly in excess."

Tolliver waited. She was sure he had a point to make. There was no need to guess why he'd come.

"We knew you were ambitious when we brought you aboard. We didn't realize how boundless your ambition is."

Tolliver replied smugly, "Takes one to know one."

A trace of a smirk crossed Cooper's lips as they lifted their glasses in mock salute.

After a moment of silence, Cooper continued. "But the 'why' isn't what matters. You compromised the mission. Which is unacceptable."

Tolliver was a bit worried, but no way in hell would she let him know that. "And what? You're going to remove me? Go ahead. Try."

"Don't fool yourself. I could get rid of you in a hot New York second," Cooper replied sternly. He paused as if he were letting her stew in that knowledge. "But the simple fact is that we can't sacrifice you now. We don't have the time to recruit and prepare someone else."

"Exactly," she said, draining the scotch from her glass and pouring another generous dollop.

The vetting process to add her to the group had been strenuous. She'd passed with ease because of her current position. When she took the next step, into the Joint Chief's role, she'd be untouchable. For a while, at least.

"We sacrificed too many assets to keep you on board. If we hadn't run interference for you, moved obstacles out of the way, sacrificed valuable personnel? You'd be dead or in prison," Cooper said calmly.

"What sacrificed assets are you talking about? Willard?" She shook her head. "That's bullshit. Willard was bent. You knew that when you funded him and put him in charge of the Boxer Group. Only one reason you would have done that. They were all expendable from the start."

"Everyone's expendable. Including you." Cooper's tone was harsh. No argument permitted.

Which was when she realized that he'd orchestrated the whole thing.

He'd found out about Bennett. She'd died eighteen months ago. He'd been holding the knowledge for a purpose, until he found a good use for it.

And Tolliver had played right into his hands.

When Emma Fonda, the second victim, turned up six months ago, Cooper might have thought Tolliver had killed Fonda, too. He'd have considered the second victim another cudgel he could use against her.

But he'd have been wrong. He wasn't God. He wasn't infallible, either.

Cooper made a mistake with Willard.

Cooper should have realized sooner that Willard never allowed Boxer Group assets to leave the organization. Willard required a lifetime commitment. Literally.

If anyone tried to leave, Willard made sure they were terminated. Simply put, no one was allowed to quit. Ever. For any reason.

Cooper would not have approved of Willard's personnel termination policies. Not even a little bit.

And then David Vaughan was killed. Tolliver had a solid alibi for that murder. Cooper was forced to point his accusatory finger somewhere else.

It took him too long to find Willard, though. If he'd connected Willard to Fonda right away, he might have saved Lydia Harmon. But he didn't.

While Cooper was distracted with other business, Willard killed Harmon.

Which must have been the point where he finally realized Willard was too erratic and uncontrollable. He had to go.

So Cooper set up the Hornet task force and put Otto on it. He probably thought Willard would remove himself. Guys like Willard always had a plan B. A secret location where he could hide out until things cooled down.

Cooper used the situation to flush Reacher, sure.

But he had never intended to leave Willard out there in the field after Harmon. Willard had been an asset for a long time. But he'd become a loose cannon. Too erratic and uncontrollable for Cooper to keep on board.

Tolliver wouldn't say any of this now. She wouldn't give him the satisfaction.

Still, good to know.

The knowledge would become useful at some point. She was sure of it.

"We're giving you a one-time pass, Tolliver. But understand this," Cooper said as he set his empty glass on the side table. "If you jeopardize our operations again, you'll be removed and replaced. Permanently."

His words sliced through the room, laying a wall of tangible tension between them.

"You think you own me, Cooper?" Her tone was calm but laced with defiance.

"No. I'm responsible for the mission," Cooper corrected, his gaze unwavering. "And *anyone* who threatens success is my responsibility. I won't allow you to destroy what has taken us so long to put in place. You're a member of the team. You're not the boss. Get your head clear on that."

Tolliver's gaze moved to the framed commendations displayed on her ego wall and then back to Cooper. "If you try to take me down, you'll see how clearheaded I can be."

Cooper leaned forward, elbows on his knees, and spoke slowly. "You're valuable, but not irreplaceable. Don't make me regret giving you a second chance."

"Trust is a two-way street," Tolliver shot back, her nerves humming like electricity through her veins.

Who the hell did he think he was talking to, anyway?

She kept her expression stoic and steady. She stopped short of threatening him in return. But she had plenty of ammunition, should he become a bigger problem than he already was.

"Then let's say, for now, we're at an impasse. You execute the mission as planned," Cooper said. "Anything goes awry before the mission is accomplished, anything at all, you're out. Are we clear?"

"Crystal," Tolliver replied, lifting her glass.

Her skin tingled with a mix of relief and rekindled determination.

Cooper was an ice-cold bastard. She was no different. Worse, probably.

"Good." Cooper nodded, breaking eye contact. He stood and let himself out while Tolliver continued her outward display of defiance until the door closed behind him.

She was relieved.

Hell, getting involved with Melody Bennett in the first place was a mistake, in retrospect. But was she supposed to live like a nun forever just because she planned to occupy the White House one day?

The double standard was alive and well in politics in America. Straight white men could have affairs and be the leader of the free world. But regardless of her long, long list of qualifications, middle-aged lesbians were not allowed the same freedom.

Killing Bennett had been a gamble that paid off.

No doubt, Tolliver had done the right thing.

Even if Bennett could have been trusted to keep Tolliver's secrets, which she couldn't, eliminating Bennett removed the risk before she became a bigger, uncontrollable problem.

Bennett would have gone to the press. Or some enterprising reporter would have discovered Tolliver's affair with Bennett. Either way, both of them would have been eaten alive.

And Tolliver's ambitions would have been derailed.

No. She felt not so much as a twinge of regret.

She drained her glass again and considered a refill.

Cooper had evidence. He'd keep it ready, just in case.

But she had to gamble that Cooper wouldn't cause her any trouble. The blowback on him would be inevitable. He was smart enough to know as much.

Which meant he might have her terminated at some point for the same reasons she couldn't allow Bennett to remain alive after their relationship ended.

Damage control.

Right now, time was on her side. There was work to be done and much of the preparations were already completed.

But when the mission was over, she would be at risk once more. There was no statute of limitations on murder.

She shrugged. Nothing she could do about that now.

As her grandfather often said, when you wrestle with pigs, you both get dirty.

Chapter 52

Sunday, June 12
Miami, FL

Kim had flown to Miami for a debrief on the way home. They were seated outside. Gaspar with his sweet coffee and cookies, Kim with a glass of red wine. She'd earned it.

"Young Jake get back to base without causing any serious problems with his CO?" Gaspar asked.

"Yeah. Vaughan called and gushed about how much help he was and how she was so grateful and yada yada yada," Kim said with a grin. "The CO didn't love how long Jake was gone, but he's back now and he'll work hard to catch up."

"He was a significant help during this case," Gaspar said. "Kind of makes you wonder how he'll turn out, doesn't it?"

Kim nodded. "He's been in contact with Reacher now and then. Which means Reacher is no longer totally off the grid. He's connected to Jake, and he seems concerned about him. Like he's keeping an eye on the kid."

Gaspar stretched his legs and crossed them at the ankles. "So Cooper's thinking if he keeps an eye on Jake, he can locate Reacher."

"That would be my guess," Kim replied.

"Which gives you an advantage," Gaspar said thoughtfully. "Jake likes you. He doesn't even know Cooper. And if Reacher is talking to him, he'll warn Jake away from Cooper, too."

"Seems like that could work," Kim replied.

"And the Boxer Group? Willard didn't own the company. I guess it will keep on keeping on," Gaspar said, and Kim simply nodded.

They sat in companionable silence for a bit. Gaspar's kids came out to say hello before Marie herded them inside for dinner. They were great kids.

Kim envied him a little bit. Not that she wanted to get married and have a brood of her own. But Gaspar seemed genuinely happy these days, which was more than okay.

"So Willard was running the Piranhas," Gaspar said, picking up the conversation again after his family left.

Kim nodded, "That's the consensus."

"And the Piranhas, following Willard's orders, killed the three Hornet victims and David Vaughan," Gaspar said, shaking his head.

"So I'm told."

"What was Willard's motive? Why kill those four people?"

"Turns out, Willard was a slimy bastard. He started raping and killing civilian Iraqi women. The members of David Vaughan's squad knew about it. Willard killed the witnesses over there. But the IED that killed his squad didn't quite do the job with David."

"So the three female Hornet victims were Willard's ex-lovers? Not drug addicts? Not homeless? He staged those crime scenes?"

"That's Cooper's theory. Some men simply won't allow a woman to leave them," Kim said, holding the Brunello on her tongue for a while before she swallowed it. "It's not like there's anyone left to confirm or deny."

Gaspar popped another guava cookie into his mouth. "Cooper must have known all that, or at least suspected, when he put you on the Hornet team and gave you the classified Piranha files back in Detroit."

"So why didn't he just bust up the crime ring? Why get the task force going, bring me on board, disclose the classified files on the Piranhas?" Kim asked, although she had her own theories.

"Because he wanted the whole mess sorted in a way that kept him out of the spotlight," Gaspar replied. "Cooper's like a rodent, running around in the dark, attacking and slinking away. You must know that by now."

Gaspar was no fan of Charles Cooper, as they were both well aware. He'd been glad to get out of the FBI when the offer from Scarlett Investigations came his way. These days, he was convinced Cooper couldn't be trusted and should never be allowed to drive any case.

But Kim hadn't given up on Cooper yet. She couldn't afford to.

She was trying to survive the Reacher assignment, finish it, and move on with her life. Gaspar kindly called her an idiot. Some days, truth be told, she couldn't fault him for the label.

"Cooper's in front of the cameras all the time. Testifying on the Hill. Making speeches to law enforcement, military, and civilians. He could have taken point on this and wrapped it all up to add to his win column," Kim said, shaking her head. "But he didn't."

"He knew Reacher was there. Or at the very least, Cooper believed he'd show up. That's always the reason he sends you instead of the rest of his Army, isn't it?" Gaspar suggested.

Kim sipped the wine and wrestled with the facts a while longer before she shrugged. "We're missing something."

"Such as?"

"Such as what kicked all this off in the first place?" Kim listed her open issues, one after the other. "Why did it take so long to figure out Bennett had been murdered? How did Willard even know her? She was Marines. He wasn't even Army anymore."

"Knowing Cooper like we do, there are layers of this thing that we'll never uncover," Gaspar said. "Whatever happened with Fonda's tattoo? Did he tell you?"

Kim shook her head. "I asked. He said it was classified and above my clearance level."

"He trots out that tired excuse whenever he knows something he doesn't want you to find out," Gaspar said with a scowl.

"Nothing I can do about that, either," she said. "But we're missing something else, too. I can feel it."

Gaspar grinned. "Yeah, Suzie Wong. We're still missing Reacher. After eight months of looking, he's still out there, thumbing his nose at you. The guy's obviously too wily for you. Are you giving up?"

She leveled a hard stare straight at him. "You've forgotten who you're talking to, Chico."

Kim was sure Gaspar's hearty laugh could be heard all the way to Hope, Colorado.

ABOUT THE AUTHOR

Diane Capri is an award-winning *New York Times*, *USA Today*, and worldwide bestselling author. She's a recovering lawyer and snowbird who divides her time between Florida and Michigan. An active member of Mystery Writers of America, Author's Guild, International Thriller Writers, Alliance of Independent Authors, Novelists, Inc., and Sisters in Crime, she loves to hear from readers. She is hard at work on her next novel.

Please connect with her online:
http://www.DianeCapri.com
Twitter: http://twitter.com/@DianeCapri
Facebook: http://www.facebook.com/Diane.Capri1
http://www.facebook.com/DianeCapriBooks